用英語說出行銷力

胥淑嵐 著

Speaking Marketing in English

以實際辦公室對話為例，活潑生動的句子讓你現學現用。

結合流行英語、時下必學的行銷手法與品牌管理概念。

你是行銷或品牌管理的職場人員，商管學院相關科系的師生，或是想增進英文的讀者，本書都是您必備的行銷英語最佳學習用書。題材充實與新穎，讓您的英語力，瞬間大增。豐富您的知識，增加您語言學習的深度和廣度，幫助您充實語言力，輕鬆學習，使用行銷英語，就是這樣得心應手。

全書分成六大主題

1. **新產品上市** — 在現實中找一條好出路
2. **促銷活動** — 增加購買力有撇步
3. **公關宣傳活動** — 如何尋找創意又符合成本
4. **廣告企劃** — 廣告說些甚麼才好
5. **顧客關係管理** — 要想乘涼先種樹，讓顧客愛上你
6. **品牌管理** — 製造一個人人愛的品牌

作者 序

在工作了一段時間後，我踏上了碩士的旅途，前往英國的行銷研究所進修；畢業後又回到熱愛的行銷領域。雖然在職場中經常會使用到英語，但是卻發現有趣生動、又貼近行銷領域真實職場所需的英語工具書實在缺乏；於是我鼓起勇氣，找上了倍斯特出版社。承蒙出版社的青睞，才有了這本書的誕生。

「用英語說出行銷力」將行銷基礎概念以英語呈現，並融入真實辦公室對話之中。翻開本書，你會發現原來行銷就在我們生活之中，原來生活與職場英語用語這麼簡單就可以表達出來！行銷概念俯拾即是，英語也應該是容易學習的。期許本書能夠協助喜愛行銷領域的讀者減少一路上的困難，讓喜歡輕鬆學英語的讀者找到樂趣。

After working for few years, I went to study abroad for my master's degree at University of Leicester, UK. I came back to the marketing domain which I love the most after my graduation. Even if English is often used in the workplace, I found it difficult to find interesting English learning book with lively dialogue as well as close to the field of marketing workplace requires. Therefore, I took courage to contact Best Books and thanks to them, now we can sit down and read it.

「Speaking Marketing in English」 presents the basic marketing concepts in English, as well as the real dialogues in the office. Open this book, you will find out that marketing is everywhere in our daily life, and it also is very easy to speak English in your daily life and workplace! Marketing concept is around each of us, and English should be easily to learn. May this book help to reduce the difficulty for marketing lovers, and let readers who love learning English in an easy way find fun and joy.

編者 序

　　〈用英語説出行銷力〉即將要出版了！在策劃本書寫作之前，眼見到市面上有關於商業財經的語言學習書的確已經不少，但看到本書的企劃案時，我不經眼睛為之一亮。因為這本書真是完美的語言學習與了解怎麼行銷的雙結合。書中教您如何在行銷領域説出一口 漂亮的英語與行話。特別是行銷領域已經是業界再也重視不過的一環，如何在此情境，以極佳的英語力來溝通協調，甚至做簡報，開行銷會議，不蓋您，本書的確有一套。也開創您學習英語的藍海，書中提出許多在行銷上，必學的相關字彙和句型，幫助您讀一本書就徹底得得到行銷英語的提升和功力，是您一定要用心細讀的絕佳行銷英語學習指南。本書也絕對是以中英雙語解説行銷情境最有系統，好學易懂的一本好書。

倍斯特編輯部

推薦 序

關鍵的一步

How're you? I'm fine, thank you. 這兩句恐怕是許多大學畢業生最有信心的英語。如果你想在業界有更多機會、人生有更多可能,你絕對不能只懂得這兩句。

在各項企業功能中,行銷功能與外界的互動最密切,因此擔任行銷相關職務者用到英語的機會也比其他職務還多,可是教導行銷英語的書籍並不多見。因此,我很高興見到胥淑嵐出版這本獨到的書籍。胥小姐擁有十餘年兩岸行銷工作經驗,並留學英國研習行銷管理,因此書中的英語非常貼近行銷實務;另外,書中對行銷的基本概念還作了一番精要解說,讓讀者可以一邊學習英語,一邊掌握正確的專業知識,可謂一箭雙雕。

如果你想跟上台灣企業國際化,想讓自己的視野與機會國際化,那麼閱讀本書將是關鍵的一步。

曾光華

中正大學行銷管理研究所副教授

目 錄 CONTENTS

Part I

New Product Launch
新產品上市

Unit 01 Analysis of Current Market-1
在現實中找一條出路

Part I
Part II
Part III
Part IV
Part V
Part VI

Steve	Hi, John. **What a coincidence!**	嗨，約翰。怎麼這麼巧！
John	Hi, Steve. How's everything?	嗨，史帝夫。怎麼樣，還好吧？
Steve	Good, and you? **What have you been up to lately**?	好啊，那你呢？最近在忙些什麼？
John	Well, nothing special. Just working on a new **product launch proposal**, I am sure you have already heard about it, didn't you?	嗯，也沒什麼特別的。正在進行一項新產品上市企劃案，我想你應該已經聽說了吧，不是嗎？
Steve	Yes, your team is responsible for the launch of new full-size luxury car.	是呀，你們團隊正負責豪華車的上市案。
John	Correct. We just finished the **market research** part.	答對了。我們才剛完成市場調查的部分。
Steve	Great! That is one of **key success factors** in a new product launch.	很好呀！那可是新品上市的成功關鍵因素。

John	No doubt about that. What about you?	無庸置疑。那你呢？
Steve	Besides market research, our team also focused on the marketing strategy we will adapt, **market positioning**, features of our new SUV car and the **competitor analysis**.	除了市調之外，我們團隊還聚焦在即將採取的行銷策略、市場定位、新 SUV 車的特色，以及競爭對手分析。
John	Competitor analysis is also **crucial** to new product launch, especially this is the first time our company decided to enter SUV market.	競爭者分析也是新品上市的重點，尤其這是公司第一次決定要進入 SUV 車市場呢。
Steve	You are absolutely right. **Since** this market is growing, we need to **grasp the opportunity**.	絕對沒錯。正因為這市場正在成長，我們應該要抓住機會才是。
John	**You bet**! So, good luck with your proposal. See you around.	那當然！所以，祝你提案好運囉。等會見。
Steve	Yes, you too. See you later.	你也是。等會見。

Part I

Part II

Part III

Part IV

Part V

Part VI

知識補給站

「不創新，便等死！（Innovation or die!）」用來描述新產品對企業的重要性，可謂不言可喻。

舉凡前所未有、革命性的創新（revolutionary innovation），改良式創新（又稱動態連續性創新 dynamically continuous innovation），局部創新（又稱連續性創新 continuous innovation），到新形象新定位（new image, new positioning）的創新，皆屬於創新的產品或服務範疇。

革命性創新的例子很多，最知名的有 Apple 電腦發明的 iPod，SONY 的隨身聽（walkman），Google 瀏覽器、臉書（Facebook）…等等，甚至愛迪生的燈泡，貝爾的電話也屬於這一類。這類產品的特徵就是「創人所未見」。改良式創新從字面上很容易了解意思，就是在既有的基礎上做改良、更新。諸如從電話到手機、傳統相機到數位相機。

局部創新屬於小幅度改變產品的使用方式與習慣，例如，印表機從兩色變成四色印刷、或者大體積變成小體積，轎車有不同汽缸數、開天窗的功能，隨身碟 (USB Flash Drive) 從 2G 變成 16G…等等。新形象新定位的創新例子不勝枚舉，例如：新形象新包裝的某飲料、店面重新改裝、藝人重新定位再出發…等等，都屬於這類例子。

Part I

Part II

Part III

Part IV

Part V

Part VI

而影響新產品或服務上市的成敗關鍵，有以下幾點：

1. 市場調查（market research）。市場調查的品質（quality）與結果分析（result analysis）的品質，會影響企業是否應該推出新產品，或者採取何種行銷策略（marketing strategy）的判斷。

2. 競爭者分析（competitor analysis）。假定市場上已經有類似或同質產品，對於既定競爭商品的分析就要準備充足；畢竟是推出新產品來搶佔市場（**seize the market**）的，競爭對手可不會默不作聲，所以有時候臆測競爭對手會進行什麼反擊（例如：降價促銷 promotion），也是新產品上市企劃的重點之一。

3. 產品品質、特色（features）與定位（positioning）。既然企業決定推出新產品或服務，就表示它有與眾不同的特點，值得消費大眾購買；這方面的描述或分析，就一定不能偷懶。反之，如果自己也不甚瞭解，又怎能期待消費者買單？貿然推出”好像還可以吧”（It seems OK.）的產品或服務，可是很危險的。

4. 市場規模與成長（market scale and growing）。意即，會買得人多不多？是不是一年比一年多？如果兩個答案都是否定的，對於是否推出新品就要再考慮考慮了。

5. 行銷策略（marketing strategy）。包含通路（channel）、包裝（packaging）、廣告（advertisement）、促銷活動（promotion events）、經銷商活動（**distributor** events）…等等，都需要面面俱到。

　　就因為新品上市企劃內容複雜（complex），有時候提案也並非一人可以獨力完成，經常要跨部門（**cross-department**）和部門內多人參與，才能減少失誤（reduce errors）。

Part I

Part II

Part III

Part IV

Part V

Part VI

Related Word 相關詞彙

1. What a coincidence! 怎麼這麼巧！

2. What have you been up to lately? 你最近在忙些什麼？

3. product launch proposal 產品上市企劃

4. market research 市場調查

5. key success factors 關鍵成功因素

6. market positioning 市場定位

7. competitor analysis 競爭者分析

8. crucial 至關重要的

   同義詞：*essential, important, indispensable, imperative, significant,*
   　　　　substantial, vital。

   文法加油站：*crucial to/for sth.* 對…來說是至關重要的
   　　　　　　　at the crucial moment 在關鍵時刻

9. Since 因為

   文法加油站：*since* 有下列三種意思：

   (1) 當從屬連接詞。既然、因為的意思。

   　　Since he was ill, he did not go to school. 因為他病了，所以沒有上學。

   (2) 當時間副詞，與完成式連用。自那時起的意思。

   　　I met her two years ago, but I haven't seen her since then. 我兩年前見
   　　過她，但此後一直沒見面。

   (3) 當介系詞。自從的意思。

   　　We have known each other since childhood. 我們從小時候就認識彼此。

10. grasp the opportunity 抓住機會

   文法加油站：可置換為 *seize the chance*.

11. You bet! 那當然！

   文法加油站：*bet* 原意是賭注。*You bet* 或 *I bet* 可以理解為 *You/I can bet*
   　　　　　　money on that，表示我有信心將錢下注在這裡的意思。*bet* 在此
   　　　　　　解作當然、一定的。

12. seize the market 搶占市場

13. distributor 經銷商

14. cross-department/trans-department 跨部門

Part I
Part II
Part III
Part IV
Part V
Part VI

Exercises 練習題

Please complete the word or sentence by filling in the blanks.

A：Hey, have you ever heard of「 ＿＿＿＿＿＿＿ ！」?

B：Sure! I will be surprised if you don't know that. It means innovation is a never-ending race, either the corporate keeps spending time or money on it or goes out of business.

A：I don't like to think new ideas, it makes me feel headache.

B：You don't really have to. You could do the ＿＿＿＿＿＿ in order to give yourself a new thought.

A：That is a great idea! Is there anything else I should to pay attention to?

B：I guess if you have done ＿＿＿＿＿＿ and ＿＿＿＿＿＿ , I think you're halfway there.

A：Thank you so much!

B：＿＿＿＿＿＿ !

Part I

Part II

Part III

Part IV

Part V

Part VI

請填空完成下面句子或單字

A：嗨，你有聽說過「不創新，就等死嗎！」?

B：當然有啊！我很驚訝你不知道耶。這句話的意思是指創新是一件永無止盡的競賽，企業要不是花時間和金錢創新，要不就是被淘汰出局。

A：我不喜歡想新的想法，這會讓我感到頭痛。

B：也不一定要自己想。你可以去做市場調查，給自己新的想法。

A：這是個好主意！還有其他我需要注意的嗎？

B：做好市場現況分析和競爭者分析，我想大概就成功一半了吧。

A：真謝謝你！

B：那當然（不客氣）！（隱含有：這點小事不言謝的意思。）

Answers to the Unit:

Innovation or die；market research；analysis of current market；competitor analysis；You bet

Unit 01 Analysis of Current Market-2
在現實中找一條出路

Background Introduction 背景介紹：

Bruce and Ada are colleagues, they both work under Duncan's management. They are talking about the internal environment analysis in their new cosmetic products which are going to be launched in one month.
布魯斯和愛達是同事，而且兩人都在鄧肯的管理之下。他們正在討論即將於一個月內上市的新化妝品的內部環境分析。

Conversation 2 對話 2

	(At the conference room)	（在會議室裡）
Duncan	So, I **suppose that** both of you have no **further** question for the new products we are going to launch.	那麼，我想你們兩位對於我們即將要上市的新品都沒有進一步問題了吧。
Bruce	I am not sure, boss. It seems that there are so many questions still **remain unanswered**.	我不太確定耶，主管。看起來好像還有很多懸而未決的問題。
Ada	I agree with Bruce. Can we **delay launch** of these new blush and pressed powder?	我同意布魯斯的話。我們可以延遲上市這些新的腮紅和粉底？

Duncan	Let's **go through** all the details and then decide what we should do later.	讓我們很快地檢查一遍所有的細節，然後稍後我們再決定該怎麼做。
Bruce	Great!　Start with me.　Our SGS testing is still on going and the results won't come out before next Friday.	好的！從我開始吧。我們的 SGS 測試還在進行中，而且結果在下週五之前都不會出來。
Ada	Financial department is still calculating the costs of these two new products, I think they won't give us answers until the middle of this month.	財務部門也還在計算兩個新品的成本，我想到月中之前他們都不會給我們答案。
Duncan	If so, we will not have enough time to print the **retail price** on the packaging.	如果是這樣的話，那我們就來不及把零售價印在包裝上了。
Ada	That's what I am talking about.	這就是我在説的。
Duncan	What else we need to check?	還有其他我們需要確認的嗎？
Bruce	Not only the price on packaging box, but also the design of packaging has not been confirmed yet.	不只是包裝上的價格，連包裝的設計都還沒被確認喔。

Part I

Part II

Part III

Part IV

Part V

Part VI

Part I　Part II　Part III　Part IV　Part V　Part VI

Duncan	I thought we **reached an agreement** last week!	我以為我們上週已經達成共識了！
Bruce	No, boss. I am afraid that General Manager has changed his mind again, and maybe he forgot to **send an email with Cc.** to you on the weekend.	沒有，主管。恐怕總經理又改變主意了，而且也許他週末寄出的信忘記寄副本給你。
Ada	Moreover, sales team also pointed out that they do not have enough part-time workers to send **giveaways** during the promotion period.	還有，銷售團隊也說了他們沒有足夠的工讀生在促銷期間發送贈品。
Duncan	I heard from last week's meeting. Haven't they solved the problem yet?	上週會議我就聽說了。他們還沒解決這問題？
Ada	I am afraid not.	恐怕沒有。
Duncan	OK, I will talk with their manager. Maybe we can ask ABC event company to help us this time.	好吧，我會和他們的經理談的。也許這次可以請 ABC 活動公司幫忙我們。

Ada	That is a good idea. I will call them and let you know what they suggest immediately.	這是個好主意。我會打電話給他們，並且讓您即刻知道他們的建議。
Duncan	Please **consult with** Bruce before you reply to the sales team.	回覆銷售團隊之前請與布魯斯商量。
Ada	Yes, I will.	我會的。
Duncan	It seems that we need to delay launch of new products this time **due to** the financial and design problem. Except that, I guess everything is good here?	看來因為財務和設計的問題需要延遲上市了。除此之外，我猜其他事都沒問題吧。
Bruce	No further questions so far.	目前為止沒有進一步問題了。
Ada	Me neither.	我也沒有。

Part I
Part II
Part III
Part IV
Part V
Part VI

知識補給站

　　從對話 3 我們可以清楚地看見，推出新產品不只是一個部門的事情，也牽涉到其他部門。

　　對話中因為財務和包裝設計的不確定（uncertainty），而必須延遲新品上市時間；銷售團隊也來不及補齊發送贈品的工讀生人手，就算上市了，也要面臨促銷期間沒有促銷活動的窘境（awkward situation）。由此可知，內部環境分析（或稱企業自身優劣勢評估）對新產品或新服務上市的重要性，不亞於外部環境的分析。

　　為了方便和快速了解新品上市的企業內部評估，下表提供一些但不僅止於此的檢視條件（viewing conditions）：

Checking Items 檢視項目	Advantages 優勢	Disadvantages 劣勢
Production skills 生產技術 ● Inventory and cost 庫存與成本 ● Scale and capacity 規模與產能 ● Just-in-time and flexible production capacity 準時與彈性生產能力		
Research and development 研究發展 ● Results and **patents** 成果與專利 ● Equipment and funding 設備與經費		
Human resources 人力資源 ● Staff selection and training 員工甄選與訓練 ● Staff quality 員工素質 ● Employee involvement 員工參與程度		

Checking Items　檢視項目	Advantages 優勢	Disadvantages 劣勢
Financial and Legal 財務與法務 ● **Gearing ratio** 資產負債比率 ● Financial stability 財務穩定性 ● Cash flow 現金流 ● Familiar with industry law 熟悉產業法律		
Marketing and Sales 行銷與銷售 ● Market share 市場占有率 ● Product margins 產品利潤 ● Product positioning 產品定位 ● Channels and retail effectively 通路與零售 　效能 ● Customer relationship 顧客關係		

　　再次提醒，檢視企業自身的條件是否對新產品或服務上是有利，需要考慮情境與競爭對手；例如，推出保養品就需要以主攻保養品的品牌為假想敵，彩妝用品則是與彩妝見長的品牌競爭，否則就是對牛彈琴（**cast pearls before swine**）。還有，必須從目標消費者（target consumers）的角度來分析自身優劣勢；如果是針對年輕族群（young people）推出的飲料口味，就應該和針對年長族群（elder people）推出的口味，甚至口感不相同。

　　最後，新品上市還需要衡量企業、品牌和產品的定位（positioning）。最簡單的例子就是，法式餐廳推出新的台菜（Taiwanese cuisine），或者訴求與當地環境共存的民宿，新開幕（new opening）時辦起夜店（night clubs）搖滾派對，都顯示定位失焦的問題。

Related Word 相關詞彙

1. internal　內部的

   文法加油站：反義詞為 external。

2. *文法加油站：suppose 還有下列兩種用法：*

   (1) 主詞＋ be 動詞＋（not）＋ supposed ＋ to V . 用以表示（不）應該做某事

   He is supposed to bring me a hot coffee.　他應該幫我帶杯熱咖啡的。

   She is not supposed to marry that guy.　她不應該嫁給那個人的。

   (2) Suppose ＋假設條件句＋主要問句用以表示 如果…的話，該怎麼辦？

   Suppose John can't make it，how will we do?　如果約翰趕不來的話，我們該怎麼辦？

3. *文法加油站：further 和 farther 都是 far 的比較級，用法稍有不同。*

   Farther 多用在形容距離上的遠；further 用在形容程度上的深入。

   Go farther and fare worse.　每況愈下。

   We inquire further into this investigation.　我們要求進一步的調查。

4. remain unanswered　有待釐清的、懸而未決的

5. delay launch　延遲上市

6. go through　很快地檢查一遍

   文法加油站：go through 延伸有下列兩意思：

   (1) Don't go through my phone!　別亂看（亂動）我的手機！

   (2) How many pairs of shoes does an NBA player go through per season?
   一位 NBA 球星一季要換多少雙球鞋？

7. retail price　零售價

8. reach an agreement　達成共識

9. giveaway　促銷贈品

10. awkward situation　尷尬的情況

11. patent　專利

12. Gearing ratio　資產與負債比率

13. cast pearls before swine 原意是丟珍珠在豬的面前，用來諷刺某人不懂得價值。亦可引伸為對牛彈琴。

Exercises 練習題

Please complete the word or sentence by filling in the blanks.

A：I heard that product Z is going to ＿＿＿＿＿＿＿ . You probably be the only one who didn't receive a ＿＿＿＿＿＿＿ copy.

B：Do you know the reason?

A：The sales and marketing teams didn't ＿＿＿＿＿＿＿ , for some kind of ＿＿＿＿＿＿＿ thing.

B：They didn't ＿＿＿＿＿＿＿ each other? Will it ＿＿＿＿＿＿＿ until new product launched?

A：I hope not.

B：Do you think these two departments are usually ＿＿＿＿＿＿＿ ? They don't understand each other's needs.

A：Tell me about it.

請填空完成下面句子或單字

A：聽説 Z 產品要延遲上市了。你可能是唯一沒有接到副本信件的人吧。

B：原因是什麼呢？

A：銷售與行銷團隊沒有達成共識，好像是為了促銷贈品的事吧。

B：難道彼此事先沒有商量？會不會一直到新品上市都還懸而未決？

A：希望不要。

B：你覺不覺得這兩個部門經常就像是對牛彈琴，彼此都無法聽懂對方要什麼？

A：就是説嘛。

Answers to the Unit:
delay launch；carbon；reach an agreement
giveaway；consult with
remain unanswered
casting pearls before swine

Part I
Part II
Part III
Part IV
Part V
Part VI

Unit 02 Target Market and Audience
準備賣給誰

Background Introduction 背景介紹：

Cindy and Jed are classmates. They are discussing their marketing assignment, which is about who should be the target audience of new juice product.

辛蒂與杰德是同學。他們正在討論一份關於誰應該是新上市果汁的目標族群的行銷作業。

Conversation 對話

Cindy	Sorry, Jed. I think I cannot agree with you in what you just said at the class.	抱歉，杰德。我想我不太能同意你剛才在課堂上講的。
Jed	About the **target audience** of new juice drinks?	關於新果汁產品的目標族群？
Cindy	Yes. You said natural juice should target teens.	對呀。你說天然果汁應該以青少年為目標。
Jed	And single males and females.	還有單身的男性與女性。
Cindy	That's right, I agree with that part.	對，這部分我同意。
Jed	But not teens? Why not?	但不認同青少年？為什麼？

Cindy	**According to FMCG** Report, recently I read, 13-17yr age group as teens replaced juice with other drinks.	根據快速流通消費品報導，最近我讀到的，13 到 17 歲青少年喝其他飲料多於喝果汁。
Jed	I see. Did the report say what kind of **beverage** they switched to?	了解。那報導有沒有說他們改喝哪一種飲料？
Cindy	It didn't show. However, do you know who is the heaviest juice consumers instead?	沒有。但是，你知道誰才是消費果汁最多的族群？
Jed	**I have no clue.**	完全沒概念。
Cindy	They are **toddlers**. What a surprise!	是嬰幼兒耶。驚訝吧！
Jed	Not really. Maybe their parents are buying for them.	也不盡然。也許是父母買給他們的。
Cindy	You are right.	對呀。

Part I
Part II
Part III
Part IV
Part V
Part VI

Jed	In other words, parents are the target audience of juice commercial while toddlers are the real consumers.	換句話說，父母才是果汁的目標族群，而嬰幼兒是真正的消費群體。
Cindy	Cross analysis of what you tended to attract and statistic from report, natural juice should target parents and single people.	交叉分析你想要吸引的和報導統計的群體，天然果汁應該以父母和單身貴族為目標對象。
Jed	It seems like that. No matter where they live or whatever their education degrees are.	看起來好像是這樣。不管他們住在哪裡或者他們的教育程度為何。
Cindy	They should all love buying **non-preservative-added** and **low-calorie** juice for themselves or children.	他們都應該喜歡買無添加的和低卡路里的果汁，給他們自己或小孩。
Jed	Indeed. Moreover, natural is a trend. Everybody loves to be considered as an **eco-friendly** consumer nowadays.	的確。而且，天然是一種趨勢。現今每個人都喜歡被視為一個環保消費者。

Cindy	You are absolutely correct. This idea is combing **psychographic variables** and **behavior variables**.	百分之百正確。這種想法結合了心理統計變數和行為變數。
Jed	Besides, this market will show a stronger growth in the future.	除此之外，這個市場未來將強勢成長。
Cindy	Which means?	你的意思是？
Jed	We should be partners together and invest in this business.	我們應該一起合夥投資這生意。
Cindy	Cut it out. I am totally **not** businessman **material**.	別鬧了。我完全不是生意人的料。
Jed	Too bad.	太可惜了。

Part I

Part II

Part III

Part IV

Part V

Part VI

知識補給站

　　無論是改良式產品或服務，還是全新推出的新品與新服務，新產品上市企劃裡，目標市場、產品定位（product positioning）、整體行銷策略（marketing strategy）是三個重要的環節。

　　目標市場即目標客群，也就是準備買這項新品或服務的消費者。我們都知道一樣商品或服務不可能全世界或全台灣的人都喜歡甚至願意買單，所以替新品找出目標族群（target market/consumer/buyer/audience）就很重要，因為他們都是會為這樣產品或服務付費的消費者。

為了描述這些目標族群，行銷提案上描述得越詳細越好。這些描述方式分別有：

1. 人口統計變數（demographic variables）：年齡（age）、性別（sexual）、職業（profession）、教育背景（education background）、所得（income）、宗教（religion）、族裔（ethic）。意即這項新產品或服務的能購買對象，是男是女？比例是多少？具有什麼教育程度？居住在什麼城市？從事著什麼工作？甚至宗教信仰？人種？要提醒的是，如果非特殊產品，一般是不需要用到宗教和人種的定位，不過我們也可以想一想，殯葬服務業（burial service）的新產品或服務，可能就需要針對不同宗教信仰和族裔而提供不同產品和服務。

2. 心理統計變數（psychographic variables）：包含人格特質（personality traits）、生活型態（lifestyle）、價值觀（values）的分析與描述。舉例來說，有巧克力廠商打出「個人獨享時刻（enjoy personal moment）」也有廠商主攻「與好朋友分享（share with friends）」的口號，就是吸引不同人格特質的消費者。還有車廠推出適合全家戶外出遊（family outdoor adventures）的車型，也有小巧玲瓏的卡通造型車款（mini cartoon style），也是為了滿足不

同生活型態的車主。

價值觀則是一種觀念，在關鍵時刻引導人做出不同是非判斷。例如：先享受後付款（play now, pay later）對某些年輕人來說沒有什麼不對，對老一輩的人來說說服力可能不大。

3. 行為變數（behavior variables）：屬於顯而於外的變數描述，不像心理統計變數，描述的是屬於內在的想法。這個變數包含消費者追求的利益（pursuit of interests）、使用時機（when to use）和使用頻率（frequency of use）。換句話說，消費者買新品或嘗試新服務，是為了滿足快速抵達目的地（選搭高鐵）還是更自由的出行方案（甲地借乙地還的租車服務），又或者是為了滿足自我實現（**self-realization**）的利益，而加入環保團體或選擇天然、有機（organic），甚至素食（vegetarian）的飲食方式。

購買時機很多元，諸如週年慶特價（Anniversary sales）、母親節、中元普渡，甚至電影的早場優惠…等等都是時機的考量與選擇。

使用頻率則是產品與服務推出的重要考量之一，一般而言，使用者經常要用到或購買的，價格會相對低一點，如果久久才用到一次，通常價格會貴一點，例如柴米油鹽和珠寶的對比。另外，公司或品牌也會針對買多一點優惠多一點的方式，刺激銷售，譬如買三送一（buy three get one free）、家庭包裝（**family pack**）…等等，就是這種考量。

Part I

Part II

Part III

Part IV

Part V

Part VI

Related Word 相關詞彙

1. target audience　目標群眾

    文法加油站：*audience* 本意是觀眾，在此已經延伸為消費者、使用者的意思。

2. According to…　根據…

    文法加油站：*according to* 的用法有下列兩種：

    (1) 表示根據某學說、期刊、法律、習慣、慣例、情況，或某人。

    Professor A's theory would be wrong if according to Professor X's.

    A 教授的理論可能是錯的，如果根據 X 教授的理論的話。

    (2) 表示隨…而定的意思。

    These watermelons have been graded according to their sizes.

    這些西瓜已經依照大小分類好了。

3. FMCG Fast Moving Consumer Goods （快速消費品）的簡稱，舉凡生活雜貨、食品飲料、日用品等經常需要購買和補貨的產品。

4. beverage　飲料

    文法加油站：*beverage* 指除了水以外的飲料，為可數名詞。，常和 *food* 並用；可以簡稱 *F&B*。

5. I have no clue　直譯為我完全沒有線索，引申為我不知道的意思。

6. toddlers1-3　歲的嬰幼兒

7. non-preservative-added　無添加的

8. low-calorie　低卡路里

9. eco-friendly　環保的，對環境友善的

10. psychographic variables　心理統計變數

11. behavior variables　行為變數

12. not…material　不是…的料

13. demographic variables　人口統計變數

14. self-realization　自我實現

15. family pack　家庭包裝

    文法加油站：國外購物時，所謂的大包裝都是指可以和家庭成員一起享用的，故以 *family* 來代替 *big* 或 *large*，理解後就更容易記憶也可以感覺到更貼近國外的生活習慣。

Exercises 練習題

Please complete the word or sentence by filling in the blanks.

A：I heard that you are working at _____ （FMCG）industry.

B：Yah, why?

A：I am wondering if you knew _____ drink is a _____ over the world?

B：_____ .

A：Made from local ingredients, _____ , and pure nature juice.

B：Oh, I see.

A：Do you want one?

B：You carry them all the time! You are really their _____ !

請填空完成下面句子或單字

A：聽說你在快速流通消費品產業上班？

B：是呀，怎麼了？

A：不曉得你知不知道環保飲料在全球掀起新風潮？

B：完全沒頭緒。

A：利用在地食材、無添加、純天然的果汁就是。

B：哦，我懂你的意思了。

A：要來一杯嗎？

B：你隨身攜帶！看來你還真是他們的目標消費者呢！

Answers to the Unit:

fast moving consumer goods

eco-friendly

trend

I have no clue

non-preservative-added

target market/consumer/buyer/audience

Part I

Part II

Part III

Part IV

Part V

Part VI

Unit 03　Product Positioning-1
商品的特色

Background Introduction 背景介紹：

Theodore is Marketing Manager and Oz is Product Manager, they are discussing the positioning of new canned coffee which is going to be launched few months later.

西奧多是行銷經理，奧茲是產品經理。他們正在討論即將上市的罐裝咖啡定位問題。

Conversation 1　對話 1

Oz	There are already so many flavors of canned coffee in the market, and I just personally think it would be difficult to **squeeze** any type of coffee **in** this market.	市面上已經有很多罐裝咖啡的口味了，我個人認為很難再把任何咖啡擠進這市場裡。
Theodore	There must be some space for **new comers**.	一定有些空間給新進入者。
Oz	All right. My opinion is we look over all canned coffee positioning, then we decide which positioning we are going to adopt.	好吧。我的意見是我們檢視一遍所有罐裝咖啡的定位，然後我們再決定要採取哪一種定位。
Theodore	It sounds great.	聽起來很棒。

Oz	We already have mocha, latte, hazelnut latte, caramel macchiato, cappuccino, **Americano** under coffee product line. What else we could come out?	在咖啡的產品線之下，我們已經有摩卡、拿鐵、榛果拿鐵、焦糖瑪奇朵、卡布奇諾和美式咖啡口味。我們還可以想出什麼其他的？
Theodore	These are only product flavors, not equal to product positioning.	這些只是產品風味，不等於產品定位。
Oz	Maybe you can explain a little further for me.	也許你可以解釋多一點給我聽。
Theodore	I am glad to. We need to find out their attributes, functions, **benefits for** consumers and personalities.	我很樂意。我們需要找出它們的屬性、功能、對消費者的利益以及個性。
Oz	I understand attributes and functions. For instances, color, size, price, quicker service, speed up **metabolism, et cetera et cetera**.	我了解屬性與功能。例如：顏色、尺寸、價格、更快的服務、加速新陳代謝…之類的。
Theodore	Yes, take our coffee for an example. Attributes could be different flavors and functions are keeping consumers awake.	是的，就拿我們咖啡為例。屬性可能是不同的風味，而功能則是提神。

Part I
Part II
Part III
Part IV
Part V
Part VI

Oz	But I don't understand the benefit or personality. It sounds strange for me if you say a canned coffee has its own personality.	但是我不懂利益和個性。如果你對我說罐裝咖啡是有自己個性的話，我會感到很奇怪。
Theodore	Product benefits are **actual factor**, such as better design or performance, or **perceived factor**, such as popularity or reputation that satisfies what a customer needs or wants. For example, product X is designed to deliver **antiperspirant** protection to make you feel fresh all the time. As personality, thinking what do you feel when I mention Red Bull?	產品利益是滿足顧客所需或所想要的實質的因素，例如更好的設計或效能，或是情感的因素，例如受歡迎或信譽良好。舉例來說，X產品是被設計來有止汗防護功效，可以使你一整天覺得清爽。至於個性，如果我提到紅牛飲料你會聯想到什麼？
Oz	Innovated, excitement and sporty.	創新的、興奮的和運動型的。
Theodore	Yes, just like describe a human being. Sometimes we buy this product or brand is because we think we have the similar or same personality with it.	對了，就像描述一個人一樣。有時候我們購買這個產品或品牌，是因為我們覺得和它之間有相似或共同的個性。

Part I
Part II
Part III
Part IV
Part V
Part VI

Oz	Now **I know where you are coming from**.	現在我懂你的意思了。
Theodore	Sometimes we use **product perceptual map** to help us positioning.	有時候我們會用產品知覺圖幫助我們定位。
Oz	How does it work?	怎麼做呢？
Theodore	Put one feature on X-axis and the other on Y-axis, and then you suppose to know what is yours and competitors' position at the market.	把一個產品特色放在 X 軸而另一個放 Y 軸，然後你就可以知道你和競爭對手在市場上的位置了。
Oz	Canned coffee for example, maybe we can compare the degree of coffee roasting and sweetness. Our products are positioning in light roasted and taste sweeter.	以罐裝咖啡為例吧，也許我們可以比較咖啡烘培程度和甜度，我們的產品都定位在輕烘培與偏甜的口感。
Theodore	Very impressive! You are a quick learner.	真令人印象深刻！你學得很快嘛。
Oz	It's **a walk in the park**.	沒什麼，輕而易舉。

Part I

Part II

Part III

Part IV

Part V

Part VI

Theodore	So, what we lack in the market now?	所以，我們在市場上還缺少什麼？
Oz	I will say stronger flavor, such as espresso or heavy roast coffee. We also can develop sugar free or special flavor, such as adding soy milk or green tea.	我會說是強烈一點的風味，例如義式濃縮或重烘培咖啡。我們也可以開發無糖或特殊風味，例如添加豆漿或綠茶。
Theodore	I think we should do it step by step.	我覺得我們應該慢慢來。
Oz	Sure, let's focus on espresso first.	當然，我們先專注在義式咖啡吧。

Part I

Part II

Part III

Part IV

Part V

Part VI

　要做好產品定位，就不能不知道品牌的四大構面（AFBP），以及善加運用產品知覺圖，或稱品牌知覺圖（brand perceptual map）。

　AFBP 是屬性（attributes）、功能（functions）、利益（benefits）、個性（personalities）的簡稱。屬性有分顯而於外的和無形的，例如：尺寸、顏色、價格高低、體積大小、氣味、設計等等。功能則是產品或品牌提供什麼實質的功用，譬如：防盜（anti-theft）、加速新陳代謝（speed up metabolism）等等。

　利益是消費者從中獲得什麼好處或者解決了什麼問題，例如：臉書（Facebook）幫助找到失散多年的小學同學、愛馬仕包讓提的人感覺周遭投射而來的羨慕（projection of envy）。個性則是在高價、涉入程度高，或是用來彰顯個人品味的產品或品牌上，較常運用的手法；例如，房仲業（real estate brokers）強調值得信賴（**trust worthy**）、某房車強調愛家的新好男人（a modern man）的選擇等等。

　產品（品牌）知覺圖則是以 X 與 Y 軸劃分出的四個象限，如下所示：

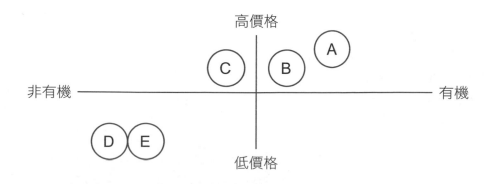

Related Word 相關詞彙

1. canned coffee　罐裝咖啡

   文法加油站：canned 後面可以加可能製成罐裝的物品，例如：canned cat food 罐裝貓食。

2. squeeze in　擠進去

   I can squeeze this meeting in my schedule. 我可以把這次面談擠進時間表裡（意即已經很忙了，但還是可以安排）。

   文法加油站：反義詞為 squeeze out，排擠的意思。

   Company A shouldn't squeeze out competitors with undue conducts of competition.

   A 公司不應該以不正當手段排擠競爭對手。

3. new comer　新進入者

4. Americano=Caffé Americano　原拼法為「美國式」的義大利文，在此指美式咖啡。

5. benefit for…　對…有利

   文法加油站：benefit 為利益、好處的意思。 benefit from 為從何得利的意思

6. metabolism　代謝

7. et cetera et cetera　之類的

   文法加油站：為拉丁原文，類似說法還有：and other things, and so on, and so forth, and the rest

8. actual factor　實質因素

9. perceived factor　情感（感性）的因素

10. antiperspirant　止汗劑

11. I know where you are coming from　（我了解）你的觀點與想法

    文法加油站：這可不是問你從哪裡來的問句。這句話是表示我知道你在想什麼或者你在表達什麼的意思，是一句相當口語的用法。

12. product perceptual map　產品知覺圖

13. a walk in the park = a piece of cake　輕而易舉的事

14. trust worthy　值得信賴的

Exercises 練習題

Please complete the word or sentence by filling in the blanks.

A：Look at this ＿＿＿＿＿＿ map here, I don't think there is any ＿＿＿＿＿＿ can ＿＿＿＿＿＿ in this market.

B：It seems like difficult. How about we ＿＿＿＿＿＿ some competitors?

A：I would love to, but how?

B：We should think any product feature which consumer can ＿＿＿＿＿＿ .

A：Right, how about anti- ＿＿＿＿＿＿ function?

B：Very impressive ！ You are a genius!

A：It is ＿＿＿＿＿＿ .

請填空完成下面句子或單字

A：看看這張產品知覺圖，我覺得市場擠不進去任何新進入者了。

B：看起好像是這樣。那不如我們擠掉一些競爭者吧？

A：我很樂意，但是怎麼做呢？

B：我們該想想任何消費者可以從中獲利的產品特色。

A：有了，止汗的功能怎麼樣？

B：太令我印象深刻了！你真是天才！

A：沒什麼，小事一樁。

Answers to the Unit:
product perceptual
new comer
squeeze
squeeze out
benefit from
perspirant
a walk in the park (a piece of cake)

Part I　Part II　Part III　Part IV　Part V　Part VI

Unit 03 Product Positioning-2
商品的特色

Part I

Part II

Part III

Part IV

Part V

Part VI

Background Introduction 背景介紹：

Dora is Al's student. One day, she asks Al about the five product levels.
朵拉是艾爾的學生。有一天，朵拉向艾爾請教關於商品的五個層次的疑問。

Conversation 2 對話2

	(Dora knocked on the door)	（朵拉敲了敲門）
Al	Yes, please come in.	是，請進。
Dora	Hello, Professor. I am sorry to bother you, but I have few questions **regarding** the five product levels you said this morning.	您好，教授。很抱歉打擾您，但我有關於今早您提到的產品五個層次的疑問想請教您。
Al	What are your questions?	你的問題是？
Dora	Could you please explain again the whole **concept** for me?	可以請您再次解釋整個概念嗎？

Al	Sure, it is easy. When you go to buy something, you are looking for some needs or wants which is waiting to be satisfied. No matter it is milk, sugar, or a birthday cake.	當然，很簡單。當你去購物的時候，你是在找某些可以滿足需求或慾望的東西。不管是買牛奶、糖，或者一個生日蛋糕。
Dora	Yes, this is easy to understand.	了解，這部份很容易懂。
Al	So, you will choose a product based on **perceived value** of it.	所以，你會根據期望的價值來選擇一項商品。
Dora	Things are getting a bit more difficult.	我想事情開始有點難度了。
Al	For example, what kind of birthday cake you will buy for your mother?	舉例來說，你會給媽媽買什麼樣的生日蛋糕？
Dora	It must look **lovely**, delicious, maybe with many flowers decorating on it.	一定是看起來討人喜歡的，可口的，也許有很多花裝飾在上面吧。

Part I

Part II

Part III

Part IV

Part V

Part VI

Part I
PartII
PartIII
PartIV
Part V
PartVI

Al	Good. So, you go to a cake shop and tell them that you are looking for this cake. Do you think they will provide you an exactly the same cake which you asked for?	很好。所以你走進一家蛋糕店，然後告訴他們你正在找這樣的蛋糕。你想他們會提供你一個正在找尋的一模一樣的蛋糕嗎？
Dora	I wish. You know, Professor, one time, my brother bought a terrible cake from the shop we usually visit. Nobody knows what happened in the shop that day.	但願如此。您知道嗎，教授，有一次我哥哥從我們經常去的蛋糕店買了一個很糟的蛋糕。沒人知道那天店裡到底發生了什麼事情。
Al	You see, you had negative experience from that shop. Would you expect more from them now?	你看，你從店裡有了負面的經驗。那麼你現在對他們還會有更多的期待嗎？
Dora	Sadly, we are thinking to find another store.	難過的是，我們考慮找另一間蛋糕店。
Al	OK. Let's suppose that you were looking for a cake shop, which is not just making delicious cakes. What else would you like them to have?	好。讓我們假設你要找一間蛋糕店，它不僅僅是製作好吃的蛋糕。你還希望它們有什麼？

Dora	Maybe different **varieties** of cakes, delivery service, some places to sit down with families or friends would also be great. Perhaps they sell not only cakes, but other sweeties.	也許是很多不同種類的蛋糕，宅配服務，可以有空間和家人與朋友坐下來的話更好。或者不只是賣蛋糕，也賣其他甜點。
Al	I guess some coffee or space for kids to play around would be nicer?	我猜來點咖啡或者有空間給小孩玩耍會更好？
Dora	Oh, isn't it too much?	喔，那樣不會要求太多了嗎？
Al	Consumers never feel satisfied. Therefore, companies need to find out different level of product to make customers happy. For example, the Core Benefit of a cake is to make family or friends happy when you share with it.	消費者永遠不會滿足的。因此，公司才需要發掘產品不同的內涵讓顧客感到快樂。例如，一個蛋糕的核心價值是分享時，讓家人或朋友們感到快樂。
Dora	**I couldn't agree with you more**.	再贊同不過了。

Al

The second point is to taste delicious, you cannot call it a cake if it was not even tasty. Which is the second product level, we call it **Generic Product**. The third part is Expected Product, which means buyers normally expect and agree to when they purchase a product. Take cake for instance, maybe beautiful packaging and candles inside, sometimes it is a reasonable price.

第二是它要嘗起來好吃，你可不能稱它是蛋糕，如果它一點也不好吃的話。這就是第二個產品層次，我們稱它為通用產品。第三部分是期待產品，意思是說購買者通常期待或同意他們要買的東西。拿蛋糕來說吧，也是許漂亮的包裝和附贈蠟燭，有時候是合理的價錢。

Dora

I see, thank you for explain so clearly to me, Professor.

我懂了，謝謝您為我解釋得那麼詳細，教授。

Al

Not finished yet, my dear. Remember we have five levels? The fourth is called **Augmented** Product, which means a product's physical attributes and the non-physical attributes that are added to increase the product's value. So, customization could be a good idea for this level.

還沒說完呢，親愛的。記得有五個層次吧。第四個稱作附加產品，意思是使產品價值提升的有形或無形的屬性。所以，客製化在這個層次裡可能是個好主意。

Dora

Like a photo cake.

就像相片蛋糕。

AI	Yes, it could be. The final level is Potential Product, which means the **augmentations** and **transformations** a product might undergo in the future.	對，可能。最後一個層次是潛在產品，表示未來產品可進行的擴建或轉換。
Dora	Just like you mentioned, the idea of combining with a coffee shop or become a childcare center?	就像您剛才提到的，（蛋糕店）結合咖啡店或成為兒童照顧中心？
AI	Not so dramatic, but any cake shop could spend time on thinking about this topic. Remember, customers are happy only if the actual value is the same or exceeds the perceived value.	也沒那麼戲劇化，但是任何一個蛋糕店可能都可以花點時間想一下這議題。記住，顧客會感到開心，只有當產品的實際價值等於或大於期待價值。
Dora	I will remember that, thank you again, Professor.	我會記住的，再次感謝您，教授。

Part I

Part II

Part III

Part IV

Part V

Part VI

知識補給站

　　根據產品的或服務的內涵層次，行銷上劃分有五個層次，這個概念來自於行銷大師——菲利浦‧科特勒（Philip Kotler）。依照同心圓的位置，最裡面為核心利益（Core Benefit），往外擴散，分別是通用產品（Generic Product，又稱實質產品 Actual Product 或基本產品 Basic Product）、期望產品（Expected Product）、附加價值（Augmented Product）、潛在產品（Potential Product）。

　　對應行銷策略上的思考，核心利益是消費者希望從中得到的好處或期望解決的問題；例如：看醫生是希望病情得到好轉或控制，買一份報紙則是希望得知新聞大事或新知。通用產品則是產品最基本包含的內容或服務，舉例來說，看醫生時至少要有醫生在，報紙則至少要有文字在紙上供閱讀。

　　期望產品很容易理解，就是消費者期望的產品或服務是什麼？看醫生時或許期望遇見和藹可親的護士或醫生，乾淨的環境…等等，報紙則是可能有搭配得宜的照片，印刷清楚或容易閱讀的文字。附加產品則是超越消費者期待（go beyond consumer expectations）或與眾不同的產品或服務；例如有些兒童診所佈置得宛如小型迪士尼樂園，有些報紙則是有很多好康優惠券（coupons），或者物超所值的訂閱贈品（**bargain** gift）…等等。潛在產品則是未來可以增進消費者利益的，例如醫師提供到府看病服務（door doctor services），雜誌推出線上電子版，可以隨時隨地下載過期內容…等等。

　　科特勒也提醒，現今眾多企業或行銷人員著眼於第二層的通用產品多於核心利益；但將核心利益放在圓心不是沒有道理。還是以蛋糕為例，核心利益是與人共享時感到快樂，那麼層層圍繞的產品層次，都應該符合快樂分享（happy to share）的主題，所以才會延伸出：可口、包裝美觀、附上蠟燭甚至刀叉、外送服務、坐下來享受的空間等等產品或服務層次。

Related Word 相關詞彙

1. regarding⋯ 關於⋯

   文法加油站：*同義詞有很多可以運用，About, Regarding, As regards, With regard to, In regard to, In terms of, Concerning, As concerns, As for⋯等都可以。*

2. concept 概念

3. perceived value 感知到的價值。是消費者自己心理認定的價值，多數時並不等於標籤上的價錢。

4. lovely 討人喜歡的

   文法加油站：*也可當作一種回應，表示太好了。*

   例如：*A：Would you like some coffee? B：Lovely. = Wonderful. = Sure.*

5. variety 多樣化

6. couldn't agree with you more 再同意不過了

   文法加油站：*more 也可置換為 anymore。*

7. generic product 通用產品

8. augmented 附加的

9. customization 客製化，訂製

10. augmentation 擴建

11. transformation 轉換，轉型

12. bargain 物超所值的

    文法加油站：*名詞為討價還價，此為形容詞。*

    名詞用法為 bargain/haggle/dicker + with + someone + over/about + something

    My mom is bargaining with the woman over the price of a handbag. 我媽正和那位女士為了一個手提包討價還價。

Part I
Part II
Part III
Part IV
Part V
Part VI

Unit 04　New Product Launch Activities-1
有什麼方式可以吸引顧客

Background Introduction 背景介紹：

Kimberly, Miranda and Ryan are checking new product launch activities checklist they have made yesterday. It seems like there are plenty of things they need to prepare for the upcoming events.

金柏莉，米蘭達與雷恩正在確認昨天擬好的新產品上市活動清單。看來為了即將到來的活動，他們有好多事情要準備。

Conversation 1 對話 1

Kimberly	I really want to **catch up on some Zs**.	我真的好想補眠。
Miranda	Me too. I am so tired now, it is all yesterday's fault. We shouldn't **stay up late** for this.	我也是。我現在好累，都是昨天的錯。我們不應該為此熬夜的。
Ryan	Pull yourselves together, please. Let's go through this as quick as possible.	振作一點，拜託。我們盡快檢視一遍吧。
Miranda	Yes, you are right. Let's **proceed**. Who wants to responsible for the **press conference** on 15th, July?	好吧，你是對的。我們繼續進行吧。誰想要負責 7 月 15 日的媒體記者會？

Kimberly	I would love to take responsibility for them again since l had more experiences here.	既然我是這裡有較多經驗的，我樂意再次負責。
Ryan	Thanks, Kimberly, you know I don't like to **deal with** these reporters.	謝啦，金柏莉，你知道我不喜歡和這些媒體們打交道。
Miranda	This means you will write **news release**, prepare press kit and work with PR event company to handle the medias on that day.	這表示你會撰寫新聞稿、準備媒體資料袋，以及和公關公司一起掌控當天到場的媒體。
Kimberly	Sure, no problem.	當然，沒問題。
Ryan	I can help in charging sales training, including training materials and explaining promotion activities we are going to proceed.	我可以幫忙負責銷售訓練，包括訓練教材以及解釋我們即將進行的促銷活動。
Miranda	Are you going to present them new product **brochures** and **flyers**?	你也將展示新產品的手冊和宣傳單給他們？
Ryan	I guess the answer would be yes.	我猜答案是對呀。

Part I

Part II

Part III

Part IV

Part V

Part VI

Kimberly	So you will on a business trip to Kaohsiung and Taichung next week?	所以你下週將會出差到高雄和台中？
Ryan	Yes, the training programs should be done before new product launch activities, otherwise our counter salespeople won't know how these activities work, will they?	是的，訓練計畫應該在新品上市活動之前就完成，否則我們的專櫃銷售人員不會知道怎麼進行這些活動，不是嗎？
Miranda	Could you also help in **following up** the progress of brochures printing?	你也可以幫忙追蹤手冊印製的進度？
Ryan	No problem. I will get it done before I travel to the South.	沒問題。我會在去南部出差之前搞定的。
Miranda	Great. I think I am going to responsible for the rest things then.	太棒了。我想我就負責其他剩下的事情吧。
Kimberly	Does that mean you will handle the **road shows** in the North and South, also online **campaign**?	這表示你也會負責北部和南部的路演，以及線上活動？

Miranda	I can do the online marketing, but not sure about the road shows. I guess I need a hand.	我可以負責網路行銷，但是不確定路演的部分。我想我需要幫忙。
Ryan	Don't look at me, **my hands are full**.	別看我，我沒空。
Kimberly	I will work with you. But since they messed up last activity, are you sure you want the PR company to join us this time?	我和你一起吧。但是因為公關公司搞砸了上次的活動，你確定這次想要公關公司再次參與嗎？
Miranda	**Hell no**. Don't worry, I will find another one.	絕不。別擔心，我會找到另外一家的。
Ryan	Did we talk about the **direct marketing** yet?	我們談到直效行銷了沒？
Kimberly	No way! I cannot believe we have so many things need to be done in three weeks. It really is a Mission Impossible.	不會吧！我不敢相信我們在三個禮拜內有那麼多需要完成的事情。這真是「不可能的任務」。

Part I

Part II

Part III

Part IV

Part V

Part VI

Part I

Part II

Part III

Part IV

Part V

Part VI

Miranda	I guess that will also under the charge of Kimberly and me, because we can do it through combining with the online campaign.	我想這也在我和金柏莉負責範圍內，因為我們可以透過結合網路活動來進行。
Kimberly	Yes, but how?	是呀，但是怎麼做呢？
Miranda	We send direct emails to the user list we gather from online campaign, and we also can use our customers' database to communicate new product launch activities during the promotion period.	我們可以寄送直郵給從網路活動蒐集到的顧客名單，在促銷期間，也可以利用我們顧客資料庫溝通新產品上市的訊息。
Kimberly	Good idea, let's do it.	好主意，我們進行吧。
Ryan	OK, I guess that's all.	好啦，我猜這是全部了吧。
Miranda	Yes, it is.	是的。

知識補給站

Part I

Part II

Part III

Part IV

Part V

Part VI

　　新產品上市，有較多行銷預算的公司或品牌，免不了舉辦試吃、試飲（testing/free to try）的活動，或者在人潮較多的路口，擺設宣傳據點，邀請民眾體驗或發送試用包（trial pack）。除了舉辦活動，也有廠商選擇回饋消費者，例如：半價（half price）、買一送一（buy one get one free）、買就送贈品（free gift）、買就抽獎（sweepstakes）…等等，都是常見的新品上市吸引顧客購買的活動。

　　實體通路（channels）的活動之外，因為網路的發達，各式各樣的網路活動（online events/campaigns/activities）甚至比實體通路的活動精彩。投票結合抽獎、特價秒殺（**SecKill**）、特價券…等等，真令人眼花撩亂（dazzling）。

　　無論舉辦哪一種活動，要留意的是，凸顯產品特色（features highlight）。舉例來說，如果有一款低熱量的飲料上市，舉辦了烤肉（BBQ）和無限暢飲（all you can drink）的活動，相信民眾應該不會留下深刻印象，因為這樣的活動無論哪一牌子的飲料都可以舉辦，烤肉和低熱量（low-calories）甚至是背道而馳。但是如果是請兩組消費者參加試驗，在相同飲食條件下，一組喝它牌飲料，另一組喝該低熱量飲料，一段時間後相互對照身材體重；活動不但話題十足，目標族群也容易留下深刻印象，下次要購買同類飲料時，指定該款低熱量飲料的機會就大增。

Related Word 相關詞彙

1. upcoming　即將到來的

2. catch up on some Zs　補眠

3. stay up late　熬夜

   文法加油站：同義詞還有 stay up all night, burn the midnight oil

4. proceed　繼續往前

   文法加油站：同義詞還有 continue, go on, keep going, keep on, move on.

5. press conference　記者會

6. deal with　安排，處理，打交道

   文法加油站：後可接人、事、物、錢。也可直接講 Deal with it. 表示說者要聽
   者想辦法解決的意思。

7. news release　新聞稿

   文法加油站：release 是釋出或發佈的意思，直譯為新聞發佈，已被廣泛為指
   新聞稿的意思。

8. brochure　手冊

9. flyer　宣傳單

10. following up　跟蹤，追蹤

11. road show　路演，指街頭的派贈、試吃試用、體驗活動等

12. campaign　原是競選活動的意思，現在也可泛指促銷活動

13. my hands are full　直譯為我的手已經滿了，引申為沒空的意思

14. hell nohell　是地獄的意思，兩個單字搭配在一起，就是寧願下地獄也不的
    意思

15. direct marketing　直效行銷，並非傳直銷。利用不同背景的顧客資料，傳
    達該族群的行銷訊息，達到分眾溝通的目的。

16. SecKill　秒殺

    文法加油站：Sec 是 second 的縮寫，兩個單字結合就是瞬間可以壓倒對方的
    意思，現在多引申為瞬間賣光的意思。

Exercises 練習題

Please complete the word or sentence by filling in the blanks.

Here is a new product launch preparation checklist:

✓ Road Show: _____ Deliver、_____

✓ Online Campaign: _____ promotion event

✓ _____

✓ News Release

✓ New Product _____

✓ Direct Marketing

請填空完成下面句子或單字

以下是一張新品上市準備物清單：

✓ 路演：發送試用包、宣傳單

✓ 網路活動：秒殺促銷活動

✓ 記者會

✓ 新聞稿

✓ 新品手冊

✓ 直效行銷

Answers to the Unit:

trial pack

flyer

SecKill

press conference

brochure

Unit 04 New Product Launch Activities-2
有什麼方式可以吸引顧客

Background Introduction 背景介紹 :

Benjamin and Juliet are checking distributor incentive program, which is one of increasing sales ways from their company.

茉麗葉與班傑明正在確認經銷商的獎勵計畫，這是他們公司提升新品上市銷售的方式之一。

Conversation 2 對話 2

Benjamin	When is the deadline to finish the **draft** of dealer incentive program?	何時是提出經銷商獎勵計畫初稿的截止期限？
Juliet	It's this Friday.	就是這週五。
Benjamin	Which means we don't have much time left, do we?	這表示我們沒有太多時間了，對吧？
Juliet	I am afraid not.	恐怕是的。
Benjamin	OK, let's check them **one by one**.	好，讓我們一個一個確認吧。
Juliet	Sure. The program period is **Q3** 2013, and the goal for each dealer is order over 15,000 pieces.	沒問題。獎計計畫期間是 2013 年的第三季，每位經銷商的目標是訂購 15,000 個以上。

Benjamin	Here we need a little adjustment. We need to down the number to 12,000 pieces, because I heard from one of our distributors, Mr. Chen, said that there will be less incentive if we made an **unachievable** number for everyone.	這裡我們需要一點調整。我們需要下修到 12,000 個，因為我從一位經銷商，陳先生那邊得知，如果我們訂了一個大家無法達到的數字，對經銷商來說也沒有獎勵的意義。
Juliet	He made a good point. I will remember to revise that part.	他說得很有道理。我會記得調整的。
Benjamin	Maybe we also can design it in three levels.	也許我們可以設計成三階段。
Juliet	What do you mean?	什麼意思呢？
Benjamin	For example, order 12,000 pieces and earn the award in level 1, order 20,000 pieces and earn the award in level 2, order 25,000 pieces and earn the award in level 3.	舉例來說，訂 12,000 個可以贏得第一級的獎品，訂 20,000 個可以贏得第二級的獎品，訂 25,000 個可以贏得第三級的獎品。
Juliet	That sounds more reasonable, isn't it?	聽起來很有道理，不是嗎？

Part I

Part II

Part III

Part IV

Part V

Part VI

Benjamin	I don't know yet, it is just our company never did this before. Maybe it's time to **try out**.	我也還不曉得,只是我們公司從來沒有這樣做過。也許是試試看的時候。
Juliet	Do you have any idea what the awards are for these distributors?	那你對經銷商的獎勵獎品有想法嗎?
Benjamin	I am thinking 5 start resort travel packages. What's in your mind?	我在想五星級的度假村旅遊行程耶。你的想法呢?
Juliet	Well, almost the same. I was thinking golf or spa packages.	嗯,差不多一致。我還在想高爾夫或 SPA 行程呢。
Benjamin	They are also not bad ideas. Should we combine them all?	也是不錯的想法。不如我們結合兩者吧。
Juliet	Don't forget **budget control**.	別忘了預算控制。
Benjamin	You are right. Maybe we **divide** them **into** three levels, just like we did to the order levels.	對。也許我們分成三階段,就像訂購數量那樣。
Juliet	You are so **brilliant**!	你真是天才!

Benjamin	So, first level is one night domestic spa package. Including hotel and roundtrip train tickets for two.	所以，第一級是一個晚上的國內 SPA 行程。包含兩人的飯店和來回火車票。
Juliet	The second level could be a three nights **oversea** Ritz-Carlton Resort package for two. Off course, return air tickets and F&B are all included.	第二級就是三晚的兩人海外麗思卡爾頓渡假村行程。當然，來回機票和餐飲都包含在內。
Benjamin	The third level is oversea golf package, including five hours golf courses, **roundtrip** air tickets for two and four nights at the Hyatt Resort.	第三級就是海外的高爾夫行程，包含五小時的高爾夫課程、兩人來回機票和四晚的凱悅度假村。
Juliet	What if the distributors want to bring the whole family?	如果經銷商們想要全家一起參加呢？
Benjamin	We will only pay for two people and the rest they need to pay themselves.	我們只能負擔兩個人的費用，剩下的他們要自己負擔。
Juliet	It sounds reasonable.	聽起來很合理。
Benjamin	What else we need to go through?	其他還有什麼要確認的嗎？

| Juliet | Sorry, can we go back to discuss the prizes again? I think I have something to add. | 抱歉，我們可以回頭再次討論一下獎品？我想我有些東西想要補充。 |

| Benjamin | No problem, what crossed your mind? | 沒問題，妳想到什麼？ |

| Juliet | Will it look fairer if we cancel the oversea golf package and then buy some home appliances as well as luxury goods, so we can courage more distributors to achieve the goal? | 如果我們取消海外高爾夫行程，然後採購家電用品和精品，會不會看起來比較公平，而且也鼓勵更多經銷商可以達成目標？ |

| Benjamin | The idea is good, however, I personally think most of them love oversea travel and enjoy the scenes outside the country. | 這個想法很好，但是，我個人覺得他們大部份還是喜歡海外旅遊同時也享受國外的景色。 |

| Juliet | Understood. I hope the one who get the first level award won't be too disappointed, it seems that there is a big gap between it and the other two. | 了解。我希望獲得第一級獎勵的經銷商們不會太失望，看起來好像和另外兩級有一大段差距。 |

Part I
Part II
Part III
Part IV
Part V
Part VI

　　如果公司有經銷商銷售管道，新品上市時，經銷商獎勵計畫是不會錯過的一個重點。用意無非就是想經銷商們認購越多商品越好，一方面是衝銷售量（increase sales volume），二方面因為下單就會有收入（income）產生，等於是立即看得見的錢入袋為安，對公司來說，當然是多多益善（the more the better）。

　　不過要留意（pay attention to）的是，經銷商獎勵計畫通常是有預算的，怎麼樣在預算之內規劃出吸引經銷商願意買單的獎勵機制（reward system），就很重要。其次，考驗行銷人員功力的還有，年年甚至季季端出不同以往，甚至不同於競爭對手的獎勵內容；試想如果是千遍一律（**There is not a pin to choose between**）的獎勵，就連小孩子都容易厭倦，更何況是身經百戰（hundreds of battles）的經銷商們。

　　現在用得較頻繁的獎勵計畫，不外乎是海內外旅遊。這其實有其原因，因為在忙碌一段時間以後，由公司做主人，招待辛苦一季或半年、一年的經銷商們一起去旅遊；不但在行程中可以增進彼此了解，也可以增進彼此情感，甚至又做成下一季或下一年度的訂單。所以對公司來說，團體旅遊可以一魚多吃（kill many birds with one stone），也是至今不敗的獎勵計畫主角。

　　當然除此之外，贈送高單價、平常不多見的禮物也是激勵的方式之一。例如：珠寶、鑽石、手錶、汽車等等，甚至公寓（apartment）、別墅（house）也曾經被拿來當成激勵計畫的一部分。

Related Word 相關詞彙

1. distributor incentive program　經銷商獎勵計畫

    文法加油站：*distributor 亦可置換為 dealer*

2. draft　草案，草稿

    文法加油站：*亦可做形容詞，初步的（設計圖，草圖，提綱…等）*

3. one by one　一個一個地

    文法加油站：*亦可置換為 one after another*

4. Q3　第三季

    文法加油站：*Q 為 quarter 的簡稱，表示季節。Q3 就是 7-9 月，以此類推。*

5. unachievable　無法實現的

    文法加油站：*un 加在形容詞、名詞之前，表示否定或缺乏的意思。*

6. try out　嘗試，試探

7. budget control　預算控制

8. divide…into…　把…分成幾等分

9. brilliant　優秀的，傑出的

    文法加油站：*亦有輝煌的、精彩、燦爛、亮晶晶的、漂亮的意思。*

10. oversea　海外的

    文法加油站：*over 有超越、超過的意思，sea 則是海洋。兩者結合即是海外的意思；同義詞還有 foreign, overseas, abroad*

11. roundtrip　來回的

    文法加油站：*round 為名詞是圓形物、一輪、巡迴的意思；作形容詞是圓的、豐滿的意思。roundtrip 就是來回票的意思；單程票為 one way ticket*

12. There is not a pin to choose between　直譯為從兩個大頭針裡二選一，比喻為沒有多大的差異。

Exercises 練習題

Please complete the word or sentence by filling in the blanks.

2013 Dealer Incentive _____

1. Program Period: _____ , 2013

2. Goal: Sell the Most units

3. Program Structure: The top 2 Dealers who sell the most units earn the _____ _____ travel package, the next 8 top Dealers earn the domestic travel package.

4. All packages are providing for two people. With _____ air tickets, 4 nights at luxury hotel, Golf courses and SPA time.

請填空完成下面句子或單字

2013 經銷商獎勵草案

1. 計畫期間：第四季，2013 年

2. 目標達成：賣出最多數量的

3. 計畫架構：排名前二名的經銷商可以贏得海外的旅遊行程，排名第三到十名的 8 位可以贏得國內的旅遊行程。

4. 所有行程都提供給兩個人（一人報名，兩人成行的意思）。包含來回機票，4 晚的奢華飯店，高爾夫課程和 SPA 時光。

Answers to the Unit:

Draft

Q4

oversea/overseas/foreign/abroad

roundtrip

Part I

Part II

Part III

Part IV

Part V

Part VI

Unit 04 New Product Launch Activities-3
有什麼方式可以吸引顧客

Background Introduction 背景介紹：

Jill is a Marketing Executive and Maisie is a web application engineer, they are working together to conduct an online lucky draw for the new product launch web campaign.

吉兒是行銷專員，梅西則是網站程式工程師，她們正一起為一個新品上市網路活動設計抽獎機制。

Conversation 3 對話 3

Jill	I am truly sorry, Maisie, my boss just **found fault with everything**.	真的很抱歉，梅西，我老闆真的很愛找碴。
Maisie	I couldn't handle it either if he is so changeable.	如果他這麼善變我也受不了喔。
Jill	I promise it is the last time.	我保證這是最後一次了。
Maisie	**Beggars can't be choosers**.	人在屋簷下，不得不低頭啊。
Jill	Don't worry, we will survive.	別擔心，我們會存活下來的。
Maisie	So, just tell me which part I need to **fix**?	好吧，就直說要我修改哪一部分吧。

Jill	OK, love you so much. First, we need to **extend** the period of this campaign from a week to a month.	好的，愛妳喔。首先，我們需要將活動從一週延長到四週。
Maisie	Let me write down first. Sure, not too difficult to adjust it.	讓我記下來。沒問題，要調整這個不會太困難。
Jill	Great! We also have to increase the frequency of the draw from one time to four times. Can you do that?	太好了！我們也要增加抽獎的頻率從一次到四次。你能做到嗎？
Maisie	Don't worry, the computer will do this.	別擔心，電腦可以做。
Jill	I am so afraid that I make you have a **heavier workload**.	我好擔心我會加重你的工作量。
Maisie	Are that all?	就這些嗎？
Jill	No, I am so sorry. I think we need to design a special mechanism which allows every joined consumer only has one chance to win the prize.	沒有，我很抱歉。我想我們需要設計一個特別的機制，讓每位參加者都只能有一次機會中獎。

Part I

Part II

Part III

Part IV

Part V

Part VI

Maisie	I see, no problem. I took the note already. How do we **notify** the winners?	了解，沒問題啊。我已經記下來了。我們該怎麼通知中獎者？
Jill	They will be notified by email, phone call and post.	他們會被通知，透過 E-Mail、電話和郵寄信函。
Maisie	My opinion is an email and a call will be enough, but it's your **boss's call**.	我的意見是一封 E-Mail 和一通電話就夠了，不過那是你老闆要決定的。
Jill	Right, he will decide. There are few more things. Could you please **announce** the prize winners list by 0:00am in the morning?	對呀，他會決定。還有一些事項。可以請你在凌晨 0 點公佈中獎者名單？
Maisie	No problem at all, just through setting the computer.	一點兒也沒問題，只要透過電腦設定就行了。
Jill	I love this computer! **Last but not least**, could you also help in putting new product catalogs and coupons on the campaign website for users to download?	我愛死這台電腦了！最後但並非最不重要，你也可以幫忙把新產品的目錄和折價券放到活動網站上，讓使用者下載嗎？
Maisie	You bet.	沒問題。

知識補給站

實體活動以外，在網路上進行新品上市活動的宣傳，已經成為現在企業不可忽視的一環（cannot be ignored）。網路活動經常舉辦的新品促銷方案，不外乎，贈品（giveaways）、新品組合價（set price）、期間限定的折扣（discount for a limited period）和抽獎（lucky draw）。

根據 PCHOME 商店街的統計，提供抽獎活動，能夠在新店開張的時候，吸引較多網友關注或購買以試試手氣（try luck）；而提供的獎品（prize）最好是非同產業的商品，舉例來說：3C 商品可以抽高檔的名牌包包（**designer handbags**），美食或化妝品就可以送 3C 周邊商品。除了在短期間吸引買家之外，最主要功用是透過抽獎活動，讓網友填寫資料後，蒐集買家名單（buyers list），以利分析和日後寄送電子促銷訊息（E-DM），讓顧客再次上門消費。

設計網路抽獎活動和在實體通路上運行的注意事項大致相同，唯因為透過電腦設計或設定功能，可以節省很多人工作業的時間。例如：抽獎時不需要從一大堆郵寄的名單中抽出中獎人，有時候書寫不清楚也會造成無法判別該中獎人資訊；排除重複中獎人（repeat winners）的資訊也不需要人工一個一個校對，只要輸入電腦就可以查找剔除重複的人或 IP。

不過就由於可以透過電腦控制，也讓許多消費者質疑是否真的是電腦隨機選中獎人，還是其實是透過「人腦」（**manually**）讓應當中獎的人中獎。無論如何，網路抽獎活動既有其誘惑力（attractive），也應該小心謹慎每一個步驟。

Part I

Part II

Part III

Part IV

Part V

Part VI

Related Word 相關詞彙

1. found fault with everything 雞蛋裡挑骨頭，吹毛求疵，老是找碴
   文法加油站：*You are always trying to find fault with me! 你老是想找我碴！*

2. Beggars can't be choosers　直譯為飢不擇食，引申為人在屋簷下，不得不低頭的意思。

3. fix　修理，調整，訂正
   文法加油站：*也有固定、安裝、奠定（establish）的意思。*

4. extend　延長
   文法加油站：*也有擴充、擴大、延伸、伸展的意思*

5. heavier workload　較重的工作量
   文法加油站：*heavy workload 也可以，比較級則是 heavier。*

6. notify　通知
   文法加油站：*亦可置換為 inform, notice*

7. boss's call　老闆要決定的事情
   文法加油站：*常聽見的口語是 You call，意即你做決定；並非通知你有電話要接聽的意思。是一句相當重要的口語。*

8. announce　公佈、宣佈

9. Last but not least　最後但並非最不重要的
   文法加油站：*口語和書寫上常用的一句話，通常到最後，聽者或讀者注意力可能不太集中了，可以用這句話來讓對方集中精神到最後。*

10. designer handbag　名牌包
    文法加油站：*很多名牌都是由設計師自創品牌，所以名牌包也稱作是設計師設計的包包。*

11. manually　人工地，手動地

Exercises 練習題

Please complete the word or sentence by filling in the blanks.

A：Could you help me to _____ David that tomorrow's meeting time is going to change?

B：To when ?

A：5PM. And the system has some problem now, ask him to download the attendance sheet _____ .

B：Anything else?

A：I will _____ something which is mainly relates to _____ the mistakes they made before.

B：Are these all?

A：What do you think I should wear for tomorrow's meeting?

B：It's _____ .

Part I
Part II
Part III
Part IV
Part V
Part VI

請填空完成下面句子或單字

A：你可以幫我通知大衛明天會議要改時間？

B：改到幾點？

A：下午五點。還有系統故障了，要請他手動下載簽到表。

B：還有其他的嗎？

A：我會公佈一些事項，主要是修正（釘正）他們之前的錯誤。

B：就這些了？

A：那你覺得我明天要穿什麼來開會好？

B：這是你自己要決定的。

Answers to the Unit:
notify/inform/notice
manually
announce
fix
your call

Unit 05　Key Points of Hosting a Meeting-1
主持會議要點

Situation 1　情境 1：

Kitty is presenting the new product proposal her wrote to her manager, and will ask him if there is there anything that can be adjusted.

凱蒂正在向部門主管簡報她撰寫的新產品上市計畫，並向主管請教是否有需要修改的地方。

Key points for your conversation 對話急救包

📎 開場白

Today, I would like to present a **brief** summary of my new product launch plan.
今天我想針對我的新產品上市計畫做簡短的摘要。
小貼士：brief 可置換為 short。

What I would like to speak to you about **this morning** is my new product launch proposal.
今天上午，我想跟您報告的是我的新產品上市企劃案。
小貼士：this morning 可置換為 this afternoon（今天下午），this evening（今天傍晚），today（今天）。

📎 說明簡報的順序

I will first introduce the analysis of current market, followed by target market and audience, and finally describe new product launch activities.
我會先介紹市場現況分析，緊接著是目標市場與客群，最後描述新品上市活動。
小貼士：followed by 可置換為 then。

Rather than describing new product launch activities, I based my presentation on new product positioning and target buyers.
我的報告會以新產品定位和目標購買者為主，而不會著墨新產品上市活動太多。

📎 提出重點

I think it would be best to start out by describing current competitors.
我想最好以討論現存競爭者開始。

I would like to make three points with respect to product features.
The first point relates to easy to carry.
The second point concerns its colorful design.
The third point is that the price is cheaper than competitors.
關於產品特色，我提出三點。
第一點是它容易攜帶。
第二點是繽紛色彩的設計。
第三點是售價比競爭者還便宜。
小貼士：詳列重點時，可用 first, second, third, fourth…last（finally）。
　　　　relate to 和 concern 可以互相對換，也可置換為 deal with。

📎 補充說明

I will give you some examples in a few minutes to illustrate the current thinking as to new product launch activities.
稍待一會兒我會提供幾個例子，來說明現階段對新品上市活動的想法。

I will say more about that in a moment.
我馬上會提供詳述。
小貼士：moment 可置換為 minute。

📎 歸納重點

Let me conclude by making an observation concerning current market analysis.
我想針對市場現況分析提出個人的觀察。
In conclusion, I would like to point out the flowing：
總之，我想要指出以下幾點：
小貼士：point out 可置換為 indicate。

Now, I would like to sum up the conclusion of my proposal.
現在，我想要總結提案的結論。
小貼士：名詞為 conclusion 為名詞；動詞是 conclude，意思是下結論。Sum up 則為概括來說的意思，通常放在總結的時候；動詞是 summarize，名詞為 summary。在接下來的篇章會看到更多用法。

Unit 05 Key Points of Hosting a Meeting-2 主持會議要點

Situation 2 情境2：

Mike is presenting the launch plan of company's new drinks to 100 distributors.

麥克正在替 100 位經銷商報告公司的新款飲料上市簡報。

Key points for your conversation 對話急救包

問候現場與自我介紹

Ladies and gentlemen：
各位先生和女士們：

Distinguished distributors and guests：
尊敬的經銷商與來賓們：

My name is Mike and is responsible for the new drinks launch plan.
我的名字是麥克，負責新飲料的上市計畫。

I would like to thank Sean for permitting me the privilege to speak to this audience.
我想要感謝西恩給我機會在此為您簡報。
小貼士：Sean 可置換為聽眾熟悉的人名。否則可以用 my company（我的公司）替代。

敘述簡報的內容

Today I will be speaking mostly about new product launch activities, but I will also cover distributor incentive program.
今天我大部份會談到關於新品上市的活動，但是我也會提到經銷商獎勵計畫。
小貼士：若會議在下午或晚上進行，today 可置換為 this afternoon 或 tonight。

The presentation I'm going to present today will describe some of the important aspects of market analysis.
今天我將進行的簡報，將敘述關於市場分析的幾個重要方面。

說明簡報方式

I would like to give this presentation in three parts.　The first part concerns market research.　The second part relates to new product features, and then the last part deals with target audiences.
我將簡報分為三個部份。首先是有關市場調查。第二部份是關於新產品特色，最後是目標客群。
小貼士：concern、relate to、deal with 可以互換。

Instead of focusing too much on product features, I intend to address myself to only one thing.　And that is distributor incentive policies.
與其聚焦太多重點在產品特色，我傾向關注在一件事情上。那就是經銷商獎勵政策。

提出論點

I should like to preface my remarks with a description of the current market analysis.
我會以敘述市場現況作為起始。

Let me quickly make two remarks.　In the first place, the price of the same product from competitors is higher than us.　The second remark I'd like to make is that we offer a better promotion activity.
容我很快地提出兩點。第一點，競爭對手提供的相同商品比我們貴。第二，我們提供更好的促銷活動。

強調論點

I must now emphasize, not only we have the better taste than competitors, but also better quality.
我必須強調，我們不只比競爭對手更好喝，品質還更好。

Where in the world would you find another company like us to give you all the support？
這世界上還有哪家公司像我們一樣給你們所有的支持？

Part I

Part II

Part III

Part IV

Part V

Part VI

Part I

Part II

Part III

Part IV

Part V

Part VI

小貼士：這句帶有半威脅性口吻的句子，如果在恰當時機點由簡報者面帶微笑以幽默
　　　　方式提出，能夠炒熱現場氣氛。否則建議不使用。

將論點簡單帶過

Without going into details, I just want to point out that market research shows that consumers are looking forward to our launch.
不多說細節，我只想點出市場調查顯示消費者正在期待我們的上市。

There are many more I could mention, but these few words will suffice.
還有很多我可以提的，但是這幾句話應該就夠了。

I am only touching on this subject for a few minutes.
我只花幾分鐘探討這個主題。
小貼士：touching on 可置換為 talking about。

停止或跳過簡報

In the interest of time, I am going to omit describing this part of my presentation.
由於時間的關係，我將省略這部份。

Maybe we can discuss this issue during the question and answer period.
或許我們可以討論這個話題，等到 Q&A 的時候。
小貼士：issue 可置換為 part，problem，chart（表），graph（圖）。

歸納與總結

I would like to close by saying that working with us is the wisest decision. Thank you for attending today.
我想作個總結，那就是和我們合作是您們最明智的決定。謝謝您們今天的出席。
小貼士：close 是動詞，名詞為 closing，作結論，總結的意思。

To sum up, I think there is room for our new drinks and together with us, we can be the number 1 in the market.
總而言之，我想我們的新飲料還是有市場空間的，而且我們一起合作，可以成為市場第一。

發問掌控

We have lots of time for discussion, so please don't hesitate to raise hands.
我們還有很多時間可以討論，所以請踴躍舉手。

Is there any specific question you would like to ask（to me）？
有沒有任何特別的問題要問（我）？

I think Sean has some final comments.
我想西恩有一些最後的總結。
小貼士：如果事先得知要上台發言的其他人名，可以使用本句。Sean 可置換為其他主
　　　　管或同事的名字。

Your question, please ？
您的問題，請説？
小貼士：當有人舉手時可使用本句。

感謝出席

If there is no further question, I would like to thank you all for attending this meeting.
如果沒有進一步的問題的話，我想感謝大家今天出席這場會議。

Thank you all for attending this meeting, our staffs would be happy to help any of you.
感謝各位出席今天的會議，我們的員工會很樂意為您解答疑惑。

Thank you very much for your attention. Please hand over the order form to any of our staffs before you left.
非常感謝各位的聆聽。請在您離開之前，將訂購單交給任何一位我們的員工。

Part II

Promotion Event
促銷活動

Unit 06 Purpose 為何要促銷

Background Introduction 背景介紹：

Ginny, Rebecca and Tess are working at the same company, but from different departments. They are arguing about what this time's promotion purposes are.

金妮，蕾貝卡和泰絲在同一家公司工作，但是來自不同部門。她們正在爭論這次促銷活動的目的為何。

Conversation 對話

Ginny	**To be honest**, I have no idea why we have to plan one promotion event after another.	老實說，我實在搞不懂為什麼我們公司要不斷地策畫促銷活動。
Rebecca	This is because we have to increase the sales volume as much as possible.	這是因為我們要盡可能增加銷售量。
Tess	It sounds a little crazy, isn't it?	這聽起來有點瘋狂，不是嗎？
Ginny	I agree. I mean, some products are unlike toilet paper, you won't always need them.	我同意。我是說，有些產品又不像是衛生紙，你不會一天到晚需要啊。

Rebecca	Sometimes promotion is not only about increasing sales numbers, but also about delivering important information from the company or the brand to customers.	有時候促銷也不只是為了增加銷售數據，而是為了從公司或品牌傳達重要的訊息給顧客知道。
Tess	Such as?	例如？
Rebecca	Suppose the company won an award or something, and they want to share the happiness with their consumers or dealers.	假設某公司贏了一個獎或什麼的，而他們想要和消費者或經銷商分享他們的喜悅。
Tess	**It makes sense** to me.	聽起來有道理。
Ginny	Yes, but all through **price reduction**?	是，沒錯，但都透過降價的方式嗎？
Rebecca	Not always, it depends on **price elasticity of demand**. High price elasticity means that when the price of a product goes up, consumers will buy less of it and when the price goes down, consumers will buy more.	不總是這樣，端看需求的價格彈性。高價格彈性表示當產品價格上揚時，消費者會買少一點；當價格下降了，消費者就會買多一點。

Part I

Part II

Part III

Part IV

Part V

Part VI

Tess	And low price elasticity **implies** the opposite, that changes in price have very little influence on their demand.	低價格彈性意味著相反囉，價格的改變對需求的影響就很小。
Rebecca	Correct.	正確。
Ginny	I see. That is why we see many **daily consumer goods** doing promotions quite often, while not many jeweler company doing the same.	我知道了。這就是為什麼日常消費用品經常做促銷，但不是很多珠寶公司會這樣做。
Rebecca	Yes, luxury brands tend to provide unique services to their customers **rather than** focusing on **price war**.	是的，奢侈品牌傾向提供他們的顧客特別的服務，而非專注在價格戰上。
Tess	Sometimes, I appreciate the products with free gifts in the same retail price. I will buy them immediately when I found them on the shelves.	有時候，我會感謝那些在同樣零售價但卻提供小贈品的商品。一旦發現它們在貨架上時我會馬上購買。
Ginny	I like them, too. It is **a great deal**, isn't it?	我也很喜歡耶。這是一筆很划算的交易，不是嗎？

Rebecca	That's true. The concept is similar to **consumer reward**. You pay the same money as usual, but get one small giveaway.	的確。這概念和消費者獎勵類似。你花和平常同樣的錢，但卻可以得到一個小贈品。
Tess	I think by doing this kind of promotion, the company or brand keeps their customers not only loyal to them, but also increase desires to purchase again and again just to collect giveaways.	我想透過這種促銷方式，公司或品牌不僅是讓顧客對他們忠誠，同時也增加再次購買的欲望，只為了要蒐集那些贈品。
Ginny	I also noticed that our company does sales promotions even during **off-season**.	我也注意到我們公司甚至在淡季時進行促銷活動。
Rebecca	Off course we do! Otherwise, how can we make money from? Not mention our salaries are all come from monthly sales.	我們當然要這樣做！否則的話，怎麼賺到錢呢？更別提我們的薪水都是從每月的銷售來的。
Tess	In other words, the more promotions, the better.	說到底，就是要越多促銷越好。

Part I

Part II

Part III

Part IV

Part V

Part VI

知識補給站

為什麼要舉辦促銷活動？答案可能有很多種。

主要的目的是為了增加銷售（increase sales），創造購買的需求（create demand）；除此以外，傳遞訊息（message delivery）或加強市場地位（strengthen market position），作出與競爭對手不同的區隔訴求，都是促銷活動舉辦的目的。

通常，促銷是短期的（short-term），主要是為了刺激某一段期間的銷售量。為了造成買氣，常用的手法有限量商品（limited edition）或售完為止（while supplies last）；促銷活動除了對一般消費者，透過經銷商販售的公司，也可以規劃對經銷商的促銷活動。

就是因為促銷給人「賺到了」的感覺，廠商除了在價格上做文章之外，額外的贈品（gifts）、雙倍的紅利積點（double bonus points）…等等，也是抓準消費者「此時不買更待何時」的心理。

不過，若企業或品牌定位的是有價值、有質感的路線，就不太適合降價促銷或買贈活動；通常是透過增加附加價值的服務，例如：終生保固（lifetime warranty）、邀請參加藝文賞析的活動（art appreciation）等，讓顧客感受與該公司或品牌相同的價值觀，藉此維繫顧客關係和加強忠誠度（strengthen loyalty）。

Related Word 相關詞彙

1. argue about… 為了…爭論

   文法加油站：argue 有下列三種用法：

   (1) argue + about/over + something，為了某事爭論

   They usually argue over kids. 他們經常為了孩子爭吵。

   (2) argue + with + someone，與某人爭論

   She is arguing with the cooker about the overcooked dish.

   (3) argue + someone + into（out of）+ doing something，說服某人做
   （不做）某事

   My mother is tired to argue me out of traveling around the world alone.
   我媽已經懶得說服我不要獨自環遊世界了。

2. To be honest 老實說

   文法加油站：同義詞還有 Frankly speaking, Honestly speaking

3. It makes sense 有道理

   文法加油站：反義詞為 It doesn't make（any）sense.

4. price reduction 降價

5. price elasticity of demand 需求的價格彈性。簡單說，彈性高代表對價格
   很敏感，小幅度漲價或降價就會造成需求的變動（例如：民生用品或忠誠
   度低的消費者），彈性低就代表不會因小幅度漲價或降價就產生需求轉換
   （例如：珠寶或忠誠度高的消費者）。

6. implies 意味著，隱含，暗示

   文法加油站：動詞原形為 imply。

7. daily consumer goods 日常消費用品

8. rather than…=but not… 而非…

   文法加油站：rather than 大致上可分為兩種用法：

   (1) 作對等連接詞時，前後的字詞和型態在結構上需平行對等，例如：He
   walked rather than ran. 他走路而非跑。

   (2) 作介系詞使用，前後結構可不對等，例如：Rather than staying home on
   a Saturday night, they went out to five different bars. 與其待在家，星
   期六晚上他們選擇去了五間不同的酒吧 / 星期六晚上他們去了五間不同酒

吧，而非待在家裡。

9. price war　價格戰

10. a great deal　一個很划算的交易

11. consumer reward　消費者獎勵

12. off-season　淡季

　　文法加油站：同義詞還有 slack season, slow season, a dead season

　　反義詞則是 the peak period, the busy season, the rush season, the boom

　　season

13. short-term　短期的

　　文法加油站：反義詞為 long-term

14. while supplies last　直譯為直到供應到最後，意思就是售（送）完為止。

15 double bonus points　雙倍紅利積點

　　文法加油站：double 除了是形容詞，也可作名詞，動詞，副詞。

Exercises 練習題

Here is a promotion advertisement, please complete the word or sentence by filling in the blanks.

Toaster Sales! A _____!

Buy 1 get 1 free, only $699!

_____.

18th~25th, AUG.

_____.

這裡是一個促銷廣告，請填空完成下面句子或單字

麵包機大特價！ 划算的交易！

買一送一，只要 $699 元！
享雙倍紅利積點。

8 月 18~25 日
售完為止。

Answers to the Unit:
great deal
double bonus points
while supplies last

Unit 07 Target Audiences 希望誰購買

Background Introduction 背景介紹：

Hannah and Calvin are arguing about who should be the target audience of a promotion activity.
漢娜與卡文正在爭論促銷活動應該對誰宣傳？

Conversation 對話

Hannah	No offense, Calvin. I just think you may need to **reconsider** who are the target audiences of this time's promotion.	毫無冒犯之意，卡文。我只是覺得你也許需要重新思考誰才是這次促銷活動的目標族群。
Calvin	Why is that?	什麼意思？
Hannah	You know sometimes the buyers are not the users of a product.	你知道有時候一個商品的買者不見得是使用者。
Calvin	Yes, I am **aware** of that.	是呀，我知道。
Hannah	Then you should target daughters or sons for Mother's Day promotion.	那你就應該把母親節的促銷目標放在女兒和兒子們上。
Calvin	The media budget is limited, I can't spend it everywhere.	媒體預算是有限的，我不能到處亂花。

Hannah	You don't need to, I am just suggesting that you may need to **shift** offline **media spend to** online.	你不需要，我只是建議你也許應該將線下的媒體花費移轉到線上。
Calvin	Shift them all to online?	全部轉移到線上媒體？
Hannah	Well, maybe 90%. You know that most young people spend almost all day long on internet, don't you? Especially, Mother's Day is the opportunity of telling children to buy gifts for their mothers.	嗯，可能 90% 吧。你也知道大部分年輕人花一整天在網上，不是嗎？尤其，母親節是個機會，藉此告訴孩子們買禮物給他們的母親。
Calvin	According to your advice, husbands should also be our **communication targets**.	根據你的建議，先生也應該是我們的溝通的目標。
Hannah	Well, you can also say so.	嗯，你也可以這樣說呀。
Calvin	**Don't be ridiculous**, Hannah! You can't target everyone, just like you can't sell one product to everybody.	別開玩笑了，漢娜！你總不能將所有人當成目標，就像你無法賣同一件商品給全部的人一樣。
Hannah	I understand where you are coming from, but…	我知道你的意思啦，可是…

Part I
Part II
Part III
Part IV
Part V
Part VI

Calvin	**It's a done deal**.	這事已經決定了。
Hannah	OK. Think about McDonald's Happy Meal.	好吧。想想麥當勞的兒童餐。
Calvin	What about it?	它們怎麼了？
Hannah	In all advertisements, they target mothers or parents instead of kids as their communication objectives.	在所有廣告中，麥當勞把母親或父母當成溝通對象，而非兒童本身。
Calvin	Right.	對。
Hannah	I am just saying that you don't need to put media budget on mothers, that's all.	我只是在說你不需要將媒體預算花在母親身上，就這樣。
Calvin	Now **I see your point**. You should (figure it out for yourself) first, honey.	現在我知道你的意思了。你自己應該先想清楚吧！

Part I
Part II
Part III
Part IV
Part V
Part VI

知識補給站

促銷活動的溝通對象（communication objectives）有時候並不見得是產品最終的使用者，如同對話中舉例的，兒童餐、母親節，類似的父親節、情人節，甚至公司團體或獎勵旅遊、福委會團購商品（**group buying**）等等，溝通的對象往往是某一群人，而最終享受到優惠的是另一群人。

這時候，促銷訊息（messages）和標語（slogan）的發想與拿捏，就很重要。通常這類型的溝通方式，是將購買的好處（the benefits of buying）點出。例如：兒童餐經常提醒父母兒童，套餐裡有水果蔬菜、牛奶或柳橙汁，可以幫助兒童攝取均衡的營養（balanced nutrition）；旅行社或渡假村則是對公司的團體旅遊規劃小組不斷地宣傳，團體旅遊可以促進團隊情感建立（improves relationships），增加工作效率（improves performance）與對公司的信任感（builds trust）。

這些訴求和直接對使用者溝通的明顯不同，如果兒童餐要對孩童宣傳好處，應該是有好吃的雞塊與薯條、冰冰涼涼的可樂和好玩的玩具；如果旅行社要對個人宣傳團體旅遊的好處，應該是團體出遊可以享受低價的飯店和機票（cheaper hotels and airfares），出遊有事先安排好的交通工具（pre-arranged transportation），甚至是邂逅同隊的異性…等等。

簡而言之，抓住一個原則：產品希望誰購買就對誰說話。

Part I

Part II

Part III

Part IV

Part V

Part VI

Related Word 相關詞彙

1. reconsider 重新考慮

   文法加油站：re 有重新，再一次的意思。

2. aware 知曉，察覺

3. shift…to…從 …轉換（挪動、移動）到…

   文法加油站：shift 有轉變、轉換、移動的意思。

   Could you help me to shift this box? 你可以幫我挪一下這箱子？

   He shifted from foot to foot. 他的腳來回交換（叉）著。

4. media spend 媒體花費，媒體預算

5. communication targets = communication objectives 溝通對象（目標）

6. Don't be ridiculous 別開玩笑了

   文法加油站：ridiculous 有諷刺人可笑或沒常識的意思，所以這句也可譯成別可笑了，或別無理取鬧了。

7. It's a done deal 此事已定，木已成舟，生米已煮成熟飯

   文法加油站：deal 有交易的意思。口語也經常聽到有人問：Deal ？意思是：說好囉或一言為定？另一人就可以回答：Deal ！

8. I see your point 我懂你的意思，我知道你的論點（觀點）

9. Figure it out for yourself 自己把事情弄清楚吧

   文法加油站：figure 有輪廓、圖解、圖像的意思，本句直譯為為你自己畫出事物的輪廓吧，其實也就是將事情弄清楚的意思。

10. group buying 團購

    文法加油站：也可置換為 collective buying。

Exercises 練習題

Please complete the word or sentence by filling in the blanks.

A：According to this report, we have spent too much on the medias.

B：Really?

A：Absolutely.

B：Maybe we should _____ to _____ .

A：Great idea. Especially, our _____ are young generations.

B：But how to do that?

A：I have no idea either. But I think before we go to boss, we need to _____

_____ .

B：You are a genius, let's do it.

請填空完成下面句子或單字

A：根據這報告，去年我們媒體預算花得太多了。

B：是嗎？

A：絕對是。

B：也許我們應該重新考慮將線下媒體預算挪到網路上。

A：好主意。尤其我們的溝通對象都是年輕人。

B：但是該怎麼做呢？

A：我也不曉得，或許我們應該在去問老闆前先試試自己弄清楚。

B：你真是聰明，就這麼辦。

Answers to the Unit:

reconsider
shift offline media spend to online
communication targets/objectives
figure it out for ourselves
a walk in the park (a piece of cake)

Part I

Part II

Part III

Part IV

Part V

Part VI

Unit 08 Period and Places-1
何時、何地舉辦

Part I
Part II
Part III
Part IV
Part V
Part VI

Background Introduction 背景介紹：

Whitney and Heath are responsible for this Chinese New Year's promotion activity, and they are discussing how long as well as where it should be held.

惠妮與希斯負責這次農曆年前的促銷活動，他們正在討論活動應該持續多久，以及應該在哪裡舉辦？

- -

Conversation 1 對話 1

Whitney	Hi, Heath, I am wondering if you have free time now?	嗨，希斯，我在想不曉得你現在有沒有空？
Heath	Yes, what I can do for you?	有啊，我可以為你做什麼嗎？
Whitney	It's just the sales team asked me to adjust the promotion period and places, so here I am.	就是銷售團隊要我調整一下促銷的期間和地點，所以我來找你。
Heath	I see, since we work on this project together. What did they said?	了解，因為我們共同負責這專案。他們說了什麼？

Whitney	They suggested maybe we can **extend** promotion period from one week to two weeks.	他們建議也許我們可以延長促銷期間，從一週到兩週。
Heath	Maybe as long as possible? They really love promotion, don't they?	也許越久越好？他們真愛促銷，不是嗎？
Whitney	In my opinion, it isn't really true.	就我而言，也不全然是這樣啦。
Heath	Whatever you say. **You were saying**?	隨你怎麼説吧。還有呢？
Whitney	Places, they also need us to contact with all our channels for supporting the Chinese New Year's promotion.	通路，他們也需要我們聯繫所有經銷商支持這次農曆春節的促銷。
Heath	Are you kidding me? That's not what they said at last week's meeting.	你開玩笑吧？這和他們上週開會時説的不一樣。
Whitney	No.	是不一樣。
Heath	What I said to you.	相信我了吧。

Part I

Part II

Part III

Part IV

Part V

Part VI

Whitney	Come on, they are not usually doing this. It is just **occasionally**.	拜託，他們也不是經常這樣。只是偶爾。
Heath	Now, thanks to them, we have to call eight headquarters of the **3C distributors** who work with us.	現在，多虧了他們，我們要打電話給合作的 3C 通路的八個總公司。
Whitney	I guess so.	我想是的。
Heath	Plus all the preparations. **Finger crossed** that we will finish it in time.	加上所有的準備。但願我們好運，能夠及時完成。
Whitney	We probably need to provide the promotion proposal in this month.	我們可能這個月要提供促銷計畫案。
Heath	Yes, usually six months ago. Then they will review it and tell us where to adjust.	是的，通常是六個月前。然後他們會審核並告訴我們要調整的地方。
Whitney	If everything goes smoothly, we need to design all the **promotion materials** in August, hopefully finish printing or production then ship to all distributors in December.	如果每件事進行順利的話，我們需要在八月設計所有的促銷製作物，希望可以完成印刷或生產，然後在十二月運到所有經銷商那邊。

Part I
Part II
Part III
Part IV
Part V
Part VI

知識補給站

促銷活動有不少細節（details）要留意，其中最主要的是開始和結束的時間（when to start or end），以及舉辦的地點。

由於前面有提過，促銷是短期的吸引，所以舉辦的期間不宜過長，通常是一～二週，百貨周年慶（Anniversary Sales）則是兩～三週左右，近年也有類似分成兩波促銷期，相加超過 40 天的周年慶檔期。

要留意的是，有時候時間或者地點因為粗心造成的錯誤（careless mistakes），例如：印製在宣傳單上的文字訊息錯誤，是會造成消費者糾紛（consumer disputes）的，因為宣傳單相當是一種書面的承諾（commitment）；保險一點的作法是印上警語（warning），例如：本公司保留隨時修改、變更或取消活動之權利並可不事先通知（The Company may change, remove, cancel, or otherwise modify the event at any time without prior notice.）。

此外，促銷涉及宣傳，亦即要讓越多該區域的消費者知道，才有機會促成較高銷售量或者讓越多目標族群知曉活動傳遞的訊息；此時，適合當地、該族群的宣傳工具（media）搭配也要留意。例如：南部和北部消費者接受資訊來源的差異，年齡層（different ages）也會影響接收來源，家庭年收入（yearly family income）的多寡可能也是宣傳工具選擇考量因素。

Part I

Part II

Part III

Part IV

Part V

Part VI

Related Word 相關詞彙

1. as well as　和

2. extend　延長

　　文法加油站：同義詞還有 prolong、lengthen。

3. You were saying?　還有呢？（你說到哪裡了？）

4. occasionally　偶爾

　　文法加油站：同義詞還有 once a while。

5. 3C distributors　3C 通路商

　　文法加油站：3C 為 Computer（電腦）、Communication（通訊設備）、
　　　　　　　　Consumer electronic（消費電子用品）為首的 3 個 C 組成；也
　　　　　　　　有一說是指 Camera（相機）、cell phone（手機）、Computer
　　　　　　　　（電腦）的 3 個 C 組成。

6. Finger crossed　期待（祝）好運

　　文法加油站：直譯為手指交叉。根據西方習俗，將中指在食指上交叉，代表十
　　　　　　　　字架，有驅魔並帶來好運的意思。是一句相當常用的口語。

7. promotion materials　促銷宣傳製作物

8. Anniversary Sales　週年慶特惠

9. consumer disputes　消費者糾紛

10. prior　預先的

11. yearly family income　家庭年收入

　　文法加油站：average monthly family income 則為平均家庭月收入。

Exercises 練習題

Please complete the word or sentence by filling in the blanks.

A：Did you finish printing _____ for the _____ ?

B：Not yet.

A：That could cause a _____ if we cannot proceed as scheduled.

B：We are doing this days and nights.

A：Then _____ we will finish it in time.

請填空完成下面句子或單字

A：周年慶特惠的促銷宣傳製作物好了嗎？

B：還沒。

A：如果不能如期展開可是會造成消費者糾紛的。

B：已經日夜趕工了。

A：那就祝我們好運可以及時完成吧。

Answers to the Unit:

promotion materials

Anniversary Sales

consumer dispute

finger crossed

Part I
Part II
Part III
Part IV
Part V
Part VI

Unit 08 Period and Places-2
何時、何地舉辦

Background Introduction 背景介紹：

Becky, Joshua and Russell are discussing how to organize a red wine group buy promotion on Facebook.

蓓琪、約書亞和羅素正在討論如何在臉書上舉辦一場紅酒團購促銷活動。

Conversation 2 對話 2

Becky	Our last month's sales volume of red wine had fallen to the bottom. It is really awful.	我們上個月的紅酒銷售量掉到谷底了。這真的很糟糕。
Joshua	Why don't we create a Fan page on Facebook? There are so many companies or brands are doing this, and consumers tend to believe what their friends or families recommended.	為什麼我們不在臉書上創建一個粉絲頁呢？現在有很多企業或品牌都正在做這件事，而且消費者也傾向相信朋友或家人推薦過的。
Russell	**Speaking of which**, I remember you said you are going to be in charge of that five weeks ago.	說到這個，我記得你五個禮拜前說過你要負責這事的。
Joshua	Me?	我？
Becky	Thank you for reminding us, Russell. Now I remember that, too.	謝謝你提醒了我們，羅素。現在我也記起來了。

Joshua	Sorry, I am so **forgetful**.	抱歉，我真是健忘。
Russell	Forget about it. **A leopard doesn't change its spots**. I think it's better that Becky **take over** from here.	算了吧。牛牽到北京還是牛。我想最好蓓琪從這接手吧。
Becky	OK, I would glad to.	好呀，我很樂意呢。
Russell	Do you know how to start it?	你知道要如何開始嗎？
Becky	I saw my sister did once, I guess I can **figure it out**.	我看過我妹做過一次，我想我能自己摸索出來的。
Joshua	What we provide for running a group buy campaign on Facebook?	那我們為臉書上的團購活動提供什麼？
Becky	I am thinking we can provide **value for money** package for fans, some good quality wine with lower price for our first try.	我在想我們可以提供物有所值的套餐給粉絲們，一些品質好但價格不昂貴的酒，作為我們第一次的試驗。
Russell	How much packages we need to prepare? Are they all red wine or mix white wine together?	我們需要準備多少套？全部是紅酒，還是要混搭一些白葡萄酒？

Part I
Part II
Part III
Part IV
Part V
Part VI

Joshua	Maybe some chocolates or different hams, cheeses also sound wonderful.	也許來點巧克力或不同的火腿,還是起司也不錯。
Becky	If we had to prepare non-wine products, we need more time for preparation. Besides, I think our members care about wine more than other things. I think at most 50 mixed packages will be attractive enough.	如果要準備非酒類的產品的話,我們就需要多一點的準備時間。而且,我想我們的會員比較在意酒而非其他東西。我想至多 50 個混合的套組就夠吸引人了。
Russell	Maybe we can combine with crystal glasses. You definitely need a glass for wine, don't you?	也許我們可以搭配水晶酒杯。喝酒一定需要一只酒杯的,不是嗎?
Becky	Good idea. Joshua, Could you **help me in this matter**?	好主意。約書亞,這件事情你可以幫我嗎?
Joshua	No problem, just remember to remind me latter.	沒問題,只是過段時間你要記得提醒我。
Russell	As the promotion period, how about three weeks?	至於促銷期間,3 週怎麼樣?
Becky	Won't it be too long?	不會太長嗎?

Joshua	I think ten days will be enough. Limited period giving people a feeling of "Do it now, before it's too late!"	我想十天就夠了。限時會給人一種「現在就下手，免得太晚了！」的感覺。
Becky	I agree with him.	我同意他説的。
Russell	I will responsible for collecting those fans data after this campaign.	那我負責活動後蒐集這些粉絲們的資料。
Becky	That would be great, we can do analysis and **focus marketing** in the future.	太好了，我們可以用來分析和未來進行焦點行銷。
Russell	All right, then. Let's **proceed separately**.	好啦。我們分頭進行吧。
Joshua	Hold on a second. How do fans pick up the packages they ordered?	等等。粉絲們要怎麼領取他們訂購的套組？
Becky	Good question, from my experiences, **pick up in store** is the most convenient and safe way, unless the fan asks us to delivery for him or her **door to door**. But in that case, we usually charge some extra fees.	好問題，從我的經驗來看，到店領取是最方便和安全的方式，除非這位粉絲要求我們幫他或她送貨到家。但這樣一來，我們通常也收取些額外費用。

Part I
Part II
Part III
Part IV
Part V
Part VI

Russell	How do we collect the money from those internet buyers?	我們要如何從網路買家那裡取得收款呢？
Joshua	We can create an internet payment system for this event and the future online wine selling business.	我們可以替這次活動和未來的線上葡萄酒銷售生意建立一個網路付款機制。
Becky	And offline payment as well, which means they also can come and pay at our store.	還有線下付款，也就是說他們也可以來店裡付款。
Russell	Online payment is convenient but sounds risky, besides, it could cost us months to get clear about the procedure since we don't have any experience in this area.	線上付款是方便但是聽起來有風險，而且，因為我們在這領域沒有經驗，可能花上數月才能弄清楚整個流程。
Joshua	What if collecting money when we delivery to the buyer's home?	如果當我們送到買家的家時收款呢？
Becky	I agree, that sounds more reasonable.	我同意，聽起來更合理。
Joshua	Perfect. **Let's party**!	太完美了。熱鬧開工吧。

Part I　Part II　Part III　Part IV　Part V　Part VI

知識補給站

臉書（Facebook）對各地企業和品牌來說，一點也不陌生了。隨著規模和市場考量，臉書也推出多種功能供企業或個人運用，像是粉絲團（Fan Pages）、社團（Groups）、應用程式（Apps）、付款（Payments）、廣告（Advertisements）。網路無遠弗屆（**far-reaching**），很多網路上的資訊，變得沒有時間和空間的限制。Google 一下，甚至還找得到十幾年前的文章或資訊，讓行銷人不得不戒慎恐懼。

網路平台相較於其他媒體，因為費用相對低廉，而且現代人上班、下班離不開電腦的生活型態，也成了許多廠商促銷活動的首選。曾經策劃每天只賣一種商品、每天定時開賣的瘋狂賣客（CrazyMike），就是網購市場（online shopping market）快速崛起的異軍。某鄉下的老店小吃，一旦躍上臉書，打卡（check in）的人多了，也可以讓老店一嘗網路爆紅（**become Internet sensation**）的滋味。

正因為網路沒有時間、空間的限制，促銷活動進行時，才更要將資訊清楚表達。常用 Google 查找資訊的人也許會發現，某些公車訊息、團購、研習會⋯等等資訊，經常是過時的。而且不同城市可能有相同地名（place name）、街名（street name），也容易造成誤解。

促銷細節環環相扣，不論在線上（online）或線下（offline）實體店面，都要小心謹慎（careful and cautious）。

Part I

Part II

Part III

Part IV

Part V

Part VI

103

Related Word 相關詞彙

1. Speaking of which　説到這個，一提到這個
   文法加油站：另一種用法為 Speaking of the devil，表示說曹操曹操到。

2. forgetful　健忘的

3. A leopard doesn't change its spots　江山易改，本性難移。牛牽到北京還是牛。
   文法加油站：leopard 是豹的意思，直譯為豹無法改變牠身上的斑點。

4. take over　接手照料

5. figure…out　搞清楚，釐清

6. value for money　物有所值
   文法加油站：物有所值有很多種說法，well worth it、well worth its value。
   　　　　　　物超所值則是 better value for money，物無所值則是 poor
   　　　　　　value for money。

7. help me in this matter　在這事情上幫我一把
   文法加油站：matter 作為名詞是議題、事情、課題的意思；作動詞則為有關係
   　　　　　　的意思，例如：It does matter.（當然有關係，表示說話的人在意
   　　　　　　這件事情）。

8. focus marketing　聚焦行銷、焦點行銷。意即針對不同目標族群的特性提供不同訊息、產品組合、價格等行銷模式。

9. proceed separately　分頭進行

10. pick up in store　到店領取

11. door to door　上門，到府

12. Let's party!　讓我們熱鬧一下
    文法加油站：此句並非真的要開派對的意思，而是借用派對的歡樂氣氛，引申
    　　　　　　為讓我們炒熱氣氛或把事情辦得熱鬧的意思。

13. far-reaching　廣大的、遠的

14. become Internet sensation　網路爆紅
    文法加油站：同義詞還有 go viral。

Exercises 練習題

Please complete the word or sentence by filling in the blanks.

Here are some questions we would like you to answer in order to help us in complete the mission of _____ .

1. Do you prefer _____ service or _____ by yourself?

2. Are you _____ ?

3. Are you always looking for things which is _____ ?

4. Will you enjoy the feeling of becoming _____ ?

請填空完成下面句子或單字

這裡有些問題我們希望您回答，以幫助我們完成焦點行銷的任務。

1. 您偏好到府服務還是自己到店領取？

2. 您是健忘的？

3. 您總是尋找物有所值的東西？

4. 您將會享受網路爆紅的滋味？

Answers to the Unit:

focus marketing

door to door

pick up in store

forgetful

value for money

Internet sensation

Unit 09　Promotion Methods Selection-1
用力促銷有撇步

Background Introduction 背景介紹：

Patricia, Sal and Danny are in the same presentation group, now they are choosing the promotion methods for hair gels.

派翠西亞、莎爾和丹尼是同一個報告小組，他們正在為髮膠產品設計促銷的方式。

Conversation 1 對話 1

Sal	I hate to say this, but it seems I am already **burned-out**.	我討厭這樣說，但是我覺得我已經精疲力盡了。
Danny	Don't say that. Come on, we are **one more step to success**.	別這麼說啊。拜託，我們離成功只差一步了。
Patricia	Let's **go over** again what we have discussed so far.	讓我們再檢視一遍剛才討論的。
Sal	OK. We have talked about free samples, coupons, **premiums**. Usually, I also get these quite often when I purchase a hair gel on supermarket.	好吧。我們談到了免費樣品、折價券、贈品。通常，當我去超市買一罐髮膠時我也會經常拿到這些。
Danny	Me, too. But we need to **think outside the box**.	我也是。但是我們需要跳脫框架去思考。

Patricia	Indeed. Hey, I have an idea. How about **patronage rewards**?	的確。咦，我有個點子。酬賓優惠怎麼樣？
Danny	I think it's a more suitable promotion tool for hair salons.	我覺得這好像是更適合美髮沙龍店的促銷工具。
Sal	Not really, it just needs more time to communicate with channel stores.	也不盡然，只是需要比較多的時間和通路店家溝通洽談。
Patricia	**Sweepstakes** and games?	抽獎活動或遊戲？
Sal	Good idea! That is what we are looking for.	好主意！這就是我們一直在找的。
Danny	Great. Let's write down how it can be done when you buy the hair gel in the supermarket.	好。讓我們寫下來可以怎麼進行，當你在超市買一罐髮膠的時候。
Patricia	My thinking is we provide a **with-pack** card, and there is a set of random number on it. At the end of promotion date, we will announce the winners on the product **official website**. How's that?	我的想法是提供隨貨包裝的卡片，這上面有一組隨機的號碼。等到促銷最後一天，我們就在產品的官方網站上公佈得獎人。怎麼樣？

Part I

Part II

Part III

Part IV

Part V

Part VI

Sal	It sounds wonderful!	聽起來很好！
Danny	The biggest advantage for us is to gather their details for other promotion events or send them direct mails.	對我們來說，最大的好處就是蒐集他們的資料，以便下次促銷活動或者寄郵件給他們。
Patricia	People tend not to **reveal** too much personal information online nowadays.	現在人們傾向不透露太多個資在網路上。
Danny	Maybe we need to provide a temptation which cannot be refused.	或許我們需要提供一個無法拒絕的誘因。
Sal	Such as a Birkin bag?	例如柏金包？
Danny	**Nice try**.	好樣的，但不是這個答案。
Patricia	But right direction, bags are always attractive for women. Let's look for some prizes like that.	但方向對了，包包對女性而言總是充滿吸引力。讓我們找這樣的獎品吧。

知識補給站

　　促銷的方式或工具（promotion methods/tools）各式各樣，根據行銷大師 Kotler 提出的行銷工具就有：減價優惠（price-off deals）、樣品（samples）、贈品（premium）、折價券（coupons）、現金回饋（cash refund）、加量不加價包裝（bonus packs）、酬賓優惠（patronage rewards）、競賽（contest）、產品保證（product warranties）、抽獎與遊戲（sweepstakes and game）、購買點陳列（point-of-purchase）。

　　方式或工具的選擇則視產品特性或企業決定。例如：食品經常看到使用贈品或加量不加價包裝的促銷，飲料市場則常看見減價優惠，或者抽獎活動，現金回饋則常用在信用卡、汽車的促銷上。競賽和購買點陳列，比較是對經銷商端的促銷方式，目的在提升進貨量（increase purchase amount），或者提供誘因給經銷商，讓他們進以往比較少進的貨。

　　隨著付款機制以及景氣的轉變，近年也常見分期付款（installment）優惠的促銷手法，像是全國電子或者網購網站。

　　促銷活動雖然能夠在短時間吸引消費者注意力，但是促銷的成本企業不可忽視，一不小心，費用高於賣出的產品所賺的獲利也有可能。如果牽涉到要花額外成本去採購的，最好加註警語：數量有限，贈（售）完為止（Limited time/quantities, while supplies last）。

Related Word 相關詞彙

1. burn-out　精疲力盡，過勞

2. one more step to success　距離成功只差一步

   文法加油站：英文諺語裡還有一句：Anger is one letter short of danger. 生氣
   離危險只差一小步，用來提醒人物三思在盛怒之下做決定。

3. go over　瀏覽一遍

   文法加油站：to go over something in someone's mind，表示某人在腦中將某
   事快速地檢視一遍。

4. premium　贈品

   文法加油站：同義詞還有 prize, reward, award。

5. think outside the box　跳脫既有框架來思考

6. patronage rewards 酬賓優惠。類似會員優惠，持認同卡或會員卡可享特殊
   優惠活動。

7. Sweepstakes　抽獎活動

8. with-pack　隨貨包裝的

9. official website　官方網站

10. reveal　透露

11. Nice try.　做得好（可惜沒成功）

    文法加油站：在某人努力嘗試某事以後，給的評語。

12. installment　分期付款

    文法加油站：亦可置換為 installment payment。Installment loan 則是指需要
    分期付款償還的貸款。

Exercises 練習題

Please complete the word or sentence by filling in the blanks.

A：I am thinking to buy a refrigerator lately.

B：Then you'd better check on the ＿＿＿＿＿＿＿ of BUYBUY.com.

A：Why?

B：Because they are offering a ＿＿＿＿＿＿＿ , ＿＿＿＿＿＿＿ of each product
and ＿＿＿＿＿＿＿ . The winner might need to pay nothing for whatever he
or she bought.

A：You must be kidding with me!

B：No, I am not.

A：Thanks, body. I go to check it now.

請填空完成下面句子或單字

A：我最近想買一台冰箱。

B：那你最好看一下買買網的官方網站。

A：為什麼？

B：他們正在進行酬賓優惠活動，每樣商品都可以分期付款，而且還提供抽獎活
動。中獎人買的東西可能一毛錢也必付。

A：開玩笑的吧？

B：不，是真的。

A：謝啦，兄弟。我這就去看看。

Answers to the Unit:

official website
patronage reward
installment
sweepstake

Part I

Part II

Part III

Part IV

Part V

Part VI

Unit 09 Promotion Methods Selection-2
用力促銷有撇步

Part I
Part II
Part III
Part IV
Part V
Part VI

Background Introduction 背景介紹：

Ingrid and Gilbert are two market researchers. *Today, they are together in a supermarket to* check out *promotion events which are organized by different chocolate's brands.*

英格麗和吉伯特是兩位市調人員，今天，他們一起來到賣場巡視各家廠牌巧克力的促銷活動。

Conversation 2 對話 2

Ingrid	Gilbert, come to have a look at this.	吉伯特，過來看看這個。
Gilbert	**Fascinating**. Many of them chose to have promotion during the same period of time.	真有趣。這些產品決定同時間進行促銷。
Ingrid	Look at their packaging.	看看它們的包裝。
Gilbert	Yes, some are providing bonus packs for consumers, others are offering **product bundling**.	對呀，有些提供加量不加價包裝給消費者，有些提供綑綁銷售。
Ingrid	I don't understand why two different brands or companies will like to sell together.	我不了解為什麼兩個不同品牌或公司會願意一起販售。

Gilbert	That is because some weaker brands or products could be sold better compare with selling alone in the market.	這是因為有些弱勢品牌或產品可以賣得更好，相較於在市場上單獨銷售。
Ingrid	So, bundling sale is made for a weaker brand?	所以，綑綁銷售是為弱勢品牌量身打造的？
Gilbert	Yes, you could say that. But why a stronger brand want to say yes to a weaker brand?	可以這麼說吧。但是為什麼一個強勢品牌同意和弱勢品牌一起銷售呢？
Ingrid	Maybe they can get more benefit from this kind of promotion tool? Or, through this way, they can sell more.	也許是他們可以從這樣的促銷工具中得到更多利益？或者通過這種方式，它們可以賣出更多數量？
Gilbert	You see, the stronger brand also **benefits from** product bundling. Image a company want to provide more complete service or products to their customers at one time, however, they cannot produce everything themselves.	你看，強勢品牌也從產品搭售中受惠。想想一家公司想要一次提供更多完整的服務或產品給他們的消費者，但是，他們無法自己生產每樣東西。
Ingrid	Like fast food industry? They sell **multiple** items which are combined into a complete meal.	就像速食業？他們販售由多樣化品項搭配成的套餐。

Part I

Part II

Part III

Part IV

Part V

Part VI

Gilbert	And most of the time, they don't produce the drinks, do they? However, a package deal not always combines with two different brands, it also happens when a company wants to sell different products at the same time.	而且大多時候，他們並不生產飲料，對吧？然而，搭售不總是結合兩個不同品牌，也適用一家公司同時想要販售不同產品時。
Ingrid	But look at what they are bundling together? Tissue, gum, candy, milk, and even a toy!	但是看看他們都綑綁些什麼啊？面紙、口香糖、糖果、牛奶、甚至玩具！
Gilbert	Yes, just try to think what you will need when you enjoying chocolates. Tissue, yes, gum and candy, why not. Milk, well, still acceptable. A toy? Definitely, for me, they are all for kids, aren't they.	是呀，就想想當你享受巧克力的時候會需要什麼吧。面紙，對呀，口香糖和糖果，為什麼不。牛奶，也還算合理啊。一個玩具？絕對的，對我而言，他們都是給孩子的，不是嗎？
Ingrid	Here is another thing. Take a look at the **POP** here.	還有另一件事。看一看這個展示陳列架。
Ingrid	I know what you mean now.	我懂你的意思了。

Part I

Part II

Part III

Part IV

Part V

Part VI

產品搭售（product bundling, tie-in sale, package deal）是在買 A 產品的時候連 B 也一起買的組合銷售模式。常見的有買電腦之外，還要另外購買相應的軟體；手機也經常和電信業者綑綁銷售；購車時如果存款不夠，可以向車商設立的貸款機構申請貸款。民生消費用品（consumer goods）諸如，不同廠家的牛奶和麥片（cereal）一起銷售、同家廠牌的柳橙汁和葡萄汁搭售…等等，都是常見的組合。

對消費者而言，搭售有好處也有壞處，端看消費者對該項產品的需求程度而定。對不懂電腦的人來説，同時買硬體（hardware）和軟體（software）可以節省不少麻煩；如果已經有門號的使用者，想要換的手機卻搭售了其他家門號時，就會覺得不方便。就連歡喝橙汁卻不喜歡喝葡萄汁的消費者，遇見綑綁銷售，也會有一種「被迫」（be forced）的感覺。

對企業來説，綑綁銷售的好處是藉由市場上已經站穩腳步的產品或品牌，來帶動新進入者的銷售，新推出的手機搭配幾家電信業者門號，就是個例子。同品牌的知名粉餅搭配新推出的唇蜜（lip gloss）產品，也是個例子。

但是不是所有的企業、品牌或商品，都適合母雞帶小雞的方式。大原則就是，想想當使用 A 產品時，消費者可能需要的其他商品或服務；例如：手機和葡萄汁似乎關連不大，價格也有一段距離。但是，啤酒和冰桶（beer and ice bucket）、書桌和桌燈（desk and lamp）…等等，就是可以考慮的綑綁銷售。

Part I

Part II

Part III

Part IV

Part V

Part VI

Related Word 相關詞彙

1. market researchers　市場調查人員

2. check out　看、檢視

   文法加油站：check out 除了有退房的意思，還有看一下（take a look at）、檢
   查、核實的意思。

   Does his saying check out?　他說的查證（核實）過了嗎？

3. Fascinating　有趣的

   文法加油站：fascinating 還有迷人的（charming）、引人入勝的
   （enchanting）的意思。

4. product bundling　綑綁銷售，產品搭售。指兩件或以上的產品組合在一
   起販售，有時候是同一間企業不同品牌之間聯合促銷，有時候是完全不同
   企業之間的聯盟銷售策略。亦寫作 package deal = tie-in sale。

5. benefit from…　從…中受惠（益）

   文法加油站：benefit 可作動詞也可作名詞。形容詞則為 beneficial，有益的。

6. multiple　多種類的

7. POP　店頭展示

   文法加油站：本詞為 point-of-purchase displays 的簡稱縮寫，指在門市擺放
   的立地宣傳牌，或者展架上的宣傳製作物。

8. lip gloss　唇蜜

   文法加油站：lip 為嘴唇的意思，與嘴唇相關的化妝品英文也採 lip 開頭。唇膏
   為 lipstick，唇筆是 lip pencil。

9. tie-in sale　搭配出售

   文法加油站：假設買 A 商品或服務搭配 B 商品銷售，A 是搭售品（tying
   product），B 就是被搭售品（tied product）。

10. ice bucket　冰桶

    文法加油站：與冰相關的英文單字也多以 ice 為開頭，ice chisel（冰鑿）、ice
    bag（冰袋）、ice boating（冰船）、ice cube（冰塊）、ice cream
    （冰淇淋）、ice hockey（冰球）、ice show（冰上表演）、ice
    dancing（冰上舞蹈）。

Part I
Part II
Part III
Part IV
Part V
Part VI

Exercises 練習題

Please complete the word or sentence by filling in the blanks.

Please complete the word or sentence by filling in the blanks.

A：_____ it _____ , the _____ says the _____

　　is on sale.

B：We do need one in summer.

A：But only purchase with a _____ . I don't need it.

B：You could give it to me. Sometimes, a _____ is pretty annoying.

A：Tell me about it.

請填空完成下面句子或單字

A：你看這裡的店頭展示寫説冰桶正在特價。

B：夏天的確需要一個。

A：但是要和唇蜜一起買才有優惠。我不需要唇蜜。

B：那送給我吧。綑綁銷售有時候是挺討厭的。

A：那還用説。

Answers to the Unit:

Check

out

POP/point-of purchase display

ice bucket

lip gloss

tie-in sale/ product bundling/package deal

Unit 09 Promotion Methods Selection-3
用力促銷有撇步

Background Introduction 背景介紹：

Wesley and Van are running an automotive repair and maintenance company together, they are discussing which promotion tools they should offer in order to attract more customers.

衛斯理和范共同經營了一家汽車維修保養廠，他們正在討論該提供哪些促銷方案，以便吸引更多消費者上門。

Conversation 3 對話 3

Wesley	We should organize some promotions in order to get more business here.	我們應該舉辦一些促銷活動以吸引更多的生意上門。
Van	**I am all ears.**	我洗耳恭聽。
Wesley	I am thinking free gifts or coupons.	我在想是不是送些免費的禮物或折價券。
Van	I don't like either of them. I mean, men are unlike women, we prefer more practical and direct benefits.	我都不喜歡這兩個。我是說，男性可不像女性，我們寧可要些實用的或直接一點的好處。

Wesley	I think they are fine, and coupon is very practical. The **opposite** ABC Car Care is giving coupons from last week.	我覺得它們很好啊，而且折價券很實用。對面的 ABC 汽車保養就從上週開始贈送折價券。
Van	If ABC is providing coupons, then we must take a **differentiation strategy**. Maybe something like the customers can use directly without waiting for the next time coming.	如果 ABC 正在提供折價券，那我們一定得採取差異化的策略。也許是一些顧客可以直接使用的，而不用等到下次光顧。
Wesley	Do you mean discount offering?	你是說提供折扣？
Van	**Cash refund** or **reduced price** is also **under consideration**.	現金返還或降價也是可以考慮的。
Wesley	I am thinking isn't there any way we can make this promotion **a hot one**?	我在想，難道沒有方法可以將促銷活動搞得火熱一點？
Van	We cannot provide free service, can we?	總不能提供免費的服務吧，對吧？

Part I

Part II

Part III

Part IV

Part V

Part VI

Wesley	What if we offer $1 bid for limited time period, I am sure many **people who is keen on gaining petty advantages** will find it interesting and willing to bid on website.	如果我們在特定的時間裡提供 $1 一元競標，我相信很多貪小便宜的人會覺得這很有趣，而且願意在網路上投標。
Van	Unfortunately, we don't have a website.	很不幸地，我們沒有網站。
Wesley	We can post the promotion event on eBay.	我們可以把促銷活動張貼到 eBay 上。
Van	Good idea. Is it free to post on it?	好主意。是免費張貼的嗎？
Wesley	I am not sure.	我不確定喔。
Van	I don't appreciate it if we have to spend money before earn it.	如果我們在賺到錢之前還要花錢，那我可不會感激的。
Wesley	**No pain, no gain.** Let's see who can attract more customers to come to our store.	沒有痛苦，哪有收穫啊。讓我們看看誰可以吸引到比較多客人到店。
Van	Don't worry, **I'll have the last laugh**.	別擔心，我一定會笑到最後的。

Part I
Part II
Part III
Part IV
Part V
Part VI

　　促銷活動玩法其實很多樣化的（various），從包裝（packaging）、搭配物（tying product）、點數積分（bonus points）到價格（price），不一而足。單從價格來看，也有折扣、現金返還、降價、一元競標（bid from $1）、分期付款…等等。

　　在價格上作文章，可以給予消費者最直接的（the most direct）感受，因為原本要付出的錢變少了。競標的設計，也給予消費者「有機會撿到好康」（has chance to buy a product with lower price）的錯覺，有助迅速累積人氣（**popularity**）。

　　還有一種另類的促銷方式，是結合公益活動（charitable activities）。將消費者消費的金額撥一小部分捐助給某慈善機構，可以讓消費者在購物同時，也覺得回饋了社會；同時可以提升對企業的好感以及認同感，有助於品牌忠誠度（brand loyalty）的形成。

　　利用價格進行促銷活動，就需要特別留意金錢的部分，例如：要打多少折扣、預估帶來多少收入、是否有隱藏成本（hidden cost）、如果還要拆帳（split），該怎麼分配…等等問題。降價促銷也有學問，例如：要降到多少錢，才不會傷害品牌形象（brand image），但是又能吸引顧客上門。

　　在行銷上，沒有絕對的答案，除了行業之間存在的差別之外，依照公司或產品定位不同、客群不同，也會有不同操作手法；最直接的方法，可能就是鎖定行業中的某產品或企業，看看人家怎麼操作的，套用看看、調整看看，就會找到最適合自己品牌、產品的促銷方式了。

Related Word 相關詞彙

1. I am all ears.　洗耳恭聽

2. opposite　對面的

   文法加油站：opposite 有形容詞和副詞兩種詞性。

   I asked the woman opposite if she would close the window for me.

   我問了（坐在）對面地女士，她是否介意幫我關窗。

   The shop is opposite the train station.

   商店是在車站對面（的）。

3. differentiation strategy　差異化的策略。意旨和競爭者不同的策略或思維、做法。

   文法加油站：亦可簡稱為 differentiation。

4. cash refund　現金返還

5. reduced price　降價

6. under consideration　在考慮的範圍內

7. a hot one　炙手可熱的

   文法加油站：亦可置換為 a hot-shot one。另外，形容一個炙手可熱的人物，可以用 a sought-after。一個重量級 A 咖人物，則可以說 a big shot。

8. people who is keen on gaining petty advantages　貪小便宜的人

   文法加油站：同義詞還有 a thirty person，形容到處尋找買一送一或使用折價券優惠的人。

9. No pain, no gain　不辛苦哪有收穫，沒有不勞而獲的

10. I'll have the last laugh　笑到最後的人是我

    文法加油站：這句英語諺語的原文是 He who laughs last, laughs longest，意即笑到最後的人，笑得最長最好；引申為鹿死誰手還不知道呢的意思。

11. popularity　人氣，受歡迎

Exercises 練習題

Please complete the word or sentence by filling in the blanks.

Idioms game, please make a line match then English and Chinese.

成語遊戲，連連看。

- a sought-after
- a thirty person
- No pain, no gain
- I'll have the last laugh
- I am all ears.

- 貪小便宜
- 笑到最後的人是我
- 洗耳恭聽
- 炙手可熱
- 沒有不勞而獲的

Answers to the Unit:

（依照英文的順序）

- 炙手可熱
- 貪小便宜
- 沒有不勞而獲的
- 笑到最後的人是我
- 洗耳恭聽

Part I

Part II

Part III

Part IV

Part V

Part VI

Unit 10 Announcing Channels and Tools
如何宣傳

Background Introduction 背景介紹：

Minnie and Olga works at the same counter at a department store. They are talking about how to promote a promotion event of female shoes.
米妮和歐嘉在同一家百貨公司的專櫃工作。她們正在談論如何宣傳女鞋產品的促銷活動。

Conversation 對話

Minnie	**I didn't mean to pry**, Olga, but I am wondering if you know how the company will promote the female shoes on our counter?	我不是有意刺探，歐嘉，但是我在想你是否知道公司會怎麼促銷我們專櫃上的女鞋？
Olga	**You got me**, Minnie. I don't know, either.	你問倒我了耶，米妮。我也不曉得。
Minnie	Well, how do you think the company will proceed it?	嗯，那你覺得公司會怎麼進行啊？
Olga	I guess pretty much like last year. Newspaper ads, radio advertising, and join the department store's joint promotion.	我猜大概和去年一樣吧。報紙廣告、電台廣告、和參加百貨公司的聯合促銷活動。
Minnie	How did them work last year?	去年成效怎麼樣呢？

Olga	Well, overall, they were not bad. Except the joint promotion on department store's DM which sent to members.	整體來説還不錯啦。除了在百貨公司發給會員的 DM 上的聯合促銷。
Minnie	What happened?	怎麼了嗎？
Olga	The counter next us provided the lowest price, so they made the most sales volume than each female shoes counters.	我們隔壁的專櫃提供了最低價，所以他們的業績是所有女鞋專櫃裡最好的。
Minnie	It was **frustrating**, wasn't it? Didn't promotion events help to increase sales?	聽了真令人沮喪，不是嗎？過去的促銷活動都沒有幫忙提升業績嗎？
Olga	Yes, one or two. But you still need to **make a living** during non-promotion periods. Maybe we just didn't find the best way to contact and communicate with our customers.	有啊，一兩次吧。但是沒有促銷的時候也要討生活的。也許我們只是沒有找到最佳的方式去和我們的顧客接觸和溝通吧。
Minnie	What are you trying to say?	你想説什麼？

Part I
Part II
Part III
Part IV
Part V
Part VI

Olga	I mean, just look at what we have done so far. Newspapers, radio stations, join promotions, what we need is something outstanding and differential.	我是說，看看我們到現在為止所做的。報紙、廣播電台、聯合促銷，我們需要的是某些令人眼睛一亮和差異化的。
Minnie	What about magazine advertising or **advertorials**? It seems posting an advertisement in the form of an editorial is quite popular among readers, because when they read it, they image they are reading a true story rather than an advertisement.	如果是雜誌廣告或廣編稿呢？以編輯稿形式刊出的廣告，好像還蠻受讀者歡迎的，因為當他們閱讀的時候，他們會想像是在讀一個真實的故事而非看一則廣告。
Olga	Besides, the cost is also cheaper than posting an ad. What a surprise, Minnie! You seem know many things on how to announce a promotion event. Why don't we tell the marketing department what we suggested since we are **frontline** sales people here?	而且，成本比刊登廣告還低廉。我的天，米妮！你好像知道很多如何宣傳促銷活動的方式。既然我們是第一線銷售員，不如我們告訴行銷部門我們的建議？
Minnie	Do you think they will listen to us?	你想他們會聽我們的嗎？
Olga	Off course, don't be so **timid**. I am sure they are not **narrow-minded**, either.	當然囉，別這麼膽小嘛。我想他們也不是這麼心胸狹窄的人啦。

Part I　Part II　Part III　Part IV　Part V　Part VI

知識補給站

促銷活動宣傳的方式，除了上一篇提到的新興的（emerging）網路廣告以外，傳統的（traditional）宣傳方式不外乎電視、報紙、雜誌、廣播電台。以往廣告形式，不外乎從自家企業或品牌的角度出發，刊登一個編輯好的畫面或者播出一段錄好的對話，最大的目標是在有限的篇幅內，把產品特色或活動特色交代清楚詳細。這種形式的缺點（disadvantage）是，廣告角度是從企業面來說話，並沒有營造和目標群體對話溝通的空間。

正由於傳統廣告的形式相對降低了民眾對於廣告的信賴感（a sense of trust），卻也因此發展出廣編稿這種報導式文章的廣告。除了廣編稿，電台主持人或者專題報導（feature story）的推薦，也相對單純的播放廣告，要能吸引聽眾的注意或激起討論興趣。

尤有甚者，置入式行銷（embedded marketing）也成為另一種促銷或廣告宣傳的模式。藉由一部收視率高的電視影集（TV series/TV program）或人氣電影，在全國甚至全球播放，都是瞬間打開人氣，促進銷售的例子。

促銷宣傳的工具只要拿捏得當，確保訊息要傳達的目標對象能夠藉由宣傳管道得知訊息，就是達成促銷任務的一半了。

Part I

Part II

Part III

Part IV

Part V

Part VI

Related Word 相關詞彙

1. I didn't mean to pry. 我不是有意刺探
2. You got me. 你難倒我了
   > 文法加油站：got 是 get 的過去式，但是這句話並不是你找到我了的意思，而是你的問題把我難倒了、困住了的意思。
3. frustrating 令人沮喪的
4. make a living 謀生，討生活
5. advertorial 廣編稿
   > 文法加油站：本詞為兩個單字的結合，分別是 advertisement（廣告）and editorial（社論），意即像報導的廣告。
6. frontline 第一線的
   > 文法加油站：第一線的員工可寫作 frontline staffs/employees。
7. timid 膽小的、懦弱的、膽怯的
   > 文法加油站：同義詞還有 cowardly。
8. narrow-minded 小心眼，心胸狹窄的
9. feature story 專題報導
   > 文法加油站：feature 是特色的意思。原意是有特色的故事，引申為專題報導、特別報導的意思。
10. embedded marketing 置入式行銷
    > 文法加油站：亦可置換為 placement marketing 或 product placement。

    最典型的例子是電影 007 系列，男主角刻意在螢幕前露出手上戴的 OMEGA 手錶，以及開的不同品牌的跑車。

Exercises 練習題

Please complete the word or sentence by filling in the blanks.

A：It is so difficult to be an advertising man these years.

B：We just try to _____ here, so stop complaining.

A：The client only provides limited budget, while asking us to buy ads, to write

an _____ and plus a _____ . Sometimes, this

job could be very _____ .

B：You could just leave this _____ staff job.

A：I am afraid I will never find a job again.

B：You are so _____ .

請填空完成下面句子或單字

A：這年頭廣告人真不好當。

B：都是為了討生活，別抱怨了。

A：客戶只有很少的預算，又要購買廣告，又要我們寫廣編稿，還要置入式行銷。
有時候這份工作真令人感到沮喪。

B：你可以辭去當第一線工作人員的工作。

A：我怕我會再也找不到工作。

B：你真膽小，對自己這麼沒信心。

Answers to the Unit:
make a living
advertorial
embedded marketing/placement marketing/product placement
frustrating
frontline
timid/cowardly

Part I

Part II

*Part III

Part IV

Part V

Part VI

Unit 11 Key Points of Hosting a Meeting-1
主持會議要點

Situation 1　情境 1：

Edmund is presenting the Father's Day Promotion Campaign of shoes and accessories for the sales team.
艾德蒙正在為銷售團隊簡報父親節鞋子與配件的促銷活動。

Key points for your conversation 對話急救包

向在座同事打招呼

Distinguished colleagues:
各位優秀的同事們：

I would like to begin my presentation by thanking you all for coming along here today.
簡報一開始，我要先感謝各位今天的參與。

Good morning, everyone. I hope it will not take too long to finish my presentation and that you will find it interesting.
早安，各位。我希望我的簡報用不了太長的時間，而且聽起來不無聊。

說明簡報順序

Now let me begin by the purpose of this event. Secondly, I will **describe** our target audiences. Thirdly, I will **talk about** promotion period and places. And finally, I will **show** you promotion contents.

現在，讓我從這次活動的目的談起。第二，我將會描述我們鎖定的目標消費族群。
第三，我會談到促銷時間和地點。最後，我會告訴各位促銷的內容。
小貼士：describe、talk about、show 可以互換。

I will to make some points on this time's promotion event. First, the purpose. Second, target market. The third point relates to period and places. The last point concerns announced channels and tools.

我想針對這次的促銷活動提幾點事項。第一，目的。第二，目標市場。第三是關於期間和地點。第四是關於宣傳的管道和工具。

歸納重點

Finally, as a summary **statement**, I would like to say that with this time's promotion strategy, an increased sales is expectable.

最後，在結論的部分，我想說透過這是的促銷策略，業績的提升是可以被預期的。

小貼士：statement 可置換為 description。

Before I close, I must say a few words about why we chose Facebook as out advertising channel.

在我結束之前，我必須針對為什麼選擇臉書作為我們廣告管道說幾句話。

To summarize, giving a discount has been used for many years in our company, and each time helped to bring significant sales volume for us.

總而言之，打折已經在我們公司行之有年，而且每次都已經帶來可觀的銷售額。

小貼士：To summarize 可置換為 To sum up、In summary。

Part I

Part II

Part III

Part IV

Part V

Part VI

1
3
1

Unit 11　Key Points of Hosting a Meeting-2
主持會議要點

Situation 2　情境2:

Fiona is giving a presentation of the 25th Brand Anniversary Promotion Event to channel partners at the conference room.
費歐娜正在會議室裡向通路商簡報這次品牌 25 周年慶的促銷活動內容。

Key points for your conversation 對話急救包

📎 自我介紹與主題說明

First, please let me welcome you. My name is Fiona and I am in charging of the 25th Brand Anniversary Promotion Event.
首先，容我歡迎各位。我的名字是費歐娜，是這次品牌 25 周年慶促銷活動的負責人。

This conference will be devoted primarily to the discussion of the various sections of the 25th Brand Anniversary Promotion Event.
這次會議主要是討論品牌 25 周年慶促銷活動的各個不同主題。

Good afternoon, Ladies and Gentlemen: I would like to welcome you all to the meeting of the 25th Brand Anniversary Promotion Event.
午安，各位女士、先生，歡迎大家參加品牌 25 周年慶促銷活動的會議。

📎 簡報內容說明

The first point I would like to make about Anniversary Promotion Event is we will list each of you on our advertisements. The next point I would like to bring up has to do with promotion materials.
關於週年慶促銷活動，第一點我想要說的是，我們將會把各位刊登在我們的廣告上。我要提到的下一點是關於促銷製作物。

Rather than giving a summary of Anniversary Promotion Event, I would prefer to emphasize certain important objectives of it.
與其對周年慶促銷活動提供摘要，我傾向強調幾個重要的項目。

分段提出重點

The first thing which I would like to discuss is our promotion contents.
我想討論的第一件事情是我們促銷的內容。

We will move on to how to display promotion materials.
我們將進行到如何陳列促銷製作物。

Your question brings me to my third point.
您的問題引出我要說的第三點。

Let's return to what each of us thinks important.
讓我們回到大家認為重要的議題上。

省略或停止現場討論

I cannot be comprehensive here in the short time available. So I would like to refer you to the documents I provided, and please send me an E-Mail if you have further questions.
由於時間的關係，我無法在此詳盡說明。所以請各位參考我提供的資料，假如您有更深入的問題，歡迎 E-Mail 給我。

I have to skip this section because of time limitation.
我必須跳過這個主題，因為時間的限制。

感謝出席

Thank you very much for your patience in listening to a long talk.
非常感謝各位耐心聽完冗長的簡報。

My last word again is how happy I am to talk before you, and I wish the result of this Anniversary event will be exceeded our expectations.
我最後幾句話是，很高興能在各位面前進行說明，我也預祝周年慶活動的結果會超出我們的預期。

Part III

Public Relations (PR) Event
公關宣傳活動

Unit 12 Situation Analysis-1
需要什麼樣的公關宣傳

Background Introduction 背景介紹：

Ian is the PR Manager of Global Company, and Kenneth is a reporter. Today, Kenneth is interviewing Ian regarding the topic of the PR activity which Global Company was conducting and helped their dealers increase sales.

伊恩是環球公司的公關經理，肯尼斯則是一位新聞採訪記者。今天，肯尼斯針對環球公司幫助旗下經銷商業績成長的公關活動，對伊恩進行訪問。

Conversation 1 對話1

Ian	Welcome, Kenneth. Have a seat, please.	歡迎，肯尼斯。請坐。
Kenneth	Thank you, Ian. It's nice to see you again.	謝謝你，伊恩。很高興再次見到你。
Ian	Sure, me too. I am sure you have already received our news release about how the PR activity helped our distributors increase their sales volume.	彼此彼此。我相信你已經收到關於我們如何透過公關活動，順利幫助了我們經銷商提升銷售量的新聞稿。
Kenneth	I did, that's why I am here to have more information about this. Can you tell me where the whole idea was from?	收到了，這也是為什麼我會在這裡想獲得更多資訊的原因。你可以告訴我這整個計畫的想法從何而來的？

Ian	I will be glad to share the whole story with you. As you may know, we **faced sales bottleneck** last year, so from the beginning of this year, my department suggested that Global Company can provide something new to help our deals.	我很高興和你分享。你或許知道，我們去年面臨了銷售上的瓶頸，所以從今年初開始，我的部門建議公司可以提供一些新作法來幫助我們的經銷商。
Kenneth	So you started the Good Neighbor Project.	所以你們就開始了「好鄰居計畫」。
Ian	Yes, through three month discussion and adjustment, we finally **reached a consensus** with our two hundred distributors.	是的，透過三個月的討論和調整，我們最終和兩百位經銷商達成共識。
Kenneth	It's a big project, wasn't it?	這真是個大工程，不是嗎？
Ian	Indeed, indeed. You see, we didn't know how it would work, however, it could be a great chance to help our dealers to enhance the relationship with local customers. **Present and potential** ones.	的確，的確。你知道嗎，其實當時我們也不確定會怎麼樣，但是，這可能是一個絕佳的機會，來幫助我們經銷商加強與當地消費者的關係。就是對目前和未來的消費者來做。
Kenneth	So Global Company decided to proceed the project.	所以全球公司決定進行這計畫。

Part I

Part II

Part III

Part IV

Part V

Part VI

Part I

Part II

Part III

Part IV

Part V

Part VI

Ian	Yes. After three months' planning and communication and three months' training, we started to help dealers to build the image of "Global Company is your good neighbor" around Taiwan.	是的。經過三個月的計畫和溝通,加上另外三個月的訓練,我們開始幫助經銷商們在台灣建立「全球公司就是你的好鄰居」的印象。
Kenneth	I heard the things your dealers were doing are quite **touching**. Would you want to tell me some more stories?	我聽說你們有些經銷商做了些令人感動事情。你想要和我分享這些故事嗎?
Ian	Sure. The employees from our dealers picked one community near by their store each weekend, and provided free checking service for **home appliances**. **On one occasion**, we found an elderly **solitary** woman passed out in her apartment and thanks to our dealer, the woman was saved after sent to the hospital.	當然。我們經銷商的員工們,每週會在他們店附近挑選一個社區,提供免費的家電用品確認服務。有一次,我們發現一個獨居的老婦人在她公寓裡昏倒了,感謝我們的經銷商,這位女士在醫院撿回了一命。
Kenneth	The story must be reported on the front page of local news. What are the other stories?	這個故事一定登上了地方新聞的頭版。還有其他故事嗎?

Ian	Not only through providing repairing service, but also helping shoppers from supermarket to help them carry the shopping goods and walk them to their cars.	不只是通過提供維修服務，還有幫助從超市購物出來的民眾提物品和陪他們走回到車旁。
Kenneth	It sounds like a shopping accompanying service.	聽起來就像是購物陪同服務一般。
Ian	Yes, you are right. But it **turned out** that everybody loved it!	對，你答對了。但是我們發現每個人都愛這項服務！
Kenneth	I bet it is. So, could you tell me how much the sales volume was increased through this project?	我相信一定是。那你可以透漏透過這個活動，銷售量上升了多少呢？
Ian	After six months hard working, our sales volume has increased 13%. We are all happy about the result.	在經過六個月的辛勤後，我們的銷售量上升了13%。大家都很滿意這個結果。
Kenneth	It seems that Global Company did not only improve the brand's image, but also brought incomes for the corporate.	看來全球公司不只是促進了品牌形象，還為企業增加了收入。

Part I

Part II

Part III

Part IV

Part V

Part VI

Ian	Very true. So, I hope you are satisfied with what we talked about today.	你說得很對。那麼,我希望你對我們今天的談話滿意。
Kenneth	Yes, thank you for your time, Ian.	滿意,謝謝你的時間,伊恩。
Ian	Not a problem. Please call me or E-Mail me if you have any question.	不客氣。如果你有任何疑問,歡迎打電話或 E-Mail 給我。
Kenneth	I will let you know. Keep in touch, goodbye.	我會讓你知道的。保持聯繫,再見。
Ian	Goodbye.	再見。

Part I
Part II
Part III
Part IV
Part V
Part VI

140

知識補給站

公關行銷（public relations marketing）簡單來說，就是替個人或企業建立（build）、改善（improve）公眾關係的一種行銷方式。建立公關的方式有：贊助公益活動（sponsored activity）、寄送企業刊物（company publication）、舉辦業內或業外活動爭取公共報導（public report）、舉辦事件行銷（**event marketing**）…等等。

公關行銷的運用操作可以回溯到 18 世紀的英國選舉，某個競選團隊在大選中利用貴族名人、媒體關係協助候選人順利當選。發展至今，面貌和手法已經相當多元，甚至在生活當中，消費者也被企業的事件行銷給消費了而不自知。

成功操作公關行銷的要點有二；第一是創造媒體與大眾都感興趣的話題（create the issues/topics which are interested by media or publics）， 第二是與時俱進，也就是要掌握社會或消費者生活型態的脈動（**grasp the pulse of consumers**），第三則是達成目標：替企業創造價值（create value）和爭取正面的曝光（get positive **media coverage**）。

最好的例子是，前一陣子流行騎腳踏車，凡是和腳踏車有關的新聞不難獲得媒體青睞；再來是台中大甲媽祖（Mazu/Matsu）成功創造地方特色行銷事件，每年三月，只要是和媽祖有關的話題，也很容易躍上媒體版面。

Part I
Part II
Part III
Part IV
Part V
Part VI

Related Word 相關詞彙

1. face sales bottleneck　遇到銷售瓶頸

   文法加油站：bottleneck 見字拆意就是瓶子的脖子，也就是瓶頸的意思。用法
   *　　　如下：*

   Do you have bottlenecks in your business?　你生意上有瓶頸嗎？

   Are you facing bottlenecks in your marriage?　你的婚姻正面臨瓶頸嗎？

2. reach a consensus　達成共識

3. present and potential　現在的和潛在的（未來有可能是的）

4. touching　令人感動的

5. home appliance　家電用品

   文法加油站：意可置換為 home electrical appliances。

6. On one occasion　有一次，一個偶然的機會下

7. solitary　獨居的

8. turn out　變成是，結果是

   文法加油站：同義詞是 become，但是 turn out 更口語一點。

9. event marketing　事件行銷。指創造或利用能夠引起社會大眾關心的議
   題，將企業或品牌與此事件進行某種關聯，以營造話題，從而在媒體報導
   與消費者參與事件時，達到提升形象與產品銷售的目的。

10. grasp the pulse of consumers　掌握消費者的脈動

    文法加油站：pulse 是脈搏的意思，在此引申為消費者喜好或習慣的動向、跳
    *　　　動的方向。*

11. media coverage　媒體曝光，媒體報導

Exercises 練習題

Please complete the word or sentence by filling in the blanks.

A：I am _____ .

B：What happen?

A：I really want to know how to become a brilliant PR person. I wanted to create as much _____ as I can for the clients, but it _____ negative.

B：That is really bad. I think the necessary condition is to _____ . I will suggest you to try again.

A：I will, thanks.

B：You bet.

請填空完成下面句子或單字

A：我工作正遭遇瓶頸。

B：怎麼了？

A：我不知道如何成為一位好的公關人。我想替客戶爭取很多正面媒體曝光，卻變成負面的。

B：真糟糕。我想掌握消費者脈動應該是必要的條件吧。建議你再試試看。

A：我會的，謝謝你。

B：不客氣。

Answers to the Unit:
facing/having bottlenecks in my business
positive media coverage
turned out
grasp the pulse of consumers

Part I

Part II

Part III

Part IV

Part V

Part VI

Unit 12 Situation Analysis-2
需要什麼樣的公關宣傳

Background Introduction 背景介紹：

Zoe, Pearce and Quincy are now talking about how to get more media coverage when the client launches the new sports shoes.
柔伊、皮爾斯和昆西正在談論客戶的新款運動鞋上市時，如何爭取媒體曝光。

Conversation 2 對話 2

Zoe	We'd better hand this PR proposal over to the client by this Friday.	我們最好在這個禮拜五之前就把公關提案交到客戶手上。
Pearce	True, I certainly don't want to be chased by them.	是的，我可不想被他們追殺。
Quincy	Where should we start it, then?	那我們從哪裡開始討論起？
Zoe	Since the mission this time is to **get** as much **media coverage** as possible, why don't we start with what the media would be interested in regards a new launched sports shoes.	既然這次任務是盡可能獲得越多媒體的報導，為什麼我們不開始討論對一款新上市的運動鞋來說，有什麼可以讓媒體感到興趣？

Pearce	I am **very impressive**, Zoe! You don't look like you just came to the company for only three months.	真令人印象深刻，柔伊！你可一點也不像進公司才三個月的。
Zoe	Well, thank you, Pearce. I tried my best to learn.	謝謝你喔，皮爾斯。我盡力學習了。
Quincy	Come back to the topic, I think we need to invite a sports star in order to get medias' attention.	回到討論的主題上，我想為了獲得媒體注意，我們需要邀請一個運動明星。
Pearce	Nice point, but do we have enough budget for this?	好主意，但是我們有沒有足夠的預算請明星？
Zoe	I guess the answer is yes. But I personally don't feel comfortable with hiring a spokesperson, you know, a stranger shouldn't represent the entire company.	我想是有的。但是我個人覺得邀請代言人有點不能接受，你也知道，一個陌生人並不能代表一整個公司。
Quincy	But this is the quickest way to **catch media's eyes**.	但是這是吸引媒體目光最快的方式。

Part I

Part II

Part III

Part IV

Part V

Part VI

Part I

Part II

Part III

Part IV

Part V

Part VI

Zoe	I am not sure, Quincy. I mean, plenty of male of female models also can do. Besides, a spokesman could have personal life issues we need to deal with during the new product launch period. It sounds very risky to me.	我不太確定耶，昆西。我是說，很多男模特或女模特也能啊。而且，在新品上市期間，代言人可能會有個人私生活的問題要我們處理喔。對我來說風險很大。
Pearce	Yes, Zoe has made a good point on this issue. Listen, why don't we **postpone this topic** and come back to it later.	對的，柔伊點出了這個議題上的重點。這樣吧，我們為什麼不延遲討論這個議題，然後待會再回來討論。
Quincy	It is fine for me. I am just saying that if we invited a sports star, then we can not only invite **lifestyle reporters**, but also entertainment reporters.	我沒問題啊。我只是想說如果我們邀請了一位運動明星，那我們就可以不只是邀請生活線記者（報導鞋子），還有娛樂線記者（報導明星）。
Pearce	I know **media attendance** is very important to us, but we need to consider the **pros and cons**.	我知道媒體出席對我們很重要，但是我們需要全盤考量優點與缺點。
Zoe	I agree. I think except a spokesman, models, we still need something different.	我同意。我想除了代言人，模特兒，我們還需要一點不一樣的東西。

Pearce	Something like an eye-catching ceremony?	例如吸引目光的儀式？
Quincy	How about an indoor sports game? The reporters are welcome to wear our sports shoes and to compete with our spokesman, the prize will be offered to the reporters who win the competition.	不如一場室內競技怎麼樣？記者們可以穿上我們的球鞋和代言人 PK，哪位記者贏了就可以獲得獎品。
Zoe	I like the idea! So we can show the new developed technology of flexibility of the shoes by our client. What do you say, Pearce?	我喜歡這個想法耶！這樣一來我們就可以秀出客戶針對鞋子新研發的彈性科技。你說呢，皮爾斯？
Pearce	Yes, why not? It seems we combine the product features and fun, I am sure we will be succeeding this time. However, did you just mentioned a spokesman, Quincy?	好呀，為什麼不呢？看來我們可以結合產品特性和娛樂，我相信這一次一定會成功的。但是，你剛才提到了代言人是嗎，昆西？
Quincy	Did I?	我有嗎？
Zoe	OK, it's time to discuss this issue, then.	好吧，那是時候來討論這個議題了。

Part I

Part II

Part III

Part IV

Part V

Part VI

Part I

Part II

Part III

Part IV

Part V

Part VI

Pearce	Why don't we vote for this, since someone ignore the consensus we had reached?	為什麼我們不乾脆投票好了，既然有人忽視剛才我們達成的共識？
Quincy	No, that would be so unprofessional. Just give me a chance to prove that I am right.	不，這聽起來不怎麼專業。給我一次機會證明我是對的嘛。
Pearce	Since we "might" invite a spokesman, why don't we confirm his time first to see if we can find the matches with the date when the most reporters can attend?	既然我們「也許」會邀請代言人，為什麼不先確認他的時間，然後再看是否能符合大多數記者能出席的日期。
Quincy	Maybe there are some other PR events during the following weeks, and I think the best way is to find out all of them so we can avoid those days.	也許接下來幾週有其他的公關活動，我想最好的方式是查出全部的活動，我們就能避開這些日期。
Zoe	That is a very good idea, perhaps you can help to do that.	很好的想法，也許你可以幫忙做這件事。
Quincy	No problem.	沒問題啊！
Zoe	You wish.	你想得美。

知識補給站

以邀請媒體參加的公關活動，常用的型態有記者會（press conference）、媒體聚會（media gathering）、專訪（interview），邀請參加的人數也相對遞減，記者會大至 200 人甚至更多（例如：奧林匹克運動會的全球記者會），專訪則一次只會有一家媒體；最大目的當然是爭取媒體曝光的版面，以及藉由媒體傳遞公司或品牌想要表達的訊息。

邀請媒體參與的公關活動想要傳遞的訊息也很多元，從新產品上市（new product launch）、產品測試（product testing）、說明公司經營策略發展方向（explain company business strategy）、打知名度（increase name recognition）、定期讓消費者了解公司或品牌動向（let consumers know the company or brand trend），甚至到向特定族群（例如政府）表達意見（express their views）…等等。

媒體在報導時，考量的重點，除了該活動本身的話題性之外，如果有名人的參與，被報導的機會也會增加；這也就是許多活動，會邀請到明星擔任代言人的目的。但是代言人的運用，對品牌或企業有正面（positive）也有負面（negative）的影響；如果不幸地，在代言期間，發生了負面的新聞或誹聞（gossip），就會連帶影響產品或公司的形象。

在眾多媒體當中，也是有次序的問題存在，通常知名媒體在公關的眼裡，會相對受到照顧和安排；通常這些記者也會有機會靠近公司高層，獲得比較特殊或第一手的消息（first-hand news）。但是，也有些產品是針對小眾群體使用的，反而知名媒體沒有報導的興趣，這時候，小眾媒體（alternative media）就是這個領域的「大咖」，值得公關們好好運用了。

Part I
Part II
Part III
Part IV
Part V
Part VI

Related Word 相關詞彙

1. get media coverage　爭取媒體報導
2. very impressive　令人刮目相看，印象深刻
3. catch media's eye　抓住媒體目光

　　文法加油站：*eye-catching* 則是引人注目的意思。

4. postpone this topic　延後討論這個議題

　　文法加油站：另一種講法是 *postpone discussion of*…，延後討論…。

5. lifestyle reporters　生活線的記者

　　文法加油站：專指報導有關生活議題的記者，舉凡美食、美酒、健康、消費用
　　　　　　　品…等等

6. media attendance　媒體出席人數，媒體出席狀況
7. pros and cons　優點和缺點

　　文法加油站：在拉丁語裡，這句話是 *pro et contra* 的簡稱，表示 *for and*
　　　　　　　against，也就是優缺點、好處與壞處的意思。

8. name recognition　知名度

　　文法加油站：*recognition* 是認出的意思，直譯的話是認出名字，引申為知名
　　　　　　　度的意思。

9. brand trend　品牌動向

　　文法加油站：*trend* 是趨勢的意思，在此引申為發展的動向（其實也隱含趨勢
　　　　　　　的意思）。

10. gossip　緋聞、八卦、流言

　　文法加油站：同義詞還有 *rumor*。

11. alternative media　小眾媒體

Exercises 練習題

Please complete the word or sentence by filling in the blanks according to the color.

media		
	media	media's
		eye
	media	

請依照不同顏色空格的提示填空完成下面句子或單字

媒體	出席狀況	抓住
小眾	媒體	媒體的
		目光
爭取	媒體	報導

Answers to the Unit:

media	attendance	catch
alternative	media	media's
		eye
get	media	coverage

Part I

Part II

Part III

Part IV

Part V

Part VI

Unit 12 Situation Analysis-3
需要什麼樣的公關宣傳

Background Introduction 背景介紹：

Yvonne and Uerica are discussing what PR activities they can hold for consumers relates to their company's products.

伊馮娜和兒瑞嘉正在討論公司產品可以針對消費者進行哪些公關活動。

Conversation 3 對話 3

Yvonne	I think we already ran out all the ideas of how to attract consumers to join our PR campaign, I wish we could **have a wild guess**.	我想我們已經用光了所有如何吸引消費者參加公關活動的點子了，我真希望我們可以瞎猜一通。
Uerica	It is so difficult, isn't it? We need to make a list about the ideas we already used, and also have a look at what competitors are doing in the market.	的確不容易，對吧？我們需要列一張關於已經用過的想法的清單，然後也看看競爭者在市場上正在做什麼。
Uerica	We already tried a new product launch press conference last year, but it didn't produce **a great deal of** immediate press coverage. How about we open a dozen of free testing kitchenware for the people who come to our counters earliest every day?	我們去年已經試過了新產品發表記者會，但是並沒有立即呈現大量的媒體曝光。不如我們開放 12 個免費試用廚房用具，給每天最早到我們專櫃上的消費者？

Yvonne	Or the Top 10 buyers during a limited period? A PR event is going to contribute to sales after all.	還是在一段時間內購物前 10 名的消費者？公關活動畢竟還是要對銷售有所貢獻。
Uerica	You also made an **excellent** point. Let's write it down first and see what boss will say.	你也提到一個絕佳的關鍵。我們寫下來然後看老闆怎麼說。
Yvonne	OK. What else?	好。還有呢？
Uerica	Since most of our kitchenware is selling to females, particularly 30 to 50 years old. So, maybe we need a handsome male here.	既然我們大多數的廚房用具都賣給女性，尤其是 30 到 50 歲的。那麼，也許我們應該要找個帥哥？
Yvonne	I like a **lady killer** too, but what is the **key message** he will deliver to our customers?	我也喜歡師奶殺手啊，但是要他傳遞給我們的消費者什麼關鍵訊息？
Uerica	Let me think. How about let the guy be a chief at our counters around Taiwan, cooks for customers and who buys under his recommendation will get an opportunity of having him to cook at the customer's home.	讓我想想。如果是讓他當我們台灣所有專櫃的一日主廚，給消費者烹飪食物，而且誰在他的推薦下購買的話，就會得到由他前往該消費者家中烹飪的機會。

Part I
Part II
Part III
Part IV
Part V
Part VI

Yvonne	Oh my God, Uerica! You are absolutely an genius! We can sell our products and build up a positive brand image and relationship with customers at the same time.	我的天啊，兒瑞嘉！你簡直就是個天才！我們可以藉此銷售產品，還可以建立同時正面的品牌形象和消費者關係。
Uerica	I just love to watch some TV programs, and the "Take Home Chief" is definitely my flavor. I am always thinking maybe one day we could take it **for reference**.	我只是愛看電視節目，「帥哥廚師到我家」絕對是我的最愛。我總是想也許有一天我們可以參考它。
Yvonne	Not bad. I will finish the proposal draft and you can check it later.	也不錯。我會完成這個提案的初稿，然後你可以稍後確認一下。
Uerica	No problem. We will **drop a bombshell** to the market.	沒問題。我們肯定會給市場投下一枚震撼彈的。

知識補給站

Part I

Part II

Part III

Part IV

Part V

Part VI

　　公關活動除了有以經銷商、媒體為對象，還有一種屬於邀請社會大眾作為參加對象的。這一類的運用不勝枚舉，諸如：縣市政府舉辦的慶典、企業或品牌邀請代言人與民同樂、唱片公司見面會、簽名會（autograph signing），甚至企業或品牌舉辦的員工、眷屬運動會…等等都是。

　　這一類公關活動與邀請經銷商或媒體參加的不同處在於，變數（variables）和危險係數（risk factors）都相對比較高，現場控制和應變能力（control and adaptability）要很好才行；換句話說，事前要考慮到的細節（details）比較繁瑣（complex）。

　　執行公關活動的好處最常被提到的事實是，運用比廣告費用還低的成本，達成媒體曝光的任務。再者，還有協助產品的銷售（help in sale）；如果參加公關活動是需要先消費（例如：購買一片歌手新推出的 CD），也會間接帶動銷售量。第三，激勵與提升員工士氣（inspiring and building staff morale）；任何一位員工，參與公司公關活動的進行，協助建立或傳遞企業在社會大眾心中的正面形象，有助於加強公司與員工之間的關係。第四，獲得大眾的支持；形象良好的企業，在需要大眾參與相關活動或者尋求政府、學術單位支援（seeking for government and higher education institutions）時，比較容易獲得青睞。

Related Word 相關詞彙

1. have a wild guess　亂猜、瞎猜

 　　文法加油站：have 亦可置換為 make 或 take。

2. a great deal of　大量的

 　　文法加油站：of 後可接名詞，a great deal 後則不限定只能接名詞。

3. excellent　絕佳的

 　　文法加油站：同義詞還有 great、fabulous、perfect。

4. lady killer　師奶殺手

5. key message　關鍵訊息、關鍵印象

6. for reference　作為參考

 　　文法加油站：這裡的 reference 作為名詞使用。動詞是 refer + to，表示參考…
 　　　　　　　的意思。

7. drop a bombshell　投下震撼彈

8. autograph signing　簽名會

 　　文法加油站：autograph 是題字、簽名的意思，動名詞同字。後面加上
 　　　　　　　signing

9. adaptability　應變能力

 　　文法加油站：adapt 是適應某人事物的意思，加上 ability 能力，就是適應力的
 　　　　　　　意思。

10. staff morale　員工士氣，員工情緒

Part I　Part II　Part III　Part IV　Part V　Part VI

Exercises 練習題

Please complete the word or sentence by filling in the blanks.

● An excellent PR person needs ＿＿＿＿＿＿＿＿＿ and keeps learning.

● Please do not ＿＿＿＿＿＿＿＿＿ , he is not that ＿＿＿＿＿＿＿＿＿ .

● I am rushing to attend a ＿＿＿＿＿＿＿＿＿ .

● Looking for correct answers from ＿＿＿＿＿＿＿＿＿ of ＿＿＿＿＿＿＿＿＿ is not an easy thing.

請填空完成下面句子或單字

● 一名優秀的公關人員需要應變能力和不斷地學習。

● 請不要亂猜，他並不是那位師奶殺手。

● 我正趕著去參加簽名會。

● 從大量的關鍵訊息中找出正確答案，真不是件容易的事。

Answers to the Unit:
adaptability
have/make/take a wild guess
lady killer
autograph signing
a great deal
key messages

Part I

Part II

Part III

Part IV

Part V

Part VI

Unit 13 Setting Goals and Objectives for the Event-1 先設定山頭，再開打

Background Introduction 背景介紹：

Abigail is a PR Manager of Z Company, and Richard is a Project Manager of Y PR Company. They are now setting the PR goals for the new skin care products launches during the upcoming Christmas season.

愛碧蓋兒是 Z 公司的公關經理，理察則是 Y 公關公司的專案經理。他們正在就聖誕節即將新上市的保養品設定公關任務目標。

Conversation 1 對話 1

Richard	Hello, Abigail. It's nice to have you here.	你好，愛碧蓋兒。很高興妳來到這裡。
Abigail	Sorry, Richard, I couldn't invite you to go to our office because it's now **under decoration**.	抱歉，理察，我們辦公室現在正在裝潢中，所以沒辦法邀請你去。
Richard	That's not a problem at all.	完全沒問題的。
Abigail	Thank you, let's begin the meeting. I am looking forward to it since last week.	謝了，我們開會吧。我從上週就開始期待了。

Richard	Sure. As you already knew our main goal for the Christmas PR event is to attract as much online and offline media as possible.	好。如同妳已經知道的，這次聖誕節公關活動的主要目的是，吸引越多的線上與線下媒體越好。
Abigail	Not only have media attendance, but also **media exposure**.	不是只有媒體出席人數，還有媒體曝光。
Richard	Off course, I am going to talk about that. The objectives are, first, successfully deliver the key message to all medias. Second, reach more than thirty media exposures.	當然，我正要談到這個。任務目標就是，第一，成功地傳遞關鍵訊息給所有媒體。第二，達到超過 30 篇曝光（報導）數量。
Abigail	On newspaper and internet?	在報紙與網路上？
Richard	Yes, also including radio and magazines.	對，還包括廣播與雜誌。
Abigail	Fantastic. Wait a minute, can we compare the media exposures with last year?	很棒。等等，我們能不能比較一下去年的媒體曝光？
Richard	Sure, here they are.	當然，在這裡。

Part I

Part II

Part III

Part IV

Part V

Part VI

Abigail	Let me see…here, we had forty five media exposures last year. I need more this year, how about we **raise the standard** to over fifty.	讓我看看,這裡,去年我們有 45 篇媒體曝光。今年我需要更多,不如提高標準到超過 50 篇吧。
Richard	You know we always will try our best, but it is hard to guarantee the exact number.	妳知道我們總是會盡最大努力達成,但是要保證確切的數字也很難。
Abigail	I understand, let's set a range then. Maybe forty five to fifty five?	我了解,我們訂個範圍好了。也許是 45 到 55 篇?
Richard	OK, I will adjust the number here.	好的,我會調整數字。
Abigail	The other thing is, since there are many young people use Facebook now, I need more online exposures and meanwhile, **raise** as much **online discussion** as you can in order to **distribute new product information**.	還有另一件事情是,既然現在有很多年輕朋友使用臉書,我需要更多的網路曝光,同時,激起越多網路討論越好,以便散佈新的產品訊息。
Richard	In this way, I can ensure you that media exposure from internet will be more than fifty.	這樣的話,我可以保證網路上的媒體曝光就會超過 50 篇了。

Part I
Part II
Part III
Part IV
Part V
Part VI

Abigail	It is good to hear that. By the way, what is the key message your team have created for the event?	很高興聽到你這樣說。對了，你們團隊為這次活動想了什麼關鍵訊息？
Richard	The key concept is to deliver a warm, joyful and amazing **atmosphere**.	主要概念是傳遞一個溫馨、愉悅的和令人感到驚喜的氛圍。
Abigail	I don't like the word "amazing" here, our new product this time has nothing to do with the word.	我不喜歡這個 " 令人感到驚喜的 " 用詞，我們新產品和這個詞一點關係也沒有。
Richard	Sorry about the misunderstanding, should we focus on warm and joyful, then?	抱歉誤會了，那我們是否應該專注在溫馨和令人愉悅的？
Abigail	I will need another word to make the whole concept more complete. Maybe you can email me your idea later.	我會需要另一個詞，讓整個概念更完整。也許你稍後 E-Mail 給我吧。
Richard	I would love to.	我很樂意。

Part I

Part II

Part III

Part IV

Part V

Part VI

Abigail	Oh, there is one thing. Look at me, **I have a head like a sieve**. We will invite a **super model** to join with us on the first day of launch.	喔，還有一件事。你看我，真是貴人多忘事。我們會邀請一位名模在上市的第一天參加我們活動。
Richard	No kidding. Then we probably need to fix the whole key concept, perhaps add some product personalities from the model's **perspective**.	不是開玩笑的吧。那我們可能需要修改整個關鍵概念了，也許是從這位名模的觀點加上一些產品特性。
Abigail	Let's see your adjusted proposal first, then we discuss further. Thank you, Richard, I guess I'll see you at the same time next week?	讓我們先看看你調整後的提案，然後再進一步討論。謝謝你，理察，下週同一個時間見？
Richard	Sure, see you until next week.	當然，下週見。

知識補給站

　　公關活動是為了解決企業問題，而與媒體或大眾進行的溝通；這些問題可能包括有：提升新產品在市場上的知名度（**increasing product awareness**）、讓大眾認識產品的某項特色（knowing product features）或政府政策（knowing government polices）、傳達企業關懷社會或環境議題、化解民眾對企業或產品誤會（**resolve misunderstandings** of companies or products）…等等。

　　要留意的是，往往公關人（a PR person）會在設定公關活動要達成的目標（objective）時，想要「一石多鳥（kill many birds with one stone）」；卻往往在檢討結果的時候，顧此失彼，被客戶檢討沒有達到當初設定的多個目標。

　　事實上，要在一個活動中傳達或達成多個目標是有相對的難度，就算目標有其相關聯性（relevance），也會隨著目標數增加而遞減達成率；假設目標間沒有很直接的關係，就不是很理想的目標組合。

　　舉例來説，「順利傳達公司是社會關懷者的印象」和「讓消費者知道產品用某某最新科技製成」就不是很有關聯性（non-relevance）的目標。公關人在企劃的時候，就需要留意這些陷阱（those **catches**）。

Part I

Part II

Part III

Part IV

Part V

Part VI

Related Word 相關詞彙

1. under decoration 裝潢中
   文法加油站：*home/office decorating* 為居家 / 辦公室裝潢的意思。

2. media exposure 媒體曝光
   文法加油站：*exposure* 為曝光的名詞。這個單詞常見於公關和廣告領域。

3. raise the standard 提升 / 高標準

4. raise online discussion 引起 / 激起網上的討論
   文法加油站：*激起網友的討論則是 raise netizens' discussion. Netizen 是由 Internet and citizen 所組成的單詞，可翻成網友或網民。*

5. distribute new product information 散佈新產品訊息

6. atmosphere 氣氛，氛圍
   文法加油站：*和氣氛相關的常用口語是 Read the air！就是要旁邊的人別再白目亂發言，讀一讀身旁的氣氛，不要說不該說的話的意思。*

7. I have a head like a sieve 貴人多忘事
   文法加油站：*sieve 是篩子的意思，直譯是頭腦像篩子一樣，漏洞百出。*

8. super model 超級名模

9. perspective 觀點
   文法加油站：*這個字也有透視圖、透視、眼界、視野的意思。另外，要表達個人觀點，可以用 From one's perspective 或 From one's point of view。*

10. increasing product awareness 提升產品知名度

11. resolve misunderstandings 化解誤會
    文法加油站：*resolve 有名詞和動詞兩種用法，作名詞為決心的意思，作動詞有解決、決議、下決心、使溶解（分解）的意思。*
    The company resolved that a four-day work week will become real from next month. 公司決議從下個月開始，實現一周上班四天的計畫。

12. catch 陷阱，圈套
    文法加油站：*catch 作動詞有抓的意思；在這裡作名詞，就有陷阱、圈套的意思。口語中常問人 What is the catch? 意即陷阱在哪裡，或要小心什麼地方？*

Exercises 練習題

Please complete the word or sentence by filling in the blanks.

A：I heard that the ＿＿＿＿＿＿＿＿＿＿ Picachu is going to come to Taiwan.

B：No kidding! When is that?

A：This Friday.

B：This gonna ＿＿＿＿＿＿＿＿＿＿ . When did you say she's going to come?

A：This Friday. You really ＿＿＿＿＿＿＿＿＿＿＿＿ .

B：Sorry, I got it now. This Thursday, right?

A：I don't want to talk to you anymore.

請填空完成下面句子或單字

A：我聽說超級名模皮卡秋要來台灣了。

B：真的！什麼時候？

A：這個星期五。好像是 M 公司為了媒體曝光量請她來的。

B：這一定會激起網友討論的。你說她什麼時候來台灣？

A：這個星期五！你真是貴人多忘事喔！

B：抱歉，這次記住了，是這個星期四，對吧。

A：我不想理你了。

Answers to the Unit:

super model

raise netizens' discussion

have a head like a sieve

Unit 13 Setting Goals and Objectives for the Event-2 先設定山頭,再開打

Background Introduction 背景介紹:

Alden and Leo are discussing how to set the goals of a PR campaign of a movie star who comes to Taiwan for promoting the film.
亞當與李奧正在討論,該如何設定電影明星來台宣傳的公關活動目標。

Conversation 2 對話2

Alden	To be honest, movie PR event is my favorite work content. I cannot wait to meet him **in person**.	老實說,電影公關活動是我最喜愛的工作內容了。我等不及要親自見到他。
Leo	You really love **rubbernecking**, aren't you?	你還真愛湊熱鬧,不是嗎?
Alden	Whatever you call me. So, what's our schedule today?	隨你怎麼說我。好啦,今天我們有那些行程?
Alden	We need to arrange some interviews from different entertainment medias, including TV, newspaper and magazines. There are also one press conference, and the meeting with Ministry of Culture.	我們需要從不同的娛樂媒體安排幾個專訪,包括電視台,報紙和雜誌。還有一場記者會和與文化部會面。

Leo	How much exposure do you think we will have?	你想我們會有多少曝光報導？
Alden	**Based on** last years' experience, I'll say around fifty to seventy.	根據去年的經驗，我會說大約 50 到 70。
Leo	They are pretty much, aren't they?	那很多了，不是嗎？.
Alden	Not so much, I just provided a **conservative estimate** so the client will not **criticize on** our objectives setting after the campaign finished.	也不是很多，我只是提供保守的估計，到時候客戶才不會在活動後批評我們的目標設定。
Leo	You really **have providence**.	你真有先見之明。
Alden	**Touché**.	說得好。
Leo	What are the objectives we need to achieve after meet with Ministry of Culture?	和文化部見面完後，我們需要達成哪些目標？
Alden	This is hard to say, but I think he can inspire the young people who have movie dreams through his own story.	這很難說，但是我想他可以透過他自身故事，激勵那些有電影夢想的年輕朋友。

Part I

Part II

Part III

Part IV

Part V

Part VI

Part I

Part II

Part III

Part IV

Part V

Part VI

Leo	But he can also talk on the press conference, **why do it all the trouble?**	但是他也可以在記者會上講這個啊，幹嘛弄得這麼麻煩？
Alden	You silly. If the meeting goes well, we'll have an extra channel to get more media exposures.	你笨蛋。如果會面安排得順利的話，我們將會有額外管道獲得更多媒體曝光嘛。
Leo	Indeed, but what if it doesn't.	的確耶，但是萬一進行不順利呢。
Alden	Then we still can let him talk on the conference. It doesn't **conflict with** anything.	那我們仍然可以安排他在記者會上說。彼此又不衝突。
Leo	I see. So, good luck with us.	我懂了。所以，祝我們好運啦。
Alden	We will, don't you worry about it.	我們會的啦，你不用擔心。

知識補給站

　　設定公關活動的目的，越明確與越少越好，如果一定要設定兩個以上目的，也要選擇有相關聯性的。至於要達成的目標，最好包含具體（specific）、可量化（measurable）、可達到（attainable）的數字或說明。

　　事前預估（estimate），事後評鑑（evaluation）。要評鑑是否達到公關目標的設定，有幾種方式：

第一，請專家打分數（Invite experts to score）。邀請相關產學領域的專家，甚至是舉辦公關活動的專家們一起評鑑，好處是從維持公平公開（keep fair and open）的審核，缺點就是學術界可能和實務界存在著差距，而其他活動公司請來的專家是否不會趁機落井下石，也很難拿捏。舉凡公部門的公關活動，較常使用這種評鑑方式。

第二，參與人員自我評分（Self-rated by participants）。好處是迅速、簡便便能得知活動的辦得怎麼樣；缺點當然就是容易自我感覺良好（self-complacency），真有要檢討的地方，也不敢提及，或者輕描淡寫地帶過（mentioned casually）。這種評鑑方式比較常見在內部檢討時使用。

第三，請參加活動的民眾填問卷（Invite joined publics to complete an questionnaire）。這種評鑑方法比較繁瑣，而且怕參與率（participation rate）不高，或者有一定的填錯比例（Incorrect rate），造成問卷無法評估；但是好處就是從參與民眾的角度出發，比較客觀。這種評鑑方式相對上述兩種來說，比較常使用。

Part I

Part II

Part III

Part IV

Part V

Part VI

Related Word 相關詞彙

1. in person　親自，本人

2. rubbernecking　湊熱鬧

    文法加油站：*rubber* 是指橡膠、定向的意思，這個單詞可以理解成脖子像橡膠一樣固定住了，也就是看熱鬧看到脖子都不會動了。

3. Based on　基於，根據

    文法加油站：經常看電影的人可能會注意到有些電影開演前，會打上 This movie is based on a true story. 字幕，意思是這部電影是根據真實故事改拍攝。

4. conservative estimate　保守的估計

    文法加油站：*conservative people* 是保守的人，*conservative ideas* 則是保守的想法。相關的詞還有保守黨 *Conservative Party*、保守主義 *Conservatism*。

5. criticize on　針對…批評

6. have providence　有先見之明

7. Touché.　好說好說，說得好

    文法加油站：此字為法文，發音類似土謝。原出處是擊劍場上，當有人擊敗另一人時，輸的人可以稱讚對方 *Touché*，意思是好樣的。運用在說話場合時，當有人提出一個論點，下一個人反擊，而原發言人不想再辯論，就會說 *Touché* 表示好了，不要再攻擊了；或者第二人是加深贊同的話，第一人也可以說這個單詞，表示說得對、說得好的意思。

8. Why do it all the trouble?　何必大費周章

    文法加油站：*do it* 亦可省略。

9. conflict with　與…衝突

10. measurable　可量化的，可測量的

    文法加油站：*measure* 可作動詞和名詞。名詞除了測量，還有手段的意思。

11. attainable　可達到的

    文法加油站：同義詞有 *achievable*、*reachable*。

12. self-complacency　自我感覺良好

    文法加油站：亦可置換為 *self-satisfied*。

Exercises 練習題

Please complete the word or sentence by filling in the blanks.

A：Based on _____ , I think there are one million people here for the show.

B：Thanks for preparing the Plan B for the raining day advanced, otherwise the joined public will definitely complain us.

A：That's because I _____ .

（After A left）

C：I think he really is the person who fells _____ all the time, isn't he?

B：Maybe we should learn from him, so we won't feel anything when we are shouted by the boss.

C：_____ .

請填空完成下面句子或單字

A：根據保守的估計，我想有 1 百萬人在這表演現場吧。

B：多虧你事先準備了雨天備案，否則在場民眾都要抱怨我們了。

A：那是因為我有先見之明啊。

（在 A 離開後）

C：我想他還真是一個總是自我感覺良好的人，對吧？

B：也許我們應該向他學習，這樣一來，等老闆像我們咆哮的時候，就不會有知覺。

C：說得真好。

Answers to the Unit:
conservative estimate
have providence
self-complacency/self-satisfied
Touché

Unit 14 PR Strategy Formulation-1
公關宣傳怎麼做

Background Introduction 背景介紹：

Judy, Lucy, and Mitchell are working at the PR department of Happy Pharmaceutical Company, and they are planning a series of PR event for their new launched cold medicine.

茱蒂、露西和米切爾三人是快樂製藥公司的公關，他們正在針對一款新上市的感冒藥規劃一系列公關活動。

Conversation 1 對話 1

Lucy	It looks like a difficult task to build an positive image for a cold medicine, isn't it?	要幫感冒藥建立正面的印象，還挺困難的，不是嗎？
Judy	We could try to build up an image of "Take me, and feel healthy again."	我們可以嘗試建立「吃我吧，感受健康重回你身」的印象。
Mitchell	That's a good idea and also nice slogan for our event. Well done, Judy.	這是個好點子而且標語也很適合我們的活動。做得好，茱蒂。

Lucy	How about we change the first two words into "Take me home"? Doesn't it sound more **approachable**, because our product is really needed to be taken home?	不如我們把前面的字改成「帶我回家吧」？是不是聽起來更平易近人，因為產品也是要被帶回家的。
Judy	You are also amazing, Lucy! I like your idea, let's do it, Mitchell?	妳也很令人吃驚，露西！我喜歡妳的想法，就這樣做吧，米切爾？
Mitchell	Yes, sure, why not. Take me home also means the consumers need to buy the item, right? So, this slogan will also contribute to our sales for sure.	可以啊，為什麼不。帶我回家也代表了消費者必須把它們買回家，不是嗎？所以，這個標語肯定也會給銷售帶來貢獻的。
Lucy	Really? You think so?	真的？你覺得是這樣？
Mitchell	Absolutely.	絕對是。
Judy	I am thinking maybe this time we should spend more budget on other medias rather than on TV commercials.	我在想也許這次我們應該花多點預算在其他媒體上，而不是電視廣告上。

Part I

Part II

Part III

Part IV

Part V

Part VI

Lucy	No TV advertisements? Then how do we **get** our **message across**?	沒有電視廣告？那我們怎麼讓消費者理解我們？
Mitchell	If we decided to give up TV commercials, we must arrange something else to **fill the gaps**.	如果我們決定要放棄電視廣告的話，我們一定要安排其他的去填補空缺。
Judy	That's exactly what I meant. I am thinking road shows around Taiwan's 319 towns and villages. Besides that, a weekly column on newspaper, a Fan Page on Facebook, and a 10-minute radio program for broadcasting the daily health information.	這正巧是我的意思。我想舉辦巡迴台灣 319 個鄉鎮的路演活動。除此之外，一週一次在報紙上的專欄、臉書上的粉絲專頁、和一個 10 分鐘的電台節目，藉此宣傳每日健康訊息。
Mitchell	What we should say on the radio program? I cannot think any of topics which relate to our new medicine.	在電台節目裡我們要說些什麼？我無法想到任何有關我們新藥品的話題耶！
Lucy	How to prevent a cold, or how to get better quickly?	例如預防感冒，或者如何好得快點的？

Judy	Yes, some tips of how to prevent a cold can be attractive, plus other information about our selected products. You know, the benefit of doing a program of this type makes **audiences** feel like they are absorbing new knowledge instead of listening an ad.	是的，如何預防感冒的小秘方可是有吸引力的，加上我們選定的產品的其他資訊。你也知道，這種節目的好處就是，讓聽眾感覺像是在吸引新知，而非聽廣告。
Mitchell	Understood. Should we **post** the same content on Facebook's Fan Page **simultaneously**?	了解。那我們是否應該同步地在臉書粉絲頁上貼文？
Judy	Yes, that is a great idea. We also can answer their questions in the radio program, so more Netizens will come to visit the Fan Page to talk again.	是的，很好的主意。我們也可以在電台中回答他們的問題，更多網友也會再次回流到粉絲頁來討論。
Lucy	Will this be lack of connection of our new product?	這和我們的新產品會不會缺乏關聯？
Judy	If we could also bring the other medicines into more sale volume, I think this event can be considered as a PR event for the company.	如果我們可以幫助其他藥品銷售得更多的話，我想這個活動可以被當成是公司的公關活動。

Part I

Part II

Part III

Part IV

Part V

Part VI

Mitchell	Then the slogan probably needs to change to "Take me home, and your family will feel happy again".	那標語可能需要改成「帶我回家，讓家人都快樂」。
Lucy	With a capital H, this is just like our company's name.	快樂就是我們公司的名字。
Judy	Yes, that would be perfect, then.	對耶，太完美。
Mitchell	I agree it, too.	我也同意。
Judy	OK, that's it. I am happy **we're in good shape**!	好的，那就這樣吧。我很高興我們狀況還不錯！
Lucy	I just hope we will not screw this up.	我只希望這次不會搞砸。
Mitchell	You could just **bite your tongue**, Lucy.	你可以忍住不說的，露西。

　　公關活動在發想的階段，可以天馬行空的發揮創意（unrestrained creativity），但是討論越到中後段的時候，最好要試著收尾，修正天馬行空的想法，找出可以執行的創意（creative idea which can be executed）。

　　許多公關事件，靠得是話題的創造，從醞釀、引爆、延續都考慮周詳。話題有可能是明星、代言人，也可能是一件（或一連串）事情或物品，當然也可能是一項調查（research）、研究報告（report）的發表（announcement）。舉例來說，每年保險套或者藥廠會公佈攸關男女「性福」的調查數據，輔以醫院醫師專業建議民眾重視問題；就是一種巧妙結合吸引人的話題，和刺激銷售量的公關議題操作。

　　其實公關活動的架構大同小異，差別就在「創意」；好的創意可以令人眼睛一亮，甚至印象深刻，最好還可以結合宣傳的產品或企業訴求，達成目的，就是成功的公關活動。而創意來自靈感（inspiration），但是許多創意大師也都表示，靈感不是僥倖（by chance），而是不斷積累和訓練之後的意外發現（an accidental discovery after continued training）。

Related Word 相關詞彙

1. approachable 　親切的，平易近人的
2. get message across 　被理解，被接受
3. fill the gap 　填補空缺

   文法加油站：gap 是空隙的意思，這句話也有填空格的意思。

   There is a big gap between us. 就是指我們之間有很大的代溝 / 鴻溝。

4. audience 　聽眾

   文法加油站：由上下文判斷，此指收聽電台節目的聽眾（listener）。其他時候，也有指電視觀眾或者民眾的意思。

5. post 　張貼

   文法加油站：此作動詞使用，也有郵寄、公告的意思。poster 則是名詞，為海報的意思。

6. simultaneously 　同步地

   文法加油站：形容詞為 simultaneous。同步翻譯（口譯）就寫作 simultaneous interpreter。

7. we're in good shape 　我們狀況還不錯

   文法加油站：shape 也有形容人身材的意思，in good shape 就是身材保持得很好的意思。

8. bite your tongue 　忍住不說
9. unrestrained creativity 　不受限制（拘束）的創意

   文法加油站：unrestrained 是不受拘束的，反義詞去掉 un 即可。un 加在名詞、形容詞和副詞之前，有否定的意思；例如：finished（完成的）/unfinished（未完成的），cooked（煮熟的）/uncooked（沒煮熟的）。

10. by chance 　僥倖的、碰巧的

    文法加油站：同義詞還有 by accent、by coincidence、occasionally。僥倖的心理則是寫作 fluke mind。

Exercises 練習題

Please complete the word or sentence by filling in the blanks.

- Susan is a _____ person, but she just cannot _____ her _____ colleagues.
- A Marketing lecturer once said, _____ doesn't come _____ . It needs a daily continue practice on thinking.
- Wife：There is a family _____ needs to be filled.

  Husband：I think _____ .

  Wife：Then, from next month, your pocket money should be canceled.

請填空完成下面句子或單字

- 蘇珊很平易近人，但是就是無法讓她的話被同事理解。
- 一位行銷老師曾經說過，天馬行空的創意並非僥倖的出現，而是需要經過每天不斷地思考練習。
- 妻子：這個月家裡有財政缺口要補上。

  丈夫：我覺得我們狀況很好。

  妻子：那麼下個月開始，你的零用錢就取消吧。

Answers to the Unit:

approachable

get, message across

unrestrained creativity

by chance

financial gap

we're in good shape

Unit 14 PR Strategy Formulation-2
公關宣傳怎麼做

Background Introduction 背景介紹：

Bridget and Hedwig are working at the PR Department of Z Bank. Now, they are checking all the details of the press conference of a credit card which will be new launched.

布莉琪與海薇兩人在 Z 銀行的公關部門工作，她們正在確認一款信用卡新上市記者會的細節。

Conversation 2 對話 2

Bridget	I cannot believe this event is coming on this Friday.	真不敢相信活動在就這週五了。
Hedwig	I don't like it either. I feel like we already went through this event a thousand times.	我也不喜歡。我覺得我們已經針對這活動討論一千次了。
Bridget	Yes, I feel the same way. Let's check everything as quickly as possible, because I don't want to be late for the date with my boyfriend tonight.	對呀，有同感。讓我們快點開始確認吧，我可不想今晚和我男朋友的約會遲到。
Hedwig	**Eat, drink, and be merry!**	及時享樂呀！

| Bridget | Indeed, I certainly will not be **died of overwork**. | 那當然，我可絕不會死於過勞死。 |

| Hedwig | So, what's the first thing we need to check now? | 那，現在要確認的第一件事是什麼呢？ |

| Bridget | I think it's the preparations of the press conference. | 我想就是記者會的準備事項。 |

| Hedwig | I have confirmed with General Manager the time, location, participants from company executives, and his talking points on his speech. What else? | 我已經和總經理確認過時間、地點、公司高層的參與者，以及他演講的大綱。還有什麼？ |

| Bridget | The news release has not confirmed yet, nor the **press kit** and who else of the **spokespeople** be except GM. | 新聞稿還沒有確認，媒體資料袋和除了總經理以外的演講人也還沒確認。 |

| Hedwig | I will check these with his secretary. Could you in charge of the rest things with Y Hotel for the equipment which they should provide on Friday? | 我會跟他秘書確認。可以麻煩妳負責和Y飯店確認週五他們要提供的設備？ |

Part I
Part II
Part III
Part IV
Part V
Part VI

Bridget	Sure. I think we will need a stage, a banner in the new credit card's shape, two microphones, a projector and one hundred and fifty chairs.	沒問題。我想我們會需要一個舞台、一張新信用卡形狀的背板、兩支麥克風,一台投影機和一百五十張椅子。
Hedwig	Three microphones would be safer, just in case. Did you mention F&B?	三支麥克風比較保險,以防萬一。妳剛才提到了食物和飲料嗎?
Bridget	Oh, no! I totally forgot! What we should do? The hotel will not be able to prepare F&B for hundred-and-fifty people in time.	喔,不會吧!我完全忘記了!該怎麼辦?飯店可能無法及時準備一百五十人份的食物和飲料。
Hedwig	OK, don't worry. I will go to ask other restaurants that can help to deliver to the hotel and you go to check with the hotel again. Don't forget to tell them if they cannot prepare in time, then allow us to buy from outside and with no extra charge for us.	好吧,別擔心。我會去問其他可以幫忙外送到飯店的餐廳,而妳去向飯店再次確認。別忘了告訴他們如果他們無法及時準備,那就要讓我們從外面買進去,而且不額外收我們費用。
Bridget	Thank you, Bridget. You are really my angel.	謝謝妳,布莉琪。妳真是我的天使。

Part I
Part II
Part III
Part IV
Part V
Part VI

Hedwig	My job is to get everything under control. Should we start to go through the Friday's **rundown** from the morning?	我的工作就是確保每件事都在控制中。現在應該確認週五從一早開始的流程了？
Bridget	Sure. Mike and I will arrive at 9am to setup for the press conference. You, GM and the other spokespeople should be the hotel around 11am for **rehearsal**. Then we take a short lunch break about 12 to 1pm, back at 1:15 for welcoming medias and you knew the rest schedules already.	好的。麥克和我會在早上九點抵達以便佈置記者會。妳、總經理和其他公司高層應該在上午 11 點鐘抵達飯店以便彩排。然後 12 點到下午 1 點是午餐休息，1 點 15 分回來接待媒體，剩下的流程妳已經知道了。
Hedwig	Perfect. So, who will be in charge at the **reception desk**?	太好了。所以，誰會負責在接待處？
Bridget	There will be Mike only.	只會有麥克 人。
Hedwig	I think one person won't be enough for welcoming one hundred and fifty people. Where will you be at that time?	我想一個人要接待一百五十個人是不夠的。妳那時候會在哪裡？

Part I

Part II

Part III

Part IV

Part V

Part VI

Bridget	I will be at backstage for preparing for the ceremony, the VIPs of **bank depositors** will need a quick guide then, so they won't make a mistake.	我會在後台為儀式作準備，銀行存戶的貴賓們會需要一個快速的導覽，才不至於出錯。
Hedwig	OK, then. I will ask the secretary to join with Mike.	好吧。我會請秘書加入麥克的行列。
Bridget	Yes, it seems a good idea. OK, that's everything.	看來是個好主意。好啦，這就是所有事情了。
Hedwig	Have a great time with your **toy boy**.	和妳的小狼狗男友玩得愉快。
Bridget	Would you promise this is only **between us**?	妳可以答應我只有妳我兩人知道這件事？
Hedwig	Sure, I have tight-lipped.	沒問題，我口風很緊的。

知識補給站

公關活動事前規劃很重要以外，現場活動的執行（implication of activity）也需要瞻前顧後（**look ahead and behind**）。通常，在活動發想之後，會針對活動的流程進行設計和規劃，諸如誰上台致詞（make a speech）、致詞順序、致詞時要說什麼重點、是否有知名人士（**celebrity**）站台、慶祝的儀式（cerebrating ceremony）是什麼…等等，都需要反覆推敲與演練。

常見的流程問題有幾個。首先是流程的安排最好是一個動態（dynamic）活動後，接著一個靜態（static）活動，反之亦可；例如：開場來一段勁歌熱舞（hot music and dancing），後面就安排主持人介紹今天活動流程。這樣安排的用意在於，讓觀眾的情緒有高低起伏，容易吸引他們關注舞台上進行的活動而不感到無聊或暴露在太過吵雜的環境。

另外，來賓致詞的優先順序（priority），通常是政府官員（government officials）、主辦單位（organizer）、協辦或贊助單位（sponsor）、嘉賓或貴賓（VIP guests）；如果不致詞，但是有特殊身分，可以請主持人介紹為列席嘉賓（不上台致詞的貴賓）。

另外，在活動前也必須針對預先設想到的特殊狀況進行沙盤推演（sand table exercise），以及針對每個重要的定點，安排足夠的人手和通訊設備（communication equipment），以利溝通協調突發狀況（unexpected situation）。

Related Word 相關詞彙

1. Eat, drink, and be merry!　及時行樂

    文法加油站：這是出自聖經的一段話，原文是 *A man hath no better thing under the sun, than to eat, and to drink, and to be merry.* 意即在大太陽底下，沒有比及時行樂更強的事了。

2. died of overwork　過勞死

    文法加油站：這句話有很幾種說法，可以用日文拼音 *karoshi* 來說，也可以說 *death from overwork* 或 *death-by-overwork*。

3. press kit　媒體資料袋。在記者會場提供給媒體記者的資料，通常包含新聞稿、相關照片、小禮品。

4. spokespeople　演講者、發言人、致詞人

    文法加油站：此為複數，單數就是 *spokesperson*。

5. rundown　流程

6. rehearsal　排演，預演

7. reception desk　接待桌，報到處

8. toy boy　小狼狗

    文法加油站：相近的詞還有小白臉 *lover boy*。

9. between us　只有我們兩人知道

10. bank depositor　銀行存戶

11. celebrity　知名人士、明星、名流、名人、

12. look ahead and behind　瞻前顧後

    文法加油站：這個形容詞也有負面的裹足不前的意思；英文可以用 *be overcautious and indecisive*，表示膽小、畏首畏尾和優柔寡斷的意思。

Exercises 練習題

Please complete the word or sentence by filling in the blanks.

Press Conference Checklist

Preparations：

✓ News release

✓ _____

✓ Gifts

Participants：

✓ 120 Medias

✓ 12 _____

_____ Time：8 月 15 日上午 11 點

Responsible for the _____：Alan and Amy

請填空完成下面句子或單字

記者會確認清單

準備物：

✓ 新聞稿

✓ 媒體資料袋

✓ 禮物

參加者：

✓ 120 位媒體

✓ 12 位知名人士

預演時間：8 月 15 日上午 11 點

報到處負責人：艾倫與艾咪

Answers to the Unit:

Press kit

Celebrities

Rehearsal

Reception desk

Part I
Part II
Part III
Part IV
Part V
Part VI

Unit 15 Planning Creative Events-1
越有創意越好

Background Introduction 背景介紹：

Darrell and Philippa are classmates in Master of City Marketing, and they are arguing how to plan a creative city PR event.

達雷爾和菲莉帕是城市行銷研究所的同班同學，他們正在爭論該如何把城市公關活動辦得有創意。

Conversation 1 對話 1

Darrell	I think we should list all the **characteristics** of this city, and then we decide what are the campaign's slogan and other details.	我想我們應該條列這個城市的特色，然後我們再決定活動的標語和其他的細節。
Philippa	OK, let's do it. This city **is known for** a variety of things, culture, food and rare animals.	好，我們開始吧。這個城市以很多東西出名，文化、美食和稀有的動物。
Darrell	I am also thinking these special animals. Should we focus on them, then?	我也正想到這些特別的動物。就以牠們為主囉？
Philippa	Sure, why not? Not so many cities in the world emphasis this, nor own such various **species**.	好呀，有何不可？世界上也不是很多城市都強調這點，而且還擁有這麼多樣化的物種。

Part I Part II Part III Part IV Part V Part VI

Darrell	But this also reminds me the campaign from Tourism Queensland's highly-successful Best Job in the World.	但這也提醒了我昆士蘭旅遊局成功舉辦的「世界上最好的工作」的活動。
Philippa	Yes, you **recalled my memories**. What a successful event, wasn't it?	對喔，你倒是喚醒了我的記憶。真是個成功的活動，不是嗎？
Darrell	Should we do it again, just **transplant** in different city?	我們應該只是移植到不同城市而已嗎？
Philippa	I think maybe focus on conservation of animals itself is often being a typical type of broadcasting a city.	我想也許專注在保護動物的本身，就是城市宣傳的最典型範例。
Darrell	What the slogan we should set for the event?	我們要幫活動取什麼標語？
Philippa	How about "The Best Job than Queensland"?	「比昆士蘭更好的工作」？
Darrell	No, you have **gotta** come up with a new idea. I think it's better not mention Queensland at all, otherwise the publics will compare us with them.	別吧，妳得要想個更好的點子。我想最好不要提到昆士蘭，免得大眾會拿我們和他們比較。

Part I

Part II

Part III

Part IV

Part V

Part VI

Philippa	All right. How about "Welcome Animal Lovers Migrate to U City"?	好吧。「歡迎動物愛好者移民 U 城市」如何？
Darrell	It sounds very close to what we are looking for. Maybe provide free apartment and food for 1 year to the top 10 immigrations?	聽起來好像很接近我們想要的感覺。也許再提供免費的公寓和一年份食物給前 10 名移民者？
Philippa	That is an incredible tempting prize.	真是不可思議的誘人獎品。
Darrell	You bet. So, **we are on the same page** now?	當然。那，我們現在都清楚彼此了？
Philippa	Yes. Oh, there is one thing. Please call in sick for me to the class tomorrow.	是呀。喔，還有一件事情。麻煩你明天的課幫我請病假。
Darrell	Again? You are really like to be **malingering**, aren't you?	又來了？妳還真是愛裝病耶，不是嗎？

知識補給站

公關活動在於展現創意，尤其是替城市做公關活動。

由於替城市做公關，對象除了駐在該城市的居民以外，也有些活動主打吸引外縣市民眾來觀光旅遊，甚至還要想辦法吸引海外的外國人，於是怎麼替城市建立清楚的形象定位，就很重要。以台北市為例，向居民訴求的是親切、好居住的城市（good city to live in）；向外地人宣傳的就是好方便（捷運）、好好玩的台北。

通常因為城市希望一年四季都有人氣（popularity），舉辦公關活動也多以12月份、四季為主，從季節中找尋可以做為主打的特色。以日本來説，行之有年的公關活動不外乎：春天賞櫻花（**cherry blossom** in Spring）、夏天看綠野（green land in Summer）、秋天看楓紅（**red leaves** in Fall）、冬天賞雪泡溫泉（hot spring and snow in Winter）。

除此之外，也有以動物、知名人物、特殊文化或事件為城市公關活動的宣傳主軸。例如：成都以熊貓的故鄉（Panda's hometown）自居，紐奧良（New Orleans）是爵士樂發源地（the **birthplace** of jazz）、義大利北方的艾維利亞（Ivrea）每年二月舉行丟橘子大賽…等等，都是令人印象深刻的城市公關行銷案例。

Part I

Part II

Part III

Part IV

Part V

Part VI

Related Word 相關詞彙

1. characteristic 特色，特點，特徵
2. is known for… 以…出名
3. specie 物種
4. recalled my memories 喚起我的記憶
5. transplant 移植

   文法加油站：trans 開頭的單詞大多有轉移、轉換的意思。例如：知名的變形金剛電影，名字就叫 Transformers。

6. gotta 必須

   文法加油站：gotta 是 got to 的口語縮寫。其他類似的還有 kinda = kind of，wanna = want to。

7. we are on the same page 互相理解彼此，我們講的是同一件事

   文法加油站：否定的用法是 we are not on the same page.

8. malingering 裝病的
9. cherry blossom 櫻花開花。多用來指賞櫻花這件事。
10. red leaves 紅色的葉子，引申為楓葉紅了（楓紅）或賞楓。
11. birthplace 發源地

Exercises 練習題

Please complete the word or sentence by filling in the blanks.

A：Do you want to go to Japan with me?

B：For what?

A：For the _____ .

B：Yes, I know that japan is _____ for that. But I don't really feel well recently.

A：I think you are just _____ .

B：Me? _____ ? Why you say thing like this?

A：Never mind. I will go even if without you.

請填空完成下面句子或單字

A：妳想跟我去日本嗎？

B：去做什麼呢？

A：賞櫻花啊。

B：是的，我知道日本是以這個出名的。但是我最近都不太舒服耶。

A：我想你是裝病的吧。

B：我？我們在講同一件事嗎？你為什麼要這樣說我呢？

A：算了。沒有你我也會去的啦。

Answers to the Unit:

cherry blossom

known for

malingering

Are we on the same page

Part I

Part II

Part III

Part IV

Part V

Part VI

Unit 15 Planning Creative Events-2
越有創意越好

Background Introduction 背景介紹：

Evelyn, Kirsten and Hugh are discussing how to design a PR event for an upcoming colored chewing gum.

伊芙琳，克麗絲坦與休正在討論如何替一款即將上市的彩色口香糖設計公關活動。

Conversation 2 對話2

Evelyn	I really like this new product, hope we will create a whole new image for it.	我真的很喜歡這個新產品，希望我們可以為它創造出全新的形象。
Kirsten	Me too. I like their colorful design, can we focus on this feature?	我也是。我喜歡它們色彩豐富的設計，我們就專注在這個特點上吧？
Hugh	It is an eye-catching feature, isn't it? How about we connect this with different personalities?	的確是個吸睛的特色，不是嗎？不如連結到不同的個性上吧？
Evelyn	Maybe combine with **star signs** are more attractive?	也許和星座連結，是不是更有吸引力？
Kirsten	**You are really a player** of this job, aren't you, Evelyn? I like your ideas always.	你可真是箇中好手喔，是不是，伊芙琳？我總是欣賞你的點子。

Hugh	That's truly an outstanding thinking, linking to the most popular topics and product characters. However, I wonder how many males will be interested in this.	的確是很不錯的想法，將產品特色與最有人氣的話題連結。但是，我懷疑有多少男性會對這個感興趣。
Evelyn	**Obviously** more females will be interested in, rather than males.	顯然更多女性會比較有興趣，而不是男性。
Kirsten	I personally fell that males are also tend to care this kind of topic, so they have something to talk with their girlfriends when they meet.	我個人覺得男性也會傾向關注這類的話題，所以當他們和女朋友見面時，才有話說。
Hugh	Goo point, Kirsten. But I still think we cannot take a risk by pointing out a **dichotomy** toward any client's products.	說得好，克麗絲坦。但是我還是認為我們不能冒險對任何客戶的產品，用一個二分法。
Evelyn	All right, so what else we can use for this colored chewing gum except various personalities?	好吧，還有什麼是我們可以替這個彩色口香糖宣傳的，除了不同的個性以外。
Hugh	Why not combine with personality and lifestyle at the same time?	為什麼不同時結合生活型態與個性呢？

Part I

Part II

Part III

Part IV

Part V

Part VI

Evelyn	Do you mean we give the each color different definition? For example, **urban life**, playboy…	你是說我們為每個顏色給定義？例如，都市生活、花花公子…
Kirsten	Or a person who **lives from paycheck to paycheck**?	或是月光族？
Hugh	You two are so creative, I was thinking something not so **ironical**.	妳們兩個還真有創意，我剛才想的是沒那麼諷刺的。
Evelyn	In my way of thinking, people can accept more **avant-garde** identities for themselves.	我的想法是，人們可以接受他們自己更前衛的身分表徵。
Kirsten	Some people even love to be considered extreme strange or **distinctive** nowadays.	現在有些人甚至喜歡被認為是特別古怪，或獨一無二的。
Hugh	How about also link to love, friendship, or, you know, that kind of emotional feelings.	或者是和愛啊、友誼，或者妳知道的，這類的情緒字眼連結。
Kirsten	I thought you didn't like to be that "dichotomy".	我還以為你不喜歡這種「二分法」咧。

Part I
Part II
Part III
Part IV
Part V
Part VI

Hugh	No, what I meant was the feeling of **lovelorn**, being betrayed, fighting with someone you love, etc. etc.	不是，我剛才的意思是說失戀的感覺、被背叛、和你愛的人吵架，等等之類的。
Evelyn	I see what you mean now, I think this will strengthen the concept of lifestyle and personality of each **individual**.	我知道你的意思了，我想這會強化個別的生活型態和個性的概念。
Kirsten	**Since you say so, I am with you two.**	既然你們這樣說了，我也贊同你們兩個囉。
Evelyn	But we still need to design some activities in order to make participants to join us online or offline, so we can express the product image of "It's colored and you are different".	但是我們還是要設計一些活動，讓參加者在線上或線下參與，以便我們把產品「它是彩色的而你是獨特的」形象傳達出去。
Kirsten	Wow, you're a terrific storyteller.	哇，你還真是個說故事高手。
Hugh	I am thinking the same thing, too. How about we recruit people from offline and online, get them together on the event day, and ask them to chew gums…	我也在想同樣一件事。不如我們在網路或現實生活裡招募人，活動當天安排他們現身，然後要求他們吃口香糖…

Part I

Part II

Part III

Part IV

Part V

Part VI

Evelyn	Cover their eyes maybe, and let them identify themselves personalities, lifestyles or feelings which are matching to our product characters. Then, if someone chose the one from the box we put in front of them and even matched the color, the winner can win a big prize, plus one year chewing gum from the brand.	把他們眼睛蒙起來，然後讓他們說說自己的個性、生活型態或和我們產品特色吻合的感覺。接著，如果有人從我們放在他們面前的箱子裡，選中了對的顏色，贏家就可以獲得獎品和一年份的口香糖。
Kirsten	It's like a match game, you know, guess if you are really match to somebody.	就像配對遊戲，妳知道的，猜猜你是否和某人配對成功。
Hugh	Good idea, this can also combine what Kirsten mentioned. Inviting some pretty girls…	好主意，這也可以和克麗絲坦提的結合。請些漂亮的女孩們…
Evelyn	Let's stop here, we really need to come up with some plans today.	先討論到這吧，我們今天真的需要寫出些提案。
Hugh	OK, you make a draft first. Kirsten and I will make an adjustment latter.	好，你先寫初稿。克麗絲坦和我會稍後幫忙調整。
Evelyn	You always pick the simplest thing to do.	你總是選最簡單的事情做。

知識補給站

Part I

Part II

Part III

Part IV

Part V

Part VI

　　由於策劃公關活動的骨架大致相同，好壞就取決於創意的發揮。

　　在發想的前期應該盡量說出或想出與眾不同的創意，第二階段再就公司的資源或限制，以及是否能和產品或品牌特色有串聯（link together），用刪去法（**process of elimination**）刪掉這次無法實現的創意。第三階段則是在剩下的答案中，安排最適當的（the most appropriate）的活動。

　　要留意的是，有些創意很好，但是和企業一直倡導的文化或產品特色，搭配不起來，結果就是，目標族群只記得活動或標語，不記得哪一家企業或主辦單位舉辦的。還有一種情形是，標語或口號十分普通，如果遮住品牌名稱，誰也不曉得是哪個品牌，這樣也沒有凸顯特色。

　　例如：「喝牛奶很健康」，就不是很有創意的口號；但是假設 Super 公司的牛奶喊出「喝 Super 牛奶 給你 Super 的健康」，既朗朗上口又容易記住，就是很有創意的口號。

Related Word 相關詞彙

1. star sign　12 星座

　　文法加油站：又稱 *Astrological sign*（黃道十二宮）。

　　分別是 Aries（牡羊座）、Taurus（金牛座）、Gemini（雙子座）、Cancer（巨蟹座）、Leo（獅子座）、Virgo（處女座）、Libra（天秤座）、Scorpio（天蠍座）、Sagittarius（射手座）、Capricorn（摩羯座）、Aquarius（水瓶座）、Pisces（雙魚座）。

2. You are really a player　你是箇中好手

3. Obviously　顯然地，明顯地

　　文法加油站：*和 apparently*（明顯地）*以及 evidently*（明顯地）*不同的地方在於，apparently 比較偏向說話者的主觀認定，obviously 則是偏向客觀角度，也隱含了眾所周知的意味，evidently 則是根據統計或數據等證據支持來看。*

4. dichotomy　二分法

5. urban life　城市生活，都市生活

6. live from paycheck to paycheck　月光族

7. ironical　諷刺的

　　文法加油站：*同義詞還有 sarcastic。*

8. avant-garde　前衛的

9. distinctive　獨特的

　　文法加油站：*同義詞還有 unique、different、unusual。*

10. lovelorn　失戀（的），害相思病（的）

　　文法加油站：同義詞還有 be out of love。

11. individual　個別的，個人的

　　文法加油站：*individually 是副詞，個別地、單獨地、逐次地的意思，相當於 one by one。*

12. Since you say so　既然你（們）這樣說的話

13. be with you　跟隨你，在你身邊

14. process of elimination　刪去法、刪除過程

Exercises 練習題

Please complete the word or sentence by filling in the blanks.

A：I heard that he was _____ .

B：Do you know why?

A：It seems like his girl said their _____ are not matched.

B：What a _____ way of saying。

A：It is quite _____ , because he is a person who _____ . It costs him more if he had a girlfriend.

B：_____ , breaking up is better for both of them.

請填空完成下面句子或單字

A：聽說他失戀了。

B：知道為什麼嗎？

A：好像是他女友說他們星座不合。

B：真是獨特的説法。

A：諷刺的是，他是月光族。交女友反而害他錢越花越多。

B：顯然地，他們還是分手的好。

Answers to the Unit:

Lovelorn/ out of love

star signs/astrological signs

distinctive/unique/different/unusual

ironical/sarcastic

lives from paycheck to paycheck

Obviously

Unit 16 Budget and Measurement-1
有多少錢做多少事

Background Introduction 背景介紹：

Cecilia is senior accounting from Accounting Department, Owen and Lester are co-workers at the PR Department. They are talking about how to save budget from PR promotion of the company Sports Day.

西西莉亞是公司的資深會計，歐文和萊斯特是公關部門的同事。他們三人正在討論公司運動會的公關宣傳該如何節省預算。

Conversation 1 對話 1

Owen	Sorry, Cecilia. I know how you hate to working during the lunch, but it's the only available time we have for the whole week.	抱歉，西西莉亞。我知道你很討厭在午休時間工作，但這是我們整個禮拜唯一的空檔。
Cecilia	That's fine, let's **get down to business** ASAP.	沒關係，我們快點談公事吧。
Lester	Sure. First of all, did you check the email I sent to you last week? Is there anything you would like to ask or talk about further?	好的。首先，妳看了上週我寄給妳的 E-Mail？有沒有任何事情是妳想要問或者深入討論的？
Cecilia	Yes, there are few things. First, how many reporters are going to attend our Sports Day?	有的，有幾件事情。第一，有多少位記者即將出席我們的運動日？

Owen	There are fifteen so far, but we have to confirm with them again one week before the event.	現在有 15 位，但是在活動一週前還會再一次確認。
Cecilia	Right, just let me know exactly one week before, because I need to buy insurance for them.	好的，就要剛好一週前讓我知道，因為我需要幫他們投保（買保險）。
Lester	Thank you for your kind reminding, I totally forgot this.	謝謝妳的好心提醒喔，我完全忘了這回事。
Cecilia	I don't blame you, honey. It's my job to do it.	不怪你，親愛的。這是我的工作呢。
Owen	Anything else?	還有其他的嗎？
Cecilia	Yes. What does "**printed matter**" mean here?	有。這個「印刷品」是什麼意思呢？
Lester	Oh, it means something like company profile, product catalogs, or press release.	哦，就是例如公司簡介、產品目錄或新聞稿之類的。
Cecilia	So, we are going to provide these to medias who come to our Sports Day?	所以，我們要提供這些給來到運動會的媒體？

Part I
Part II
Part III
Part IV
Part V
Part VI

Owen	Yes, so they have better understanding of our company and what we are doing or what going to do in the future.	是的，所以他們會對我們公司更了解，以及我們現在在做什麼或未來要往哪裡去。
Cecilia	That makes sense.	很有道理。
Lester	So everything is good here?	所以沒問題了？
Cecilia	**What's the rush**, young man? You said there will be fifteen reporters going to attend, then why we need to buy one hundred gifts for them?	急什麼，年輕人？你說會有 15 位記者要出席，那為什麼我們需要買 100 份禮物給他們呢？
Owen	I said there are already fifteen who confirmed that they will attend, but there will be more. We had fifty-two medias attended **successively** on the Sports Day last year, so totally one hundred and four gifts gave away.	我是說已經有 15 位記者確認要出席，但是還會有更多的。我們去年有 52 家媒體陸續地抵達，所以總共發出了 104 份禮物。
Cecilia	I am so confused right now.	我聽得很混亂。

Lester	One gift for the journalist and the other for the photographer, so fifty-two **times** two equals one hundred and four.	一個禮物給文字記者，一個禮物給攝影記者，所以 52 乘以 2 就等於 104。
Cecilia	I see. So basically, two gifts for one media company then.	懂了。所以基本上，一家媒體給兩個禮物囉。
Owen	Yes, sometimes three or four. But usually two.	對，有時候是三或四個。但是通常是兩個。
Cecilia	Do we also need to hire photographers by ourselves? Cannot we ask some media to do this for us for free?	我們也需要自己請攝影師？不能請哪個媒體免費幫我們？
Owen	No, it won't be **appropriate**. Besides, it won't cost too much for hiring two of them.	不好，這樣不是很恰當。而且，請兩個攝影師也不是很貴。
Cecilia	Tell me again why do we need two of them?	再講一次為什麼我們需要兩個人？

Part I

Part II

Part III

Part IV

Part V

Part VI

Lester	One for photo shooting and the other is for film taking. So, after the event, we can put those photos or films on our company website.	一個是拍照的，另一個是攝影的。在活動結束後，我們就可以把照片或影片放到公司網站上。
Cecilia	That's a wonderful idea, isn't it?	這是個很棒的點子呢，不是嗎？
Owen	Yes, it is.	是的。
Cecilia	OK, I am all good here. You two can **go ahead with your stuff**.	好啦，我沒問題了。你們兩個去忙吧。
Lester	Thanks, Cecilia. Love you.	謝啦，西西莉亞。愛妳。
Owen	Let me buy you a sandwich or some?	讓我請你吃個三明治或什麼吧？
Cecilia	No need, I'm on a diet recently.	不用了，我最近在節食。
Owen	Too bad. Take care, see you around.	那太可惜了。保重喔，回頭見。

知識補給站

Part I
Part II
Part III
Part IV
Part V
Part VI

雖然預算編列的篇章，往往在提案的後段才會展示出來，但是其實預算和任務、目標一樣重要。

以政府機關的活動或公關案標案來說，通常會有幾個提案必備條件（限制），諸如：活動名稱（name）、活動發想概念（concept）、活動目標（goals and objectives）、行銷策略（marketing strategy）、經費明細（budget plan）、預期效益（**expected benefits**）、工作時間表（working schedule）、工作團隊組織架構（team based structure）、團隊過往實績（past performance）…等等。

預算的多寡會影響活動的硬體和軟體表現，這是主辦單位必須要體認到的一點。但是公關人的價值，也就體現在「在有限的預算內發揮最大的公關效益（**budget-maximizing**）」。

在檢視預算的時候，必須留意是否總金額超過了客戶的預算。還有，如果有更好的建議，但是會超過預算一點點，也可作為備案（Plan B），提出來和客戶討論。很多時候，客戶往往能夠接受多花一點錢，但是達到更好的效益的方案。

Related Word 相關詞彙

1. save budget 節省預算

    文法加油站：另一種寫法是 *budget saving*，整個作為名詞使用。

2. get down to business 談（辦）正（公）事

3. printed matter 印刷物（品）

    文法加油站：同義詞還有 *printed material（s）*。

4. What's the rush 急什麼

    文法加油站：*rush* 亦可置換為 *hurry*。

5. successively 陸續地

    文法加油站：同義詞還有 *one after another*。

6. times 乘

    文法加油站：數學中的加減乘除，用英語表示分別是 *plus*、*minus*、*times*、
    divided by。

    One plus one is（equals）two. 1 加 1 等於 2。

    Twenty divided by four is（equals）five. 20 除以 4 等於 5。

7. appropriate 適當的，恰當的

8. go ahead with your stuff 你去忙吧

    文法加油站：亦可置換 *go on with your work, go ahead with what you are*
    （were）doing。

9. expected benefits 預期效益

    文法加油站：其他提案相關字詞還有主辦單位（*Organizer*）、協辦單位
    （*coordinator*）、評估標準（*Evaluation Standard*）、追蹤
    （*tracking*）。

10. budget-maximizing 預算最大化

Exercises 練習題

Please complete the word or sentence by filling in the blanks.

A：I have a question for you.

B：Go ahead.

A：How do you evaluate a PR event is successful or not?

B：It's easy. Whether it achieve a ＿＿＿＿＿＿＿ or not.

A：And?

B：Whether it achieve the ＿＿＿＿＿＿＿ . Why?

A：Nothing, just ＿＿＿＿＿＿＿＿＿＿＿ .

B：＿＿＿＿＿＿＿ ? Now, it's my turn to ask you some things.

Part I

Part II

Part III

Part IV

Part V

Part VI

請填空完成下面句子或單字

A：我想問你個問題。

B：問吧。

A：你怎麼評估一個成功的公關案？

B：很簡單，是否達到預算最大化。

A：還有呢？

B：是否達到預期效益。怎麼了？

A：沒事，你去忙你的吧。

B：急什麼？換我有事情要問你了呢。

Answers to the Unit:

budget-maximizing

expected benefits

go ahead with your stuff/go on with your work/go ahead with what you are （were) doing

What's the rush

Unit 16 Budget and Measurement-2
有多少錢做多少事

Background Introduction 背景介紹：

Tracy and Stephanie are discussing how to host a press conference with limited budget.

崔西和史蒂芬妮正在商量該怎麼在有限的預算裡舉辦記者會。

Conversation 2 對話2

Tracy	I just came back from the meeting with the client, and they want to cut their budget of the press conference.	我剛才和客戶見面了，他們想要刪減這次記者會的預算。
Stephanie	I feel **my luck ran out**. So, what did they say?	我覺得我運氣用光了。所以，他們說了什麼？
Tracy	They only have one million instead of two for this event.	他們只有一百萬，而不是兩百萬給這個活動。
Stephanie	What? That's only half of the original budget. I already **have a very bad feeling about this**.	什麼？那只有原來預算的一半。我已經有很糟糕的預感了。
Tracy	Things still need to get done.	事情還是要做的啦。

Stephanie	**I know it by heart.** Let me back to my seat and bring the budget list to you. Could you wait at the conference room, and **I will be right with you**.	我牢記在心。讓我回座位拿一下預算表給妳。妳可以在會議室等我,我馬上回來。
Tracy	Sure.	沒問題。
	(Five minutes later)	(5 分鐘後)
Stephanie	Basically, there is a **fundamental change** we need to make.	基本上,我們需要做一個根本的改變。
Tracy	Which is?	那就是?
Stephanie	We need to hire a person from **B-list**, instead of A-list.	我們需要放棄原先的 A 咖級人物,請一個 B 咖級的人了。
Tracy	I think the client could accept that, but never suggest a **comedian** or an **entertainer**.	我想客戶可以接受的,但是不要建議用搞笑藝人或者綜藝咖。
Stephanie	I am aware of that. So, this changes everything, from **venue**, F&B, the decoration, the size of the stage etc. etc.	我知道的。所以,這也會改變每件事,從場地、食物與飲料、裝潢、舞台的大小…等等。

Part I

Part II

Part III

Part IV

Part V

Part VI

Tracy	I hope the client will not be very disappointed with this arrangement.	我希望客戶對這安排不會太失望。
Stephanie	How's that? You know what, they shouldn't create this kind of mess to us.	怎麼會？妳也知道，他們不應該製造這種混亂給我們的。
Tracy	Everything will be fine, just control yourself.	沒事的，控制一下妳自己。
Stephanie	I am OK. Can we also adjust the expected benefits of this event?	我很好。我們也可以調整這次活動的預期效益吧？
Tracy	I think so. You also know a person from the B-list is much less attractive for some medias.	我想可以。妳也知道 B 咖級人物對某些媒體來說就是少了吸引力。
Stephanie	Maybe you could also tell them to stop treating us like a **pushover**?	也許妳也可以告訴他們，別再把我們當軟柿子吃了？
Tracy	Just go back to work. I'll pretend I never heard that.	回去工作吧。我會假裝沒有聽到的。

Part I

Part II

Part III

Part IV

Part V

Part VI

　　從上述對話中，就可以看得出來，預算的事先告知對活動影響有多大；當然，也包括預算的調整。更動預算，就會造成活動在軟硬體安排上的落差，可能連帶影響民眾或媒體的觀感，所以很少會有主辦單位或企業臨時刪減預算（temporary budget cuts），通常都是追加預算（supplementary budget）的情況比較多。

　　如何在有限的預算裡完成任務，又達到一定的媒體曝光量，在有經驗的公關公司或公關人心裡，自然有一套計算公式。通常是靠著多年與協力廠商（third-party/subcontractor/partner）的配合，知道哪一家的預算、品質如何；怎麼樣品質的記者會，能吸引怎麼樣的媒體曝光，同樣也是掌握在經驗豐富的公關人手裡。

　　通常預算會花費在的幾個大項目有：場地、代言人／明星、場地布置、舞台、音效（sound effect）、燈光（lighting）、食物或酒水等等。其他還有人員薪水（salary）、顧問費（consulting fee）、交通費（transportation cost）、雜支（**miscellaneous** expense）等等。

Related Word 相關詞彙

1. my luck run out　我運氣用完了，我好日子不再了

   文法加油站：還有一種常見的講法是 Today is not my day（今天不是我的好日子），如果想要強調晚上，可以改成 It is not my night（我今晚運氣不好）。

2. have a very bad feeling about this　有很不好的預感，感覺這事不對勁

3. I know it by heart　我牢記在心，我清楚得很

4. I will be right with you.　我馬上回來

5. fundamental change　根本上的改變

   文法加油站：同義詞還有 basic、main、key、foremost、prime、essential。

6. B-list　B 咖

   文法加油站：所謂的大牌小牌，就是按照排名先後，所以用 list（名單、列名）來作為一個象徵。A-list 就是 A 咖級的，以此類推，可以講到 D-list。

7. comedian　搞笑藝人、喜劇演員

   文法加油站：喜劇片則寫作 comedy。

8. entertainer　綜藝咖、藝人

9. venue　場地

   文法加油站：常用來指活動舉辦的地點。

10. pushover　軟柿子

    文法加油站：這個單詞是用來形容好欺負的人。水果的柿子則是 persimmon。

11. miscellaneous　雜項

Exercises 練習題

Please complete the word or sentence by filling in the blanks.

A：Look! Isn't he that actor on the _____ ?

B：I think he is the _____ .

A：No, he is also the _____ who always dressed like the President on TV.

B：I really don't have a clue.

A：_____ him _____ .

請填空完成下面句子或單字

A：你看！他不就是那個 A 咖演員嗎？

B：他是那個搞笑藝人吧。

A：不是，他也是電視上老是扮成總統的藝人啊。

B：我實在想不起來。

A：我可是打從心底記得他呢。

Answers to the Unit:
A-list
comedian
entertainer
I know, by heart

Unit 17　Key Points of Hosting a Meeting-1 主持會議要點

Situation 1　情境 1：

Abby is a PR Manager, and she is hosting a press conference of a new launched watch.

愛比是一位公關部經理，她現在正在主持一款新上市手錶的記者會。

Key points for your conversation 對話急救包

📎 記者會開始前

Ladies and gentlemen：Please be seat yourself for the Press Conference on Launch of New X Watches, which follows in five minutes.

各位女士、先生，請入座參加 X 手錶新上市記者會，記者會將在 5 分鐘內開始。

The Press Conference on Launch of New X Watches will be held here immediately. **Will** all participants **please** remain seated？

X 手錶新上市記者會即將開始，請所有與會人員就座。

小貼士：Will⋯please？的內容多為請求對方配合，所以句尾可以用句號代替。

May I have your attention, please！ The Press Conference on Launch of New X Watches will be held in ten minutes, please be seated as soon as possible.

請各位注意，X 手錶新上市記者會將在 10 分鐘內開始，請各位盡速就座。

📎 致歡迎詞

Good afternoon, everyone. My name is Abby Lin, the PR Manager of X Watch Company. **It is a great pleasure for me** to welcome you to this Press Conference on Launch of New X Watches.

各位午安，我的名字是林愛比，X 手錶公司的公關經理。我很榮幸歡迎各位來參加這次的 X 手錶新上市記者會。

小貼士：亦 可 置 換 為 I am happy、It gives me pleasure、I am privileged、It is a privilege。

Let me introduce myself. I am Abby Lin from X Watch Company. We have gathered in this hall today to learn the latest news from X Watch.
請容我自我介紹，我是 X 手錶公司的林愛比。我們今天聚集在這間會議廳裡，是為了獲得關於 X 手錶的最新消息。
小貼士：亦可置換為 Allow me、Permit me to。

This afternoon we are **privileged** to have with us a wonderful show which will be presented by A Model Company to demonstrate the features of the new launched watches from X Watch.
今天下午我們很榮幸請到 A 模特兒公司帶來的精彩走秀，以展示新上市的 X 手錶的嶄新特色。
小貼士：亦可置換為 happy、honored。

介紹在場貴賓

I am very pleased to be able to introduce John Chen, our General Manager, and Mr. Don Huang, one of our sealers.
我非常高興為各位介紹陳約翰，我們總經理，以及黃堂先生，我們其中一位經銷商。

I would like to introduce our one hundred and fifty distributors here, as you know, their hard working makes where X Watch is today in the market.
我想要介紹我們在場的一百五十位經銷商，如同各位知道的，他們的努力造就了 X 手錶今日在市場上的地位。

記者會開始

The Press Conference on Launch of New X Watches is now called to order.
X 手錶新上市記者會現在開始。

Now, Ladies and Gentlemen, **I would like to introduce** our General Manager, Mr. John Chen.
現在，各位女士與先生，容我介紹我們的總經理，陳約翰先生。
小貼士：亦可置換為 may I present to you。

It is now a pleasure to turn the conference over to Mr. Don Huang, one of our dealers' representatives.
現在我很榮幸將記者會交給黃堂先生，我們其中一位經銷商代表，來進行。

📎 記者會儀式舉行

I am now present to you the ceremony of this conference, please welcome our General Manager and our dealers to come to the stage.
現在我們將為您呈現記者會的儀式，請歡迎我們的總經理與經銷商們到台上來。

Could all the photojournalists please come up to the front ？
麻煩所有攝影記者到台前來好嗎？

Thanks for all the VIPs on the stage, let's give them a round of applause.
感謝台上的貴賓們，讓我們給予他們熱烈的掌聲。

📎 現場 Q&A 掌控

We have fifteen minutes on hand for questions. I think most of the reporters are still here in the audience, so if anyone would like to ask any question about this afternoon's press conference, please feel free to do so. Anyone, please ？
我們還有 15 分鐘的回答時間。我想現場還有許多在座的媒體，所以如果有任何一位想要針對今天下午的記者會發問的話，請自由發問。請問有沒有人呢？

I am afraid we will have only five minutes for **Q&A**, because time is running out.
因為時間不夠，恐怕我們只能用 5 分鐘時間來進行問答。
小貼士：Q&A 是 questions and answers 的縮寫，表示問問題以及給予回答。

Could you please speak into the microphone and identify yourself, so that everyone here can hear you well.
請您對著麥克風發言並說明身分，好讓全場的人都可以清楚聽到您。

Yes, the gentleman in the **first row**, your question is ？
是的，第一排的先生，您的問題是？
小貼士：可以置換為 two row、third row，或 at the back（後面）。

Does anybody of the conference wish to ask any question further ？
還有沒有任何來賓想要詢問其他問題？

Allow me remind you that we just have three minutes left, and we would like to have another one question only.
請容我提醒各位我們只剩下三分鐘，可以再問一個問題。

We must now end the press conference up for lack of time.
由於時間的關係，現在我們必須結束記者會了。

📎 散會

Allow me thank you all again and, with this, close the Press Conference on Launch of New X Watches. If you need an interview, please come to the front and our staffs will help you.
請容我再次感謝在場的每一位，並且宣佈 X 手錶新上市記者會到此結束。如果您需要專訪，請到台前，我們的工作人員會協助您。

I would like to thank our dealers and the presses for making this press conference a success.
我想感謝我們的經銷商和媒體朋友們的出席，使得這次記者會如此成功。

Thank you all to attend this conference, please feel free to contact me if you have any question regards today's press conference.
感謝出席這場記者會的每一位，如果您有關於今天記者會的任何疑問，歡迎與我聯繫。

Unit 17 Key Points of Hosting a Meeting-2 主持會議要點

Situation 2 情境 2：

Veronica is presenting her crisis communication management plan for company executives.
維妮卡正在向公司高層報告她的危機溝通管理計畫。

Key points for your conversation 對話急救包

📎 說明會議目的

This meeting is planned and organized on the topic of Crisis Communication Management. It was felt that this kind of meeting should **regularly** proceed in order to set the stage for a sudden crisis.
這次會議是針對危機溝通管理所規劃和籌備的。這類會議有感於應該經常地進行，以便為突然到來的危機做準備。
小貼士：亦可置換為 often, frequently, regularly, constantly。

The purpose of this meeting is to bring into focus the problem and solution of crisis management. It is hoped that this meeting will answer many of the problem.
本次會議的目的在於著重於危機管理的問題與解決方法。希望這些問題可以在這次會議中找到答案。

📎 提出與詳述簡報內容

I would like to start with an introduction of Crisis Communication Management.
我想從介紹危機溝通管理作開場。

Today, I would like to talk about the general problem of the Crisis Communication Management. I am not going to discuss the reason of why crisis occur, but to focus on the solutions of this problem.
今天，我將要談到危機溝通管理的一般問題。我不會探討危機發生的起因，而是會專注在問題的解決之道。

What we would like to consider at this topic is that who is going to be the contact window and spokesman when a crisis happens.
我們要討論的重點是當危機發生時，誰來當聯繫的窗口和發言人。

I would like to **enlarge** on this issue with more slides.
我想針對這個議題，以更多 PPT 畫面呈現。
小貼士：亦可置換為 expand、elaborate。

The first thing I want to talk about is a brief of what is Crisis Communication Management, and I will limit my presentation to crisis prevention and crisis mitigation.
我想談論的第一件事是簡介何謂危機溝通管理，然後我將專注在危機預防和危機解除的議題上。

The next issue I would like to address myself to is prevention、detection and correction of crisis management.
下一個我想談論的議題是危機管理的預防、偵測和矯正。

歸納與總結

In my opinion, there is no other issue of equal importance to the future of preventing crisis than how we go about preparing the training of company executives in the skills that are necessary in dealing with that kind of issue.
我認為，除了讓公司高層接受專業的技能訓練之外，沒有比預防危機更重要的議題了。
小貼上：亦可置換為 As far as I can see、In my view, In my judgment。

My conclusion will be that many technological tools now become more helpful and available for controlling crisis.
我的結論是現在有很多科技工具，在控制危機上變得更有幫助和更方便。

I would like to close my presentation this morning by saying that as soon we start the project of Crisis Communication Management the better.
我想總結今天上午我的簡報，那就是越快開始危機溝通管理專案越好。

Part I
Part II
Part III
Part IV
Part V
Part VI

Part IV

Advertising Planning
廣告企劃

Unit 18 Situation Analysis and Goals of Planning-1 希望廣告解決什麼困境

Background Introduction 背景介紹 :

Stuart is Marketing Manager of S Company and Bernard is Creative Director of M Advertising Company. They are talking on the phone about what advertising goals should be achieved.

史都華是 S 公司的行銷主管，伯納德是 M 廣告公司的創意總監。他們正在電話上討論廣告應該達成什麼目標。

Conversation 1 對話 1

Stuart	Hi, Bernard, do you think how long it will take for this conversation?	嗨，伯納德，你想我們會談多久？
Bernard	You have another meeting? It won't take long.	你有另一場會議嗎？應該不會很久。
Stuart	OK. It's my daughter, she ate some bad food this morning, and now she has really bad **diarrhea**.	好。是我女兒，她早上吃了壞掉的食物，現在在拉肚子。
Bernard	Oh, that's really bad. Let us start as quickly as possible.	喔，真是糟糕。那我們盡快開始吧。

Stuart	Sure. As you already knew it, this advertising is going to be an **institutional advertising**, so we are expecting a whole new image for the company from your team.	好的。如同你已經知道的，這支廣告會是一個機構廣告，所以我們期望你們團隊為公司打造一個全新的形象。
Bernard	You have my words that we are going to make you surprised.	我保證一定會讓你們驚訝的。
Stuart	That would be wonderful, then.	那就太好了。
Bernard	But I still need to confirm few things before we start to plan.	但是在計劃之前，我還是有些事情需要確認。
Stuart	What are they?	是什麼？
Bernard	You know there are thousands of ways to show an ad. It could be playing music, creating an image, with fun or humor, or even focus on telling scientific evidence.	你知道有成千種方式來表現一則廣告。可以是透過音樂、營造一種形象、用好笑或幽默的方式，或者甚至專注在講些科學證據。

Part I
Part II
Part III
Part IV
Part V
Part VI

Stuart	You absolutely pointed out one of the key point which I want to discuss with you. Can we just focus on creating a warm and positive image, since the **economic depression** recently we have.	你完全點出我想和你討論的要點。最近經濟低迷的緣故，我們是否可以專注在建立一種溫馨和正面的形象？
Bernard	So, should we shoot a silent TV commercial?	所以，我們應該拍一支無聲的電視廣告嗎？
Stuart	No. Please don't. I am thinking some warm music.	不。千萬不要。我在想一些溫馨的音樂。
Bernard	Sure. Music has a certain **intrinsic** value which can help in increasing the **persuasiveness** of the advertisement.	當然。音樂具有一定的內在價值，可以幫助增加廣告的說服力。
Stuart	It sounds terrific, doesn't it?	聽起來很棒，不是嗎？
Bernard	What image should we build or create for S Company in this commercial?	在這支廣告裡，我們該替 S 公司建立或創造什麼形象？
Stuart	How about combining **emotional and rational appeals** together?	結合情感和理性的訴求怎麼樣？

Part I　Part II　Part III　Part IV　Part V　Part VI

Bernard	Don't you think these two appeals are conflict?	你難道不覺得這兩種訴求是衝突的？
Stuart	Like I said, we need to **cheer the society**, however, the past commercials of our company tend to appeal rational appeals. So, I am thinking how to combine them together.	就像我說的，我們需要替社會打氣，但是，我們公司過往的廣告傾向理性的訴求。所以，我才想如何把兩者結合。
Pearce	Since we "might" invite a spokesman, why don't we confirm his time first to see if we can find the matches with the date when the most reporters can attend?	既然我們「也許」會邀請代言人，為什麼不先確認他的時間，然後再看是否能符合大多數記者能出席的日期。
Quincy	Maybe there are some other PR events during the following weeks, and I think the best way is to find out all of them so we can avoid those days.	也許接下來幾週有其他的公關活動，我想最好的方式是查出全部的活動，我們就能避開這些日期。
Zoe	That is a very good idea, perhaps you can help to do that.	很好的想法，也許你可以幫忙做這件事。
Quincy	No problem.	沒問題啊。

Part I
Part II
Part III
Part IV
Part V
Part VI

Bernard	In one commercial, that could be a problem. You know, there are only thirty seconds for a TV commercial, this makes it difficult to tell a complex story.	在同一支廣告裡的話,可能會是個問題。你知道的,一支電視廣告也就 只有 30 秒鐘,這很難講述一個複雜的故事。
Stuart	You are right. I shouldn't think too much.	你是對的。我不應該想太多。
Bernard	I will see what our team can come out, and I will let you know ASAP.	我會看看我們團隊可以想出什麼辦法,然後盡快讓你知道。
Stuart	Sure, thanks.	好的,謝了。
Bernard	Hey, we should hang out sometime. You know what, never forget to **stop and smell the roses**.	嘿,我們哪天應該一起出來。你知道的嘛,永遠別忘記停下腳步享受生活。
Stuart	After this project, I will.	在這專案之後吧,我想。

知識補給站

Part I
Part II
Part III
Part IV
Part V
Part VI

　　為什麼要廣告？目的可能有兩個：第一，為了新產品上市（new product launch）告知，或者推出了新的活動（new campaign）；第二，為了企業或機構的形象宣傳（image ad）。

　　為了形象宣傳目的製作的廣告，稱為機構廣告（institutional advertising）；另一個則稱作產品廣告（product advertising）。機構廣告可以簡單理解為形象廣告，例如，中國信託銀行旗下的基金會每年舉辦點燃生命之火的公益活動（**nonprofit activity**），並且透過電視廣告、銀行櫃檯（bank counter）放置傳單（**leaflet**）、郵寄銀行／信用卡客戶活動訊息…等等，都是一種透過形象宣傳方式，增加民眾、目標族群對其好感的一種機構廣告。

　　而在廣告中，因應不同目的也會有不同表現手法。舉例來說，好幾年前安泰人壽的死神上門廣告，宣傳不買保險的風險很高，很容易被死神盯上，就是利用消費者恐懼（fear）的心理訴求呈現廣告，這類廣告也常見於健康宣導（health promotion）的訊息（常抽菸容易死於肺癌、性生活複雜易罹患愛滋病）。另外還有以生活片段（fragments of life）引起共鳴的（汽車產品常見手法），以幽默（humor）方式呈現產品特色（孟姜女哭倒長城後需要一顆喉糖），還有強調科學證據（scientific evidence）的（生髮產品或醫藥產品常見手法），甚至請代言人（spokesman）站台的…等等，類型相當多元。

　　會發展出各式各樣的訴求，也是因為每個族群有其特色，再加上配合產品定位，所以發展出對不同人說不同話的廣告型態（type of ad）。

Related Word 相關詞彙

1. diarrhea 腹瀉

   文法加油站：腹部的英文是 *abdomen*，所以肚子痛可以說成 *abdominal pain*。

2. institutional advertising 機構廣告。用來傳達企業、組織理念的宣傳方式，目的在提升組織的形象或商譽，不會直接訴求銷售的訊息。

3. economic depression 經濟低迷

   文法加油站：類似的單詞還有 *financial crisis*（金融危機）、*economic slump*（經濟不景氣）、*economic downturn*（經濟衰退）、*economic stagnation*（經濟停滯）。相反的話，則可用 *economic boom*（經濟繁榮）或 *economic turnaround*（經濟好轉）。

4. intrinsic 內在的，固有的，本質的

5. persuasiveness 說服力

6. emotional and rational appeal 情感與理性的訴求。依照廣告內容，大致分為這兩個領域，情感訴求是以驅動消費者的情感或衝動來做吸引購買，理性訴求則是強調產品的功能或購買之後的好處。

7. cheer the society 為社會打氣

   文法加油站：*cheer* 作動詞是加油打氣的意思，作名詞有歡呼、喝采、愉快的意思。對某人說 *Cheer up!* 就是要對方振作、打起精神來。替比賽隊伍加油的啦啦隊長就寫作 *cheerleader*。

8. stop and smell the roses 停下腳步享受生活

   文法加油站：直譯是停下來聞聞玫瑰花香，比喻在忙碌生活中應停下腳步，享受身邊美好事物的說法。

9. nonprofit activity 公益活動，非營利活動

   文法加油站：同義詞還有 *charity event*。所以 *charity* 有公益組織或慈善機構的意思，另外 *nonprofit organization*（簡稱 *NPO*）也是代表公益團體或非營利的組織／團體的意思。

10. leaflet 傳單

    文法加油站：同義詞還有 *fryer*、*handbill*。

Exercises 練習題

Please complete the word or sentence by filling in the blanks.

A：It seems we are having a _____ recently.

B：I went to a _____ today, it seemed people were lacking energy.

A：Yap.

B：There should be more people stand out for _____ at this moment.

A：You are one of them.

B：I am just _____ in my busy life. I think I will continue to go there and help tomorrow.

請填空完成下面句子或單字

A：最近景氣真低迷。

B：我今天去幫一個公益活動發宣傳單，感覺大家很沒有活力。

A：是呀。

B：這個時刻應該有更多人站出來替這個社會加油打氣。

A：你就是一個了。

B：我只是在忙碌的生活中停下腳步享受生活而已。看來明天我再繼續去吧。

Answers to the Unit:
economic depression/economic slump/economic downturn
nonprofit activity/
cheering the society
stopping and smell the roses

Part I

Part II

Part III

Part IV

Part V

Part VI

Unit 18 Situation Analysis and Goals of Planning-2 希望廣告解決什麼困境

Background Introduction 背景介紹：

Mimi and Isaac are discussing the advertising contents for the new diaper product which is going to be launched by their company.
美美和艾薩克正在為公司即將上市的紙尿褲產品發想廣告內容。

Conversation 2 對話 2

Mimi	I **feel like** my work is repeated every day, which I don't like it at all.	我感覺我的工作好像一直在重複做著，而我一點也不喜歡。
Isaac	You got to **carry on**. Do you know that we are going to launch a new type of diaper?	你一定要撐下去。你知道我們即將要上市一款新的尿布？
Mimi	I know that, but I don't know where is the difference between the new one and the old ones we have now.	我知道這件事，但我不知道新的和我們現在舊的有什麼不同？
Isaac	Well, they are pretty much different. For example, the new one has **bio-based** corn/wheat blend in **super-absorbent** core, and stylized designs for boys and girls.	嗯，還有蠻多不同處的。舉例來說，新的有用天然成份玉米與小麥混合而成的超強吸收核心，和針對女孩與男孩的個性化設計。

Mimi	Does the new one still use natural **odor-inhibitors**?	新的也有使用天然的氣味抑制劑？
Isaac	Yes, it does.	有的。
Mimi	From the way I see it, we should emphasis on the feature of the product's personality.	我的觀點是，我們應該強調產品個性的特點上。
Isaac	Which means?	那也就是説？
Mimi	We should strengthen our competitive advantages through emphasizing on the stylized designs, because **as far as I know**, there is no competitors are selling this kind of product.	我們應該強化我們競爭優勢，透過強調個性化的設計，因為就我知道，還沒有哪一個競爭者正在賣這樣的產品。
Isaac	You probably right. How about we focus on showing parents how to use our new product?	你可能是對的。如果我們專注在告訴父母們如何使用我們的新產品呢？
Mimi	Does it have a new function design?	它有新的功能設計嗎？

Part I
Part II
Part III
Part IV
Part V
Part VI

233

Isaac	Not really, OK, a bad idea. How about we show some statistics?	不太算，好吧，壞主意。不如我們展示一些統計數據？
Mimi	Good idea, but about what?	好方法，但是關於什麼的？
Isaac	We can use statistics or figures to display aspects of the product and its popularity in particular.	我們可以用統計數字或圖表展現產品，以及它受歡迎的程度。
Isaac	Can we invite a celebrity or well-known person to **endorse** our product?	那我們可以邀請一位名流或知名人士來為我們產品站台？
Isaac	Yes, I think so. We strengthen the product characteristics on the commercial, so we can deliver our differentiation through it.	我想是的。我們在廣告上強調產品的特性，透過它傳達我們的差異化。
Mimi	It seems a strong proposal now. By the way, could you write the proposal this time? I will take **personal leave** this afternoon.	現在看起來是個夠強的提案了。對了，可以麻煩你這次寫提案？下午我要請事假。
Isaac	Sure, you can **leave it to me**.	沒問題，你可以交給我。

Part I
Part II
Part III
Part IV
Part V
Part VI

知識補給站

　　為新產品上市策畫廣告，有幾項可能會遇到的困難，最顯而易見的（obvious）就是，既然是新產品，可能會有新的使用方法（a new way to use it）、新的鎖定對象（new audiences）、與既有競爭者有何不同…等等問題，需要在短短 30 甚至 15 秒廣告中展現出來。

　　克服的手法也有很多，例如，產品使用示範（**product demonstration**）適合需要教育使用者的產品，像是兒童玩具或者 3C 產品是常見的廣告方式。產品個性化，有的時候也和品牌個性結合，像是精品（luxury goods）、烈酒（spirit）或鎖定特定族群的商品就常用這種強調百年工藝（century crafts）、獨一無二（unique）、勇於突破（**the courage to break**）和做自己…等等的個性宣言。此外，用名人現身說法（talk from their own experiences），也是新產品上市廣告常用的手法，藉由名人的知名度和高度，讓消費者產生信賴的好感，進而願意購買嘗試看看（try it）。

　　還有一種特殊表現手法，是利用卡通明星或動畫，有時候不見得是給小朋友看，而是因為企業本身的代言人就是這些卡通明星；例如香港迪士尼樂園的廣告，和花蓮海洋公園的廣告。還有一種強調想像（imagination）的手法，像是蠻牛飲料或喝完以後會飛走的紅牛飲料（Red Bull），運用這類手法，能瞬間吸引觀眾注意，也能和產品功能 / 利益（product functions/benefits）相連結。

Part I

Part II

Part III

Part IV

Part V

Part VI

Related Word 相關詞彙

1. feel like　感覺好像是
2. carry on　撐下去，繼續下去
   文法加油站：carry on 還有一句經典台詞，那就是 Keep calm and carry on
   （保持冷靜，堅持下去）
3. bio-based　天然成份，生質機質的
4. super-absorbent　高吸收性
   文法加油站：absorbent 作形容詞是吸收性佳、能吸收的意思，名詞則是吸
   收、吸收劑、吸附的意思。
5. odor-inhibitor　氣味抑制劑
   文法加油站：這是由兩個單詞組成的單字，odor 代表氣味，inhibitor 則是抑
   制劑的意思。
6. as far as I know　就我所知
7. endorse　擁護，支持
   文法加油站：此為動詞，同義詞還有 support；名詞寫作 endorsement，有擁
   護、支持和背書的意思。
8. take personal leave　請事假
   文法加油站：請假的理由有以下幾種講法：
   (1) take sick leave　請病假
   (2) take annual leave　請年假
   (3) take maternity leave　請產假
   (4) take funeral leave　請喪假
   (5) take paid/unpaid leave　請支薪／不支薪假
9. leave it to me　把事情留（交）給我，讓我來
10. product demonstration　產品使用示範
    文法加油站：亦可簡稱為 product demo。
11. the courage to break　勇於突破
    文法加油站：還有一種說法是後面加上 out of your comfort zone，意思是
    勇於突破走出你的舒適圈。另外，勇於和某人分手，則是 the
    courage to break up with someone。

Exercises 練習題

Please complete the word or sentence by filling in the blanks.

● Please don't always take _____ nor _____ your

　work _____ .

● This is the newly developed _____ .

● You should have the _____ .

● A：I feel like _____ .

　B：No, you have to _____ .

請填空完成下面句子或單字

● 請不要老是請事假，也不要把你的工作留給我做。

● 這是新開發的天然成份氣味抑制劑。

● 你應該勇於突破走出你的舒適圈。

● A：我想要辭職。

　B：不行，你要堅持下去。

Answers to the Unit:

personal leave, leave, to me

bio-based odor-inhibitor

courage to break out of your comfort zone

resigning

carry on

Part I

Part II

Part III

Part IV

Part V

Part VI

Unit 19 Advertising Appeals-1
廣告說什麼好

Background Introduction 背景介紹：

Vanessa is the Marketing Director of T Company, Kirk is the Account Manager from X Advertising Agency and Eugene is the Art Director. They are now discussing how to shoot the men's skin care product advertisement for T Company.

凡妮莎是 T 公司的行銷總監，柯克是 X 廣告代理商的客戶經理，尤金則是美術指導。他們三人正在討論 T 公司的男士保養品廣告，應該怎麼拍攝才好。

Conversation 1 對話 1

Kirk	So, should we start to talk about which type of **advertising appeal** we should adapt?	我們是不是先討論要採用哪一種廣告訴求？
Vanessa	OK, let's begin with deciding what type of **product advertising** we are going to choose in the commercial?	可以，那就先決定要在廣告裡播放哪一種型的產品廣告？
Eugene	In my opinion, **informative advertising** seems more suitable for the product at this stage.	我的意見是，告知式的廣告在這個階段好像比較適合我們的產品。
Kirk	I am thinking maybe we should try **comparison ad**, you know, compare us with the other competitors.	我在想也許我們應該嘗試比較式廣告，你知道的，拿我們和其他競爭者比較。

Eugene	In comparison advertising, we can show **the newest formulas** of our product which are not other brands have in the current market.	在比較式廣告裡，我們可以表現，現在市場上競爭對手沒有的產品最新配方。
Vanessa	Cannot we find something more attractive? I mean a really strong feeling that kind of telling the audiences you must have this.	不能想些更有吸引力的點子嗎？我是説一個真的很強烈的感覺，就像是告訴觀眾你非買不可。
Kirk	Right, I have an idea. How about we display the attraction between one man and a woman? We can emphasis that once you bought the skin care product, it will improve your romantic or love life.	這樣吧，我有個想法。不如我們展示一個男人對一個女人的吸引力？我們可以強調，只要你買了我們的護膚產品，就可以增進你的浪漫史或愛情生活。
Eugene	Unfortunately, I think P brand already used that kind of appeal in their last month's advertising.	不幸地，我想 P 品牌已經在上個月的廣告裡用了這類的訴求。
Vanessa	**What a pity**, I found it quite sexy.	真可惜，我倒覺得還蠻性感的。
Eugene	Maybe we can try with **youth appeal**?	也許我們可以試試回到青春的訴求？

Kirk	Good point, skin care or cosmetic product usually makes use of this appeal.	說得好，保養品或化妝品經常使用這類訴求。
Vanessa	But our product doesn't reflect youth, therefore, I think we have to give up this type of appeal.	但是我們產品沒有反映年輕化，所以，我想我們必須放棄這類的訴求。
Eugene	**What a shame**, since this kind of appeal is my favor.	可惜啊，這類訴求可是我的最愛呢。
Kirk	I'll **make it up to you** someday.	改天我會補償你的。
Vanessa	I guess we have to go back and choose the **romance appeal** then, and based on this, make it an informative ad seems a more relevant decision.	我想我們就必須回到浪漫訴求了，基於這思路，用告知式廣告手法似乎是比較相關的決定了。
Eugene	It fits our goal in this project, so I think it's a wise choice.	還是符合我們專案的目標，所以我想是個明智的決定。
Vanessa	OK, gentlemen, wish our **pleasant cooperation** in future!	好啦，紳士們，希望未來合作於愉快！
Kirk/ Eugene	Sure!	一定的！

Part I Part II Part III Part IV Part V Part VI

知識補給站

產品廣告（相對於機構廣告所拍攝的主要是形象）是以產品為主角進行拍攝，舉凡訴求產品特性、產品好處、促銷…等以產品為主角的廣告，都可以稱作產品廣告。大致分成三種拍攝內容，第一種是以告知式廣告為主題，第二種是說服式廣告，第三種是提醒式廣告（reminder advertising）。

告知式廣告大多出現在產品剛問市，或者有改良後的新品所使用的廣告手法，廣告中會表現產品如何使用、有哪些最新的配方／技術（the newest formulas/techniques）、第一家推出（the first to launch）、風行全球多年（has been sold around the world for many years）…等等告知式的訊息。例如，吉列刮鬍刀推出五層刀片的新產品，廣告中放大刀片構造，加強說明帶來前所未有的舒適感…等等，都是告知式廣告的手法。

說服式廣告（persuasive advertising）大多運用在產品已經推出好一段時間，目的在說服更多消費者來購買（convince more consumers to purchase）、加強品牌偏好感（strengthen brand preference），著重在產品優點（advantages）和特色（features），像是提到「限量」就是一個例子；有時候也會拿其他競爭對手做比較，強調自己的好，稱為比較式廣告。比較式廣告最著名的例子是，金頂電池的粉紅兔子，牠總是跑得比較快、比較遠，不管對手有幾隻兔子接力，牠總是領先到終點。還有像「比一般市售商品多了…（more than other products in the market）」的這種宣傳台詞，也屬於比較式廣告的特色。

提醒式廣告是當品牌或產品已經歷久不衰，但是也沒有特殊新品上市時，所播放的廣告手法；海尼根（打開海尼根，精彩你的世界）、可口可樂（走跳辦桌）都拍過這類型廣告。

Related Word 相關詞彙

1. advertising appeal　廣告訴求。意思是用什麼內容或創意，鼓勵或刺激消費者採取某些行動，或者影響消費者對某些產品或服務的態度。

2. product advertising　產品廣告

3. informative advertising　告知式廣告

4. comparison ad（vertising）　比較式廣告

5. the newest formula　最新配方

6. What a pity. = What a shame.　真可惜

   文法加油站：pity 可作動詞和名詞都是憐憫、可憐、慈悲的意思，形容詞則是 pitiful。

7. youth appeal　青春 / 年輕化訴求

8. make it up to you　補償你

9. romance appeal　浪漫訴求

10. pleasant cooperation　合作愉快

11. reminder advertising　提醒式廣告

Part I

Part II

Part III

Part IV

Part V

Part VI

Exercises 練習題

Please make a line match then English and Chinese.

連連看。

- comparison advertising
- romance appeal
- informative advertising
- youth appeal
- reminder advertising

- 青春訴求
- 提醒式廣告
- 浪漫訴求
- 比較式廣告
- 告知式廣告

Answers to the Unit:

（依照英文的順序）

- 比較式廣告
- 浪漫訴求
- 告知式廣告
- 青春訴求
- 提醒式廣告

Part I

Part II

Part III

Part IV

Part V

Part VI

Unit 19 Advertising Appeals-2
廣告說什麼好

Background Introduction 背景介紹：

Nora is Account Executive and Willa is Account Manager, they are thinking a new advertisement for their client's yogurt product.

諾拉是廣告公司的業務執行，而威娜是客戶經理，她們正在替客戶的優酪乳商品發想一個新的廣告內容。

Conversation 2 對話 2

Nora	Have you heard that Amy and David are **seeing each other** recently?	你有沒有聽說艾咪和大衛最近在交往？
Willa	I am sure it's just **kid stuff**.	我確信他們只是兒戲罷了。
Nora	You are really a **mean** person.	你真是一個很刻薄的人。
Willa	Well, we can make a bet on this.	那好，我們來打賭。
Nora	I will never do that. Anyway, let's start to talk about the thing I emailed you yesterday.	我永遠不會這樣做的。好吧，讓我們開始討論我昨天發信給妳的事情。
Willa	Right. You said the client didn't satisfy with the proposal we sent to them?	好的。妳提到客戶不滿意我們寄給他們的提案計畫。

Nora	No. They asked us to make an adjustment as soon as possible.	的確。他們要求我們盡快調整。
Willa	Where are they unhappy about?	他們不高興哪一點呢？
Nora	They think we didn't make a clear image for the yogurt in the proposal.	他們覺得我們在計畫書裡沒有為優酪乳建立一個清楚的形象。
Willa	OK, let's go through the ad again. This product is targeting **adult male** market, and since it has lower calories than other competitor products, we provided a combination of statistic and **health appeal**.	好吧，我們再檢視這支廣告一遍。產品是以成年男性為目標市場，而且卡路里比其他競爭產品低，所以我們綜合了統計數據和健康訴求。
Nora	They said they want to see more emotional appeal, rather than rational appeal.	他們說想要看到更多情感的，而不是理性的訴求。
Willa	Well, I think we need to confirm all the clients with this kind of question at the very beginning in the future.	好吧，我想未來我們需要和所有客戶在初期階段就確認類似這樣的問題。

Part I
Part II
Part III
Part IV
Part V
Part VI

Nora	You probably right, since this isn't the first time we heard from our clients.	妳大概是對了，因為這不是第一次我們聽到客戶這樣説了。
Willa	How about we use **humor appeal**? Like use a comic character or an adult to make fun with the yogurt.	如果我們使用幽默訴求呢？像是用漫畫角色，或成年人拿優酪乳開點玩笑。
Nora	Actually, I am thinking maybe we should try **less than perfect appeal**. You know, people who will pay attention to their weight are our target audiences, aren't they? So, we could show an overweight guy who is standing on a scale and the product on the corner of the screen, says "Looking for something?".	其實，我在想也許我們應該試試看不完美訴求。妳知道的，在意體重的人是我們的目標族群，不是嗎？所以，我們讓一個過重的男士站在體重計上，然後讓產品出現在電視機角落，寫上「在找什麼嗎？」。
Willa	This means our product is exactly what they are looking for?	意思是我們的產品正好是他們在找的？
Nora	Yes! What do you say?	對！妳説好嗎？
Willa	Doesn't this **imply** that our buyer is an overweight person?	這不就是暗示我們的購買者是超重的人？

Nora	What if we change the image to a slim young man? Will it look like we are suggesting that the person who buys our product can enjoy a healthy and happy life?	那如果把人換成一個瘦的年輕人？是不是就會看起來像，我們在暗示買我們產品的人可以享受健康和快樂的生活？
Willa	Maybe not so slim, just with an average weight.	可能也不是很瘦的人，就是中等體重的。
Nora	Sure.	當然。
Willa	Anything else?	還有別的事嗎？
Nora	Yes, the client also wanted to confirm where the ad will be announced?	有的，客戶還想知道廣告會在哪裡播放？
Willa	Except TV, there are radio stations, magazines and new paper.	除了電視。還有廣播電台、雜誌和報紙。
Nora	On which or what kind of program?	在哪個或什麼樣的節目？

Part I
Part II
Part III
Part IV
Part V
Part VI

Willa	It is usually based upon program ratings or the audience measurement of a station or network. So, I will suggest the programs which is targeting as the same audiences as our product buyers.	通常是根據節目的收視率或電視台的觀眾人數測量。所以，我會建議鎖定和我們目標購買者一樣的視聽群眾收看的節目。
Nora	Which means some kind of sports programs and magazines, as well as men's magazines, such as Men's Uno or Golf?	就是說是些體育節目和雜誌，還有男性雜誌，例如男人誌或高爾夫雜誌？
Willa	That's correct.	是的。
Nora	And the length?	長度呢？
Willa	Either thirty or sixty seconds on television, and fifteen, thirty or sixty seconds on radio.	電視的話不是 30 秒就是 60 秒，廣播是 15、30 或 60 秒。
Nora	No online medias?	沒有網路媒體？
Willa	They haven't confirmed yet, maybe you should ask them again.	他們還沒有確認，也許妳應該再問他們一次。
Nora	I think I asked too many questions and now I'm **paying for it**.	我想我問太多問題了，而且正在受現世報。
Willa	How's that? That is you job!	怎麼會？這是妳的工作耶！

Part I
Part II
Part III
Part IV
Part V
Part VI

　　產品廣告的三種類型之下，還區分有許多拍攝的手法，或稱訴求（appeal），簡單說，就是透露什麼訊息給目標族群。

　　給在意年紀、外表的族群看的話，可能用青春訴求（youth appeal）容易打動他們的心；給理性購物的人看，用理性訴求（rational appeal）或統計數據（statistic）比較受到他們青睞；感性訴求（emotional appeal）適合要傳達愛、歡樂、愛家…等等情感面的產品；健康訴求（health appeal）則經常用在食品、藥品、健身相關的產品上，強調天然、自然風味、食用／使用後能帶來健康…等等。

　　幽默訴求（humor appeal）則利用真人或卡通、動畫（animation），營造會心一笑的情境，讓消費者在輕鬆之餘接受了產品傳達的訊息，像卡紙的機器令人抓狂，所以要使用某品牌的紙張、人生隨時有突發狀況，所以要買保險，都是這類型的訴求。不完美訴求（Less than perfect appeal）也經常在化妝品、保養品、醫美或塑身廣告上看見，利用廣告點出某些缺陷，暗示購買了產品或服務後將可以改善。

　　還有一些特殊族群，適合稀少性訴求（scarcity appeal），例如對限量、參加抽獎、有機會…等字眼特別敏感的人。孤傲訴求（snob appeal）經常被用來與威士忌酒、精品品牌或高級車款愛好者對話，因為這群人可能對被他人羨慕、是行業頂尖者的形象更能產生認同感。還有一種稱為冒險訴求（adventure appeal），可能是旅遊產品，或者某台被定位為城市冒險家的車款，他們溝通的對象是正在渴望藉由這項產品改變生活型態（lifestyle changes）、增添生活樂趣（add fun to life）的人。

Related Word 相關詞彙

1. seeing each other　交往中

     文法加油站：如果詢問對方是否正在交往中，就是 Are you seeing someone?

2. kid stuff　兒戲

     文法加油站：直譯也有小孩子的玩具的意思，在此為引申的意思。

3. mean　刻薄的

     文法加油站：同義詞還有 sharp and unkind（尖酸刻薄）、harsh（嚴苛的）。

4. adult male　成年男性

     文法加油站：成年女性寫作 adult female，兒童市場寫作 kid's market。

5. health appeal　健康訴求

6. humor appeal　幽默訴求

7. less than perfect appeal　不完美訴求

8. imply　暗示

     文法加油站：同義詞還有 hint、suggest、insinuate、intimate。

9. paying for it　現世報，還債

10. scarcity appeal　稀少性訴求

     文法加油站：scarcity 也可以譯成匱乏、稀缺的意思。

11. snob appeal　孤傲訴求

Part I
Part II
Part III
Part IV
Part V
Part VI

Exercises 練習題

Please make a line match then English and Chinese.
連連看。

scarcity appeal ●　　　　　　　　● 不完美訴求

less than perfect appeal ●　　　　● 健康訴求

snob appeal ●　　　　　　　　　● 稀少性訴求

humor appeal ●　　　　　　　　● 幽默訴求

health appeal ●　　　　　　　　● 孤傲訴求

Answers to the Unit:
（依照英文的順序）
● 稀少性訴求
● 不完美訴求
● 孤傲訴求
● 幽默訴求
● 健康訴求

Unit 20 Media Selection-1
選擇在哪裡廣告

Part I
Part II
Part III
Part IV
Part V
Part VI

Background Introduction 背景介紹：

Felicia and Gary are talking about their group assignment, which is where a new launched real estate project should advertise.

范麗西亞和蓋瑞正在討論他們的小組作業，那就是新推出的房地產專案應該在哪裡刊登廣告。

Conversation 1 對話 1

Felicia	I think what the Professor said in the class was totally **over my head**.	我覺得剛才教授在課堂上講的，超出我的理解範圍了。
Gary	It's not so difficult to understand, actually.	其實也不是那麼難理解。
Felicia	I am glad that we are at the same group, I think I can **count on you**.	我很高興和你同一組，我想我可以依靠你。
Gary	The only thing we need to do is coming out with a reasonable plan, since Professor is a **down-to-earth person**.	我們唯一需要做的事就是想出一個合理的提案，因為教授可是一個很實際的人。
Felicia	No problem, where should we start?	沒問題，我們應該從哪裡開始？

Gary	What is our project's topic?	我們的專案題目是什麼？
Felicia	"Where should a new launched real estate project advertise?"	「新推出的房地產專案應該在哪裡刊登廣告？」
Gary	OK. Is this real estate targets high-end or middle-end class buyers?	好的。這個房地產是鎖定高端還是中端層級的買家？
Felicia	Middle-class buyers and some personal investors.	中產階級買家和其他個人投資客。
Gary	Great, then the answer is clear. They should spend budget on **outdoor billboard, Sunday supplement** and real estate magazines.	太好了，那答案很清楚。他們應該把預算花在戶外看板、報紙的週日特刊和房地產雜誌上。
Felicia	Basically, those are all **print media** and outdoor media.	基本上，這些都是印刷媒體和戶外媒體。
Gary	Maybe some budgets on TV commercial.	也許花點預算在電視廣告上吧。
Felicia	Are these all national advertising?	都是全國性的廣告嗎？

Part I
Part II
Part III
Part IV
Part V
Part VI

Part I

Part II

Part III

Part IV

Part V

Part VI

Gary	Oh, no, honey. I think they are local advertising only.	哦,不,親愛的。我想他們只是地方性的廣告。
Felicia	OK. Should we try something new? I bet the other groups will come out with some more creative plans on advertising.	好吧。是不是應該試試新的方法?我打賭其他小組會想出更多有創意的廣告方法。
Gary	You really love to compete, don't you?	你真的很愛競爭耶,不是嗎?
Felicia	I just don't want to **overlook** anything.	我只是不想漏掉任何一件事。
Gary	You are right. How about **electric spectaculars**? They are outdoor signs or billboards that are composed electrical components or largely of lighting.	你是對的。如果是霓虹燈廣告怎麼樣?就是戶外的標誌或看板,由電子儀器或大型燈光組成的。
Felicia	Isn't that a bit of **worldliness**?	那不是有點俗氣嗎?
Gary	But this fits the target market. Or you have some other better ideas?	但是這想法符合目標市場。或者你有其他更好的想法?

Felicia	How about **car card**? It's an advertising message designed for display inside public transportations, such as trains, buses, or subway cars.	車廂廣告怎麼樣？就是一種廣告形式，設計來展現在公共交通工具上的，例如火車、巴士或地鐵車廂。
Gary	I know what car card is, but from my point of view, it doesn't suitable for our target people.	我知道車廂廣告是什麼，但是以我看來，它們並不適合我們的目標族群。
Felicia	What we can do now? We could argue this until tomorrow morning.	那現在怎麼辦？我們大可以爭論到明天早上。
Gary	No, we won't. The only thing we need to do is combining them together, and making a reasonable proposal to convince the Professor.	不用，我們不需要。只要把這些整合在一起，然後製作一份合理的提案說服教授就好啦。
Felicia	So, let me make a quick conclusion here. We agree to buy local TV ads, local print and outdoor media, and car card.	好，我快速結論一下。我們同意投放地方性的電視廣告、地方性的平面和戶外媒體，和車廂廣告。

Part I

Part II

Part III

Part IV

Part V

Part VI

Gary	Perfect. Do we need to decide how to arrange the budget in detail?	完美。我們需要決定怎麼詳細安排預算嗎？
Felicia	What do you mean?	什麼意思？
Gary	I mean the size of the advertisement. For example, full, half or one-quarter of where we want to put the ad on.	我是說廣告的尺寸。例如，是我們要刊登廣告的位置的全部、一半或四分之一版面。
Felicia	Oh, not now, please. I think I have a headache and need some rest immediately.	喔，不要現在，拜託。我想我頭痛，而且需要立刻休息一會兒。
Gary	Whatever you said. So, see you around.	隨你怎麼說吧。好吧，回頭見。
Felicia	Sure, you know where to find me if you need to discuss this assignment further.	當然，你知道去哪裡找我，如果你需要深入討論這份作業的話。

知識補給站

選擇在哪裡投放廣告會影響活動成敗，以下提供各種媒體管道的優缺點參考。

印刷媒體（print media）包含報紙、雜誌和新聞期刊。選擇報紙的優點是即時反應活動訴求（helps to reflect the changing market conditions）、閱讀群眾廣泛（reach a huge number of people）、有分享傳閱的機會（to be shared between friends）；但是缺點就是壽命短（short life）、印刷不夠精緻（not an extraordinary printing quality）、版面過於擁擠（too crowded **layout**）、容易分散讀者注意力（disperse the readers' attention easily）。

雜誌的優點是目標讀者群準確（easier to concentrate on a particular market segment）、廣告壽命長（longevity of the ad）、印刷品質比其他印刷媒體精美（physical quality also higher than in other print media）、可以分享傳閱；缺點就是價格昂貴（costly）、廣告時間太長（long lead time）不容易即時反應活動需求、版面位置容易受前後文影響，或被前後其他廣告分散注意力（lacking of flexibility on placement）。

戶外媒體，包含招牌、電子顯示屏（electronic signs）、公車亭（bus station）、大型看板…等等的優點是，可以提供區域性的告知（advertise locally）、成本相對比較低（lower cost）、重複出現頻率高（high frequency repeat）；但是缺點就是沒有目標族群針對性（non-specific target groups）、有時候會破壞景觀（landscape damage），甚至造成安全上的疑慮（cause safety issue）。

Related Word 相關詞彙

1. over my head　超出我的理解

   文法加油站：相同說法還可以用 I have no idea what that is、I have problem
   understanding what you mean、My brain doesn't work、
   What are you talking about?

2. count on you　依靠你，依賴你

   文法加油站：county 作動詞有依賴的意思，同義詞為 rely；另外還有計算
   （calculate）的意思。

3. down-to-earth person　實際的人

4. outdoor billboard　戶外廣告路牌

5. Sunday supplement　週日發行的特刊

6. print media　印刷媒體

7. overlook　忽視，忽略

   文法加油站：overlook 作動詞還有俯視（look down）、忘記（forget）、監視
   （keep watch over）、高聳（stand tall）的意思。作名詞使用還
   有漠視（disregard）的意思。

8. electric spectacular　霓虹燈廣告

9. worldliness　俗氣

   文法加油站：關於俗氣有幾種講法，名詞有 cheesy，形容詞可以用 corny
   （也可以當誇張的、肉麻的）、tacky（俗氣的、花俏的）、out of
   taste（沒有品味的）。

10. car card　車廂廣告

11. layout　版面，佈局，設計

Part I
Part II
Part III
Part IV
Part V
Part VI

Exercises 練習題

Please choose correct numbers to match the titles.

- Outdoor Media: _____
- Print Media: _____
- Electronic Media: _____

1. Car card
2. Electric spectacular
3. News paper
4. Sunday supplement
5. Electronic sign
6. Magazine

請選出正確的號碼與標題配對

- 戶外媒體：_____
- 印刷媒體：_____
- 電子媒體：_____

1. 車廂廣告
2. 霓虹燈廣告
3. 報紙
4. 週日特刊
5. 電子顯示屏
6. 雜誌

Answers to the Unit:
- 戶外媒體：1、2、5
- 印刷媒體：3、4、6
- 電子媒體：2、5

Part I

Part II

Part III

Part IV

Part V

Part VI

Unit 20 Media Selection-2
選擇在哪裡廣告

Background Introduction 背景介紹：

Norm is the Product Manager of W Online Game Company, Oliver and William are co-workers from Marketing Department. They are discussing where to announce their next season's advertisements.

諾姆是 W 線上遊戲公司的產品經理，奧利佛和威廉是行銷部的同事，他們正在討論應該在哪裡刊登下一季的廣告。

Conversation 2 對話 2

Norm	Hi, guys, **what's up**?	嗨，你們好，最近怎麼樣啊？
Oliver	Norm! How nice to see you here, could you do us a favor?	諾姆！在這遇見你真好，你可以幫我們一個忙嗎？
Norm	Sure, how can I help?	好啊，能幫什麼忙？
William	We were arguing where to spend the next season's media budget on. We think you may be able to help us to figure something out, since you are the Product Manager.	我們正在討論下一季的媒體預算應該花在哪裡。也許你可以幫我們釐清一些部份，因為你是產品經理。
Norm	My pleasure. So, go on, who wants to start talking here?	我很榮幸。好吧，開始吧，誰要開始提問呢？

Oliver	You know that we spend a **substantial** budget on TV commercial for the Taiwan Empire Online Game this season, however, we didn't find it **cost effective**.	你知道我們這一季花了一筆可觀的預算替台灣帝國線上遊戲打電視廣告，但是，我們認為並不符合成本效益。
William	Therefore, we are considering switching from offline to online media.	所以，我們正在考慮用線上媒體替代線下媒體。
Norm	Well, it sounds reasonable, isn't it? Our players can use internet to watch movies, listen music, and even watch TV programs. I don't understand why we spent money on offline media, seriously.	嗯，聽起來很合理，不是嗎？我們的玩家可以用網路看電影、聽音樂、甚至看電視節目。我不懂為什麼我們要花錢在線下媒體，真的。
Oliver	Because this season we launched this game, and we chose to create a strong **product awareness**, that's why.	因為這一季我們才發表這個遊戲，而我們選擇要建立一個夠強的產品知名度，這就是為什麼。
Norm	Sure, I respect your profession. So, do you still have the same amount to be used for the next season?	當然，我尊重你們的專業。那麼，你們仍然有同樣的預算用在下一個季度？

Part I

Part II

Part III

Part IV

Part V

Part VI

William	Not really, the first season for the new product always gets the most amounts. That is also why we are thinking to advertise on online media, they are less expensive than TV commercials.	不盡然，新產品的第一季總是會有最大的預算。這也是為什麼我們在思考要在網路上做廣告，它們比電視廣告便宜些。
Norm	Have you guys thought about the **radio advertising**?	你們考慮過電台廣告嗎？
Oliver	Why you think it will help to gain more users for the game?	你為什麼認為它可以替遊戲帶來更多使用者呢？
Norm	Because of my nephew, he's always playing online games and listening music at the same time.	因為我的姪子，他總是一邊玩線上遊戲一邊聽音樂。
William	Maybe it's not from a radio station, it's **a sort of** online music platform which allows listeners to choose or download what they love to listen.	可能不是電台，它是一種線上音樂平台，可以讓聽眾選擇或下載他們喜愛的音樂。
Norm	Can we advertise on them?	我們可以在上面打廣告嗎？
Oliver	Off course, we will find out how to work with them.	當然可以，我們會找出該怎麼合作的方法。
Norm	Oh, the other thing is, you probably heard of **viral marketing**?	喔，還有一件事情，你們也許聽過病毒式行銷？

William	Yes, why?	聽過呀，怎麼了？
Norm	I saw an article from a business magazine, and it says that viral marketing is cheaper and more effective way if you are considering online advertising.	我從一本商業雜誌上看到一篇文章，裡面提到病毒式行銷是比較便宜和有效果的方式，如果想要利用網路廣告的話。
Oliver	It is true, because you only pay for your advertising based on the number of people it reaches.	是真的，因為你只需要針對你觸及到的人群付廣告費用。
William	Besides we can place banner ads of various sizes, **pop-up**, text and streaming audio and video ads if we advertise on internet.	除此以外，我們可以置放不同尺寸的橫幅廣告，或是彈出式廣告、文字廣告和音樂以及影片廣告，如果我們在網路上投放廣告的話。
Norm	I know that keyword advertising refers to any advertising that is linked to specific words or phrases. Common forms of keyword advertising are known by many other terms including pay per click.	我知道關鍵字廣告就是與特定字或句子產生關連的任何廣告。形式有很多，按照每次點擊付費的廣告形式是最常見的。
Oliver	You are right, and I think we can add this ad channel as well. Did we talk about Facebook?	對的，我想我們也可以增加這種廣告管道。我們剛才討論過臉書了？

Part I
Part II
Part III
Part IV
Part V
Part VI

William	Not yet, but nice one! There are billions of people are using it right now, it does provide a great opportunity for ad buyers to not just simply put ads, but also make connections with fans through these ads.	還沒有，但是好提議！有成千上百萬人正在使用臉書，它也的確提供一個絕佳的機會給廣告主，不只是簡單的放置廣告，透過廣告還可以和粉絲們產生連結。
Norm	And they are all affordable for ad buyers?	而且對廣告主來說都是經濟實惠的？
Oliver	Most of them, yes. But not banners or full sized advertisements, basically they charge based on how large or what size your ad is. Normally, it cost you more if the size is larger.	大部份，是的。除了橫幅或全版的廣告，基本上收費是按照你的廣告有多大或是什麼尺寸。通常，越大的越貴。
Norm	I guess the answer is obvious clear, then. Sorry, but I got to go. Hope this conversation helps, and good luck with you guys.	我猜答案已經很明顯了。抱歉，我得要離開了。希望這個對話有點用處，還有，祝你們好運。
Oliver	OK, thank you for your time, we really appreciate that.	好的，謝謝你的時間，我們真的很感謝。
William	Bye for now, Norm.	再見，諾姆。

Part I
Part II
Part III
Part IV
Part V
Part VI

知識補給站

　　透過電視播放廣告的優點是，觸及群眾相當廣泛（communicate with a very large audience）、同時兼具聲音和影像畫面的多感官吸引力（multi-sensory appeal），吸引觀眾觀看廣告概念和訴求；相對的，缺點就是成本高（costly）、播放時間短，無法完整表達產品概念（do not express much about the product）、拍攝時牽涉較複雜的過程（involves complicated procedure）。

　　透過廣播電台傳達廣告也有其優缺點，最明顯的缺點是，收聽廣播的群眾大多時候是一邊做事情一邊聽廣播，所以很容易分心（distraction），不會特別專注在收聽廣告訊息上；優點是相較印刷和電視廣告便宜（cheaper than print and TV advertising）、相對其他媒體管道必須眼睛盯著看，廣播具有可移動性（portability），不管在戶外修剪花草或在室內煮飯，都可以收聽。

　　另外，新興的網路媒介也給了企業主更多選擇刊登廣告的管道。網路行上中的病毒式行銷利用的是戶口碑傳播的原理，像病毒一樣迅速蔓延，因此病毒式行銷被視為一種高效的信息傳播方式；而且，有些是用戶之間自發進行的，網友們經常是此種口碑推薦為較具信賴度的（trustworthy）。整體來說，網路廣告刊登的速度更快（online advertising is much faster than offline advertising）、覆蓋範圍更廣（wider coverage）、易於跟蹤和測量成效（easy to track and measure conversion）等等。舉例而言，台灣有一個經營外銷的廠商，如果鎖定在臉書上針對海外使用者廣告，只要按照步驟上傳圖文，選擇哪一群人可以觀看到廣告，付費完成後，廣告馬上就會出現，前後也許不到 30 分鐘的過程。

　　網路創造便利，卻也製造不可磨滅性（indelible）。電視、廣播廣告可能播過就結束了，印刷媒體如果過期了，也不容易找到，但是網路上的留言卻很難刪除；所以在處理上更需要小心謹慎（cautious）。

Related Word 相關詞彙

1. What's up?　最近好嗎？有什麼事？
   文法加油站：這是一句相當口語的打招呼用語。其他相似用法還有 How are you doing、How are you、How's going。

2. substantial　可觀的，優渥的

3. cost effective　成本效益

4. product awareness　產品知名度

5. radio advertising　廣播廣告

6. a sort of　一種
   文法加油站：同義詞還有 a kind of, a type of。

7. viral marketing　病毒式行銷。
   文法加油站：virus 是病毒的名詞，viral 則是形容詞。

8. pop-up　彈出式
   文法加油站：此指瀏覽網頁時，有時候會突然跳出的廣告框；另外立體卡片或立體書的英文就簡稱叫 pop-up，取其一翻開就躍入眼簾的意思。

9. multi-sensory　多重感官
   文法加油站：multi 有多重、多種的意思，後可接名詞或形容詞；例如，multi-ethnic（多民族的）、multi-cultural（多文化的）、multi-function（多功能）。

10. distraction　分心
    文法加油站：此為名詞，另外也有娛樂、消遣、精神渙散的意思。

11. trustworthy　可信賴的

Exercises 練習題

Please choose correct numbers to match the titles.

● TV advertising: _____

● Radio: _____

● Online advertising: _____

1. Portability

2. Easy to track and measure conversion

3. Multi-sensory appeal

4. Indelible

5. Involves complicated procedure

6. Easily distracted

7. Do not express much about the product

請選出正確的號碼與標題配對

● 電視廣告：_____

● 廣播廣告：_____

● 網路廣告：_____

1. 具有可移動性

2. 容易追蹤和測量成效

3. 多重感官吸引力

4. 不可磨滅性

5. 牽涉較複雜的過程

6. 容易被分心

7. 無法完整表達產品概念

Answers to the Unit:

● 電視廣告：3、5、7

● 廣播廣告：1、6

● 網路廣告：2、4

Part I

Part II

Part III

Part IV

Part V

Part VI

Unit 21　Performance Measurement-1
播完廣告，然後呢

Background Introduction 背景介紹：

Kelly and Matthew are classmates of Master in Advertising, and they are talking about evaluating the effectiveness of advertising in which method.
凱莉和馬修是兩位行廣告學研究所的同學，他們正在談論用哪一種方法評估廣告的成效。

Conversation 1　對話 1

Kelly	Hi, Matthew, how's your thesis going?	嗨，馬修，你的論文進行得怎麼樣了？
Matthew	Not so well, you?	不是很順利，你呢？
Kelly	I think I am doing well. If you need my help, I will be glad to help.	我想我還可以。如果你需要幫忙的話，我會很樂意的。
Matthew	Thanks, but I **prefer** doing alone.	謝謝，但是我比較想自己進行。
Kelly	So, have you proceeded to how to measure or evaluate the effectiveness of advertising?	你進行到如何測量或衡量廣告效益了嗎？

Matthew	I think I did some research online yesterday, but haven't decided which method I am going to adapt.	我想我昨天上網查了一下，但是還沒有決定我要採用哪一種方式。
Kelly	Are you considering a **qualitative** or **quantitative** method?	你想用定性的還是定量的方法？
Matthew	I don't know yet. How about you?	我還不知道，你呢？
Kelly	I think I will choose to combine **laboratory testing** and **portfolio testing**.	我想我會選擇結合實驗室測試和組合測試的方式。
Matthew	Are they quantitative research method?	它們是定量的研究方法嗎？
Kelly	No, they are both qualitative methods.	不是，它們兩個都是定性的方法。
Matthew	Oh, sorry, I never understand.	喔，抱歉，我從來沒搞懂過。

Part I

Part II

Part III

Part IV

Part V

Part VI

Kelly	It's easy. Quantitative research involves analysis of numerical data, while the other is involves analysis of data such as pictures or words.	很簡單。定量的研究涵蓋數字資料的分析，但是另一個就牽涉圖片或文字的分析。
Matthew	I see, I will try to remember that. I think I will choose quantitative analysis, then. Only analysis numbers or data doesn't seem very difficult.	懂了，我會試著記得的。我想我會選擇定量的分析吧。光是分析數字和資料似乎不是很困難。
Kelly	Not necessary. First of all, you need to design a **questionnaire**.	也不盡然。首先，你需要設計一份問卷。
Matthew	OK, I can do that.	好呀，我可以做到。
Kelly	Then you need to do **sampling**, gather the data, make codes, analyze with SPSS software, and…	然後你需要選樣本、蒐集資料、編碼、用 SPSS 軟體分析，還有…
Matthew	Hold on, hold on, I have to do all of them if I go to a quantitative method?	等等，等等，如果我選擇定量的方法就需要作全部這些？

Kelly	Sure. But I tell you if you chose a qualitative method, it doesn't mean too much easier work.	那當然。但是我告訴你啊，如果你選擇定性的方法，也不代表是份輕鬆的工作。
Matthew	How's that?	怎麼説呢？
Kelly	You will need to organize **focus groups** or **key informant interviews**, in order to get information from the participants and then analyze how they feel about the advertisements you showed to them.	你會需要組織焦點團體或關鍵人物訪談，以便從參與者身上蒐集資訊，然後分析他們對你拿給他們看的廣告有什麼意見。
Matthew	Jesus! I guess I will never finish my thesis, what should I do?	老天爺！我猜我永遠也完成不了我的論文了，我該怎麼辦？
Kelly	Calm down first. Tell me what you are good at, dealing with numbers or talk to people?	先冷靜點。告訴我你擅長什麼，是處理數字還是和人説話？
Matthew	I guess I like to talk with different people, I don't like to deal with numbers at all, they makes me headache.	我猜我喜歡和不同的人説話，我一點也不喜歡處理數字，它們讓我頭痛。

Part I

Part II

Part III

Part IV

Part V

Part VI

Kelly	Then you should choose quantitative research method, just like I do. Actually, we can do it together. There are some researches also published by **multiple** authors.	那你應該選擇定量的研究方法，就像我一樣。事實上，我們可以一起做。有些研究也是由多位作者一起發表的。
Matthew	Do you mean that I can copy your thesis?	是不是表示我可以抄你的論文啊？
Kelly	**Not in your life time**.	你這輩子都別想。

Part I

Part II

Part III

Part IV

Part V

Part VI

　　廣告播出前，有廠商會尋求測試以協助決定播出哪一則廣告。下面是常用的幾種方法：

　　實驗室測試，在實驗室裡透過儀器或觀察，測試受試者對廣告的反應是否達到預期；例如，播放巧克力廣告時，受試者視覺焦點是否集中在巧克力上，還是其他地方。此種方式只限於測試受試者對廣告的注意程度（degree of attention），無法測試喜好（like）、理解（understanding）或記憶程度（degree of memory）。

　　組合測試，讓目標消費者在無時間限制之下，閱讀完廣告，然後測試受試者是否記得廣告的內容。組合測試可以測出廣告是否容易記憶和理解。直接評分（direct rating），屬於定量性研究的一種，讓目標消費者直接對廣告給予不同程度的評分；例如，「廣告是否具有吸引力？」、「廣告內容是否清晰？」。

　　廣告播出後，如果要測試目標消費者對廣告的觀感，也有下列方法可以使用：

　　辨識測試（recognition test），主要在測試目標消費族群是否能辨認廣告中的品牌、產品、廣告內容…等等。回想測試（recall test），又區分為有提示的回想（aided recall test），和沒有提示（unaided recall test）的回想；前者如「最近是否有看過白熊洗碗精的廣告？」，後者則是「最近有沒有看過哪一個廠牌的洗碗精廣告？」

　　廣告效果預測和評估，有助於廠商減少錯誤（reduce error）和金錢損失（loss of money），某種程度上也幫助廣告更有效的推廣給對的人群，在行銷上也是重要的一環。

Related Word 相關詞彙

1. prefer 比較（更）喜歡，情願

   文法加油站：*prefer 用法很廣泛，大致上可以分為下列幾種，意思都是更喜歡，或傾向某事物：*

   (1) prefer ＋名詞或動名詞

   Do you love playing golf? 你喜歡打高爾夫球嗎？

   Yes, but I prefer tennis. 喜歡，但是更喜歡網球。

   (2) prefer ＋不定詞

   I prefer to be alone on weekends. 我周末喜歡一個人待在家

   (3) prefer A to B

   He prefers cats to dogs. 他喜歡貓勝於狗

   (4) prefer someone to do something

   Her father prefers she comes home before 7pm every day. 她爸爸希望她每天晚上七點前回到家

   (5) prefer ＋不定式＋ rather than ＋不定式

   I prefer to eat out rather than to cook at home on Sunday nights.
   週日晚上我比較喜歡去外面吃，而不是在家煮。

2. qualitative 定性的

   文法加油站：*quality 是質量的意思，所以此單詞也翻作質性的；簡單說就是利用訪問調查，分析受訪者的回答。*

3. quantitative 定量的

   文法加油站：*quantity 是數量的意思，此單詞也翻作量化的；簡單說就是用大量的問卷得到數據，交叉分析後得出研究結論。*

4. laboratory testing 實驗室測試

5. portfolio testing 組合測試

6. questionnaire 問卷，調查表

7. sampling 抽樣，取樣

8. focus group 焦點團體

9. key informant interview 關鍵人物訪談

10. multiple 眾多的

11. Not in your life time. 你這輩子都別想

Exercises 練習題

Please make a line match then English and Chinese.

Quantitative ●

● Focus group
● Direct rating
● Questionnaire
● Sampling

Qualitative ●

● Key informant interview
● Make codes

連連看。

定量的 ●

● 焦點團體
● 直接評分
● 問卷
● 抽樣

定性的 ●

● 關鍵人物訪談
● 編碼

Answers to the Unit:
定量的：直接評分、問卷、抽樣、編碼
定性的：焦點團體、關鍵人物訪談

Part I

Part II

Part III

Part IV

Part V

Part VI

Unit 21 Performance Measurement-2
播完廣告，然後呢

Background Introduction 背景介紹：

Emily is the Media Planner from Q Advertising Company, Ruth and Georgina are the Account Managers at the same company as Emily. Today, they are talking about how to measure the effectiveness of advertising for Ruth's client.

艾蜜莉是 Q 廣告公司的媒體策畫，露絲和喬治娜則是 Q 公司的客戶經理。這一天，她們三人正在為露絲的客戶擬定廣告的成效評估方式。

Conversation 2 對話 2

Ruth	Hi, Georgina. Do you have a minute?	嗨，喬治娜。妳有空嗎？
Georgina	Hang on a second, let me finish this. Now. Sure, what I can do for you?	等等，讓我結束這個。好了。當然有空，我可以幫妳什麼？
Ruth	It's just I don't know how to provide a method of performance measurement for my client, so I am thinking maybe you can give me some suggestions.	就是我不太清楚該如何為客戶提供成效評量的方法，所以我想妳可能可以給我些建議。

Georgina	I am happy to, but since Emily is the Media Planner for your project, how about we go to her together?	我很高興幫忙，但是既然艾蜜莉是妳專案的媒體策畫，不如我們一起去找她吧。
Ruth	Totally agree.	完全同意。
	(At the cubicle where Emily seats)	（在艾蜜莉座位的辦公室隔間）
Emily	Hi, both of you. How's everything going?	嗨，兩位。妳們都還好吧？
Ruth	Hi, Emily, everything is fine. I just want to ask you about how to evaluate the effectiveness of advertising?	嗨，艾蜜莉，我們都好。我想要請問妳關於如何評估廣告成效的問題。
Georgina	You see, her client's case is also under your responsibility of planning where to place their advertisements, that's why we think it will be helpful if she comes to you directly.	妳看喔，她的客戶也是妳負責規劃在哪裡投放廣告的，這就是為什麼我們想如果她直接來找妳比較有幫助的原因。

Part I

Part II

Part III

Part IV

Part V

Part VI

Emily	Off course. We usually use **gross rating point** to measure the size of an audience reached by a specific media or schedule, for example, TV or radio.	沒問題。我們通常會用毛評點來衡量特定媒體，例如電視或廣播，接觸到的觀眾數量。
Ruth	Why do you measure the gross rating point?	為什麼要使用毛評點來測量呢？
Emily	The purpose is to measure impressions in relation to the audiences for an advertising campaign.	目的是為了衡量觀眾對一個廣告的印象。
Georgina	I also heard of **reach** and **frequency**, what are they?	我也聽過接觸率和頻率，它們是什麼意思？
Emily	Reach times frequency is gross rating point.	接觸率乘以頻率就是毛評點了。
Ruth	I see. Anything else I should know?	我懂了。還有其他的我需要知道的嗎。
Emily	There are plenty, honey. But I just talk about few, otherwise you will get **confused** soon.	還有很多呢，親愛的。但是我就談一些，否則妳很快就會感到困惑的。

Ruth	Thank you, Emily.	謝謝妳喔，艾蜜莉。
Emily	Except the effectiveness, you will also need to pay attention on the costs of your advertising. It is also a method to evaluate whether your budget is spent wisely or not.	除了成效，妳也需要注意廣告的成本。這也是一種評估妳的預算是不是花得到位的一種方法。
Georgina	It sounds very reasonable, so what are those methods?	聽起來很有道理，是哪些方法呢？
Emily	For example, **cost per impression**, also known as CPI, it refers to the cost of internet marketing where advertisers pay for every time an ad is displayed.	舉例來說，每千人印象成本，也稱作 CPI，它指的是廣告客戶支付每次網路廣告顯示的成本。
Georgina	What else?	還有呢？
Emily	The **cost per thousand**, we call it CPM **in short**, is a commonly used measurement in advertising. CPM means the cost of per 1000 estimated views of the advertisement.	每千人成本，我們稱它作 CPM，經常被使用在廣告評估上。CPM 表示每千人觀看廣告的成本。

Part I

Part II

Part III

Part IV

Part V

Part VI

Ruth	Yes, I have heart of it.	是的，我聽過這個名詞。
Emily	It is useful in comparing the **relative** efficiency of different advertising media and in measuring the costs of overall campaigns.	對比較不同廣告媒體的相關效益和評估整體活動的成本來說，它很有用處。
Ruth	I guess I had a rough picture about what I am looking for.	我想對我正在找的事情，已經有了粗略的概念。
Emily	I am glad to help. Georgina, may I confirm one of your clients' proposal?	我很高興有幫到妳。喬治娜，我可以和妳確認一下妳其中一位客戶的提案？
Georgina	No problem, which one you are talking about?	沒問題，妳說哪一位客戶？
Ruth	I just leave you two to discuss, thanks again, Emily.	我就讓妳們兩位繼續討論吧，謝啦，艾蜜莉。
Emily	No problem at all.	一點也不用謝。

知識補給站

評估廣告是否有效，除了訪問目標消費者的質化（qualitative）方法以外，還有其他量化（quantitative）指標：

接觸率，只在一定期間內，接觸到廣告的人數百分比（percentage）；例如 7 月 1 日到 2 日上午 10 點 ~12 點某廣告可以接觸到 45% 的南部家庭主婦，45% 在此就代表接觸率。

頻率，指一定期間內，接觸到廣告的平均次數。

總收視率，又稱毛評點，就是以上兩者相乘的結果。當毛評點值越大時，代表接觸到的人越多或頻率越高，廣告就越有滲透力（**penetration**）。但是相對也表示，花費的成本很高。

媒體刊登的成本也是評估效益的標準，如果花得錢越多可是 GPR 很低，就表示廣告費用花錯地方了。媒體成本常以每千人成本（CPM）表示，意思是某廣告投放期間，聽到或看到的每千人平均分擔到多少廣告成本。

CPI 則是每千人印象成本，表示顯示一千次（代表一千人看到）的費用，現在已經成為網路廣告收費慣例。網路廣告還有 CPC（**cost per click**），代表每次點擊的成本，Google 廣告就是使用這種收費方法，廣告主只需要支付被目標群眾點擊的廣告費用即可，甚至可以自行設計一天的花費上限。

Part I

Part II

Part III

Part IV

Part V

Part VI

Related Word 相關詞彙

1. cubicle　辦公室隔間

2. gross rating point　毛評點，總收視率

3. reach　接觸率

4. frequency　頻率

5. confused　困惑的

　　文法加油站：此為形容詞，除了困惑的意思以外，還有迷糊的、暈的、亂糟糟
　　　　　　　的意思。名詞為 confusion。

6. cost per impression　每千人印象成本

7. cost per thousand　每千人成本

　　文法加油站：此句英文不簡稱 CPT 而簡稱 CPM 是因為原文為 cost of mille，
　　　　　　　mille 在古英文裡是千（thousand）的意思，所以簡稱 CPM。

8. in short　簡稱

9. relative　相關的

10. penetration　滲透力

11. cost per click　每次點擊成本

Exercises 練習題

Please write down the full English words for the abbreviation.

請將縮寫英文寫下英文全稱。

CPI　＝_____

CPC　＝_____

CPM　＝_____

GPR　＝_____

Answers to the Unit:

cost per impression

cost per click

cost per thousand/mille

gross rating point

Part I

Part II

Part III

Part IV

Part V

Part VI

283

Unit 22　Key Points of Hosting a Meeting-1
主持會議要點

Situation 1　情境 1：

Jasper is making a presentation of his advertising proposal to his colleagues from the same department. After that, he needs to integrate the suggestions which are given from his colleagues.

賈斯伯正在向部門同事介紹他的廣告企劃提案。會後，他必須整合同事們給予他的建議。

Key points for your conversation 對話急救包

介紹簡報流程

I would like to start by making few statements about my plan, and which are that it can gain more exposures, as well as saving more costs. Now, let us spend some time on discussing my plan.

我想以關於這個企畫的幾句話做開場白，那就是它可以達到比以往更好的曝光效果，以及費用更省。現在，讓我們花一點時間來討論我的提案

I would like to divide my presentation into four parts. First, situation analysis. Second, advertising appeals. Third, media selection. Last but not least, performance measurement.

我今天的簡報會分成四部份。第一，情況分析。第二，廣告表現的內容。第三，媒體的選擇。最後但並非不重要的是，效益衡量。

強調重點

Only in this **way** can we make lasting contributions to the benefit-maximizing for our client.

只有以這種方式，才能不斷地為客戶貢獻最大利益。

小貼士：亦可置換為 method。

The important thing to notice here is that we must **take** online media **into consideration**.
在這裡要注意的是，我們一定要把網路媒體納入考慮。
小貼士：亦可置換為 take into account。

I must emphasize, I will provide an overview picture of advertising appeals because of its importance.
我必須強調，因為廣告表現手法的重要性，所以我將提供全面的介紹。

結束簡報

In concluding my presentation, I would like to comment on performance measurement.
我想評論（廣告）效益衡量來結束我的簡報。
小貼士：亦可置換為 To Conclude⋯、In conclusion,⋯。

In summary, I have talked about media selection, which will provide channels for effective communication to target audiences.
總結來說，我已經提過媒體的選擇，將針對目標族群提供有效溝通的管道。

Thank you very much for your patience. Is there any specific question about my presentation?
謝謝各位的耐心。針對我的簡報，有沒有特別的疑問？

激起討論

I wonder if **there is anyone** would like to comment on situation analysis.
我在想有沒有在座任何一位願意對此發表評論？
小貼士：亦可置換為 any of you。

May I ask each of you to make a suggestion on this topic?
可否請你們每一位都針對這個議題提供建議？

Let's focus on which goals we want to achieve through this advertisement.
讓我們先專注於討論我們想透過這支廣告達成哪些目標。
小貼士：亦可置換為 Why don't we⋯+ 問號。表示提議的意思。

Unit 22 Key Points of Hosting a Meeting-2 主持會議要點

Situation 2 情境 2：

Deborah is giving a presentation of the advertising proposal which prepared by her team, and negotiating with the client for the details.
黛博拉正在向客戶簡報她團隊的廣告提案，並與客戶談判相關的細節。

Key points for your conversation 對話急救包

敘述簡報主旨與內容

There are a number of reasons why we need to take action. One reason is fighting back against competitors. The second reason is sales decline.
有幾點原因說明為何我們需要採取行動。第一個理由是反擊競爭對手。第二個理由是銷售量下滑。

I will go through the next four points **quickly**.
我會盡快地說明接下來的四個要點。
小貼士：亦可置換為 briefly（簡短地）。

Time permits only reference to the two points in my presentation this afternoon.
時間的關係，今天下午我的簡報只能提到兩個要點。

將焦點拉回現場或轉移

We seem to be getting off the subject. Can I bring the discussion back in the direction of media selection?
看起來我們是偏離主題了。可以容我將討論帶回媒體選擇上嗎？

I am sorry, that's the answer to another question. The original question was what else we need to add on situation analysis.
我很抱歉，這些答案可能是回應另一個問題的。原先的問題是我們還需要替現況分析增加什麼嗎？
小貼士：用在現場有人討論起其他問題的時候。

Perhaps we could return to that point in a moment.
也許我們稍後可以回到這個議題上。

談判話術

I suggest we focus on budget now.
我建議我們現在應該專注在預算上。

Maybe another option would be reducing some budget on radio.
也許另一項作法（另一個選項）是刪減廣播廣告的一些預算。

I think it might be better to adjust the method of measuring cost effective.
我認為調整一下成本效益衡量的方法，也許會更好一些。

It sounds like a reasonable idea, but I think our team needs time to think through.
聽起來好像是合理的提議，但是我想我們團隊需要時間全面考慮。

給予保證或承諾

Let me assure you that the advertising will be successful, if we could solve all these problems.
我向您們保證這支廣告會很成功，如果我們可以解決這裡所有問題的話。

I am sure that we will see a trend of how technology affects advertising.
我確定我們將會看到科技是如何影響廣告的新趨勢。

You can be sure your suggestions will receive our earnest attention.
我保證您的建議將會受到我們深切的關注。

Our team will try better to make this happen **one way or another**.
無論如何，我們的團隊都會盡力讓事情達成。
小貼士：亦可置換為 no matter what。

Part V

Customer Relationship Management（CRM）
顧客關係管理

Unit 23 Customer Segmentation
顧客也分好幾種？

Background Introduction 背景介紹：

Fred and Cliff are colleagues of Customer Relationship Department of N Company. They are discussing on how to classify customers and the reason of why they need to do that.

弗雷德和克里夫是 N 公司的顧客關係管理部門同事。他們正在討論如何對顧客進行分類，以及分類的理由。

Conversation 對話

Fred	Hi, Cliff. May I speak with you for few minutes?	嗨，克里夫。我可以耽誤你幾分鐘時間嗎？
Cliff	What's up, Fred. **You are looking really good**!	你好啊，佛雷德。你看起來氣色真好！
Fred	You think so? I just **keep early hours**.	是嗎？我只是早睡早起罷了。
Cliff	I should learn from you. So, what do you want to talk about?	我也應該學學你。所以，你想要聊些什麼呢？
Fred	I am wondering why we **classify** our customers. You know, aren't they all our buyers?	我在想，為什麼我們要將顧客分類。你知道的，他們不都是我們的購買者嗎？

Cliff	Yes, they all bought our products or services before. However, the concept of customer segmentation isn't that simple.	是的，他們都曾經買過我們的產品或服務。但是，顧客區隔並不是那麼簡單的概念。
Fred	Maybe you can tell me more about it.	也許你能告訴我多一些。
Cliff	Sure. For example, we separate our customers into different kinds or classes.	沒問題。舉例來說，我們將顧客區分為幾個等級。
Fred	I know that, such as new customers, which means who just bought our products in these two months. We also create the Loyal Club for our key customers or **frequent buyers**.	這個我曉得，例如，新客戶就是在兩個月內剛購買我們產品的人。我們也為重要顧客或經常性買家建立了「忠誠俱樂部」。
Cliff	Correct! You are a quick learner.	答對了！你學得挺快的。
Fred	But I don't understand why we need to classify them?	但是我不明白為什麼我們要將他們分類？

Part I
Part II
Part III
Part IV
Part V
Part VI

Cliff	Each customer contributes differently to the company, that's why we need to analyze and classify them. For instance, a loyal customer may purchase a lot a year or even introduce other customers to us. Don't you think he or she deserves a special care from the company? Besides, each person is different, knowing who he is can **personalize** promotions and advertisements.	每一個顧客對公司有不同貢獻，這就是為什麼我們需要分類。舉例來說，忠誠的顧客一年中會買很多，或甚至介紹其他顧客給我們。你不覺得他或她值得公司特別對待嗎？此外，每個人是不一樣的，瞭解顧客是誰有助於客製化促銷和廣告方式。
Fred	I see. Then yes, the loyal customers are important to us.	我懂了。那麼肯定的，忠誠的顧客對我們是很重要。
Cliff	Not only the loyal clients, but also **potential customers**, or even the customers who leave us.	也不只是忠誠的顧客啦，還有潛在顧客，或甚至離開我們的顧客。
Fred	If the customers leave us, then they are no longer contributing to our sales. Why we should care about them?	如果顧客都離開我們了，那就不再對我們的銷售有貢獻了。為什麼我們應該關注他們？

Cliff	My dear friend, you are **inexperienced**. There are more than fifty percent customers leave because of **indifference** to them. If we keep pay less attention to find out why these people leave, we will lose more of them.	親愛的朋友啊，你還真涉世未深。有超過 50% 的顧客是因為企業對他們默不關心而離開。如果我們不留意他們為什麼離開的話，那我們會失去更多顧客。
Fred	Now I understood. So, if we already lost them, how can we win them back again?	原來如此。所以，如果我們已經失去他們了，應該怎麼把他們贏回來？
Cliff	That's a good question! In fact, there are three main methods which help us to gain more customers. They are trying to gain new customers, keeping the current ones and letting the **former** customers to introduce new buyers for us.	好問題！事實上，主要有三種方式幫助我們獲得更多的顧客。分別是爭取新顧客、留住原有的顧客，以及讓舊顧客介紹新顧客。
Fred	I see. I think keeping the current customers is easier than the other two ways.	了解。我想留住原有的顧客比另外兩個還簡單。

Part I
Part II
Part III
Part IV
Part V
Part VI

Cliff	You are absolutely correct. You see, there is six to seven times more expensive to acquire a new customer than keeping an exist one.	非常正確。你知道嗎，爭取一個新顧客的花費是留住原顧客的 6 至 7 倍呢。
Fred	I didn't know that, it is quite expensive if we lose one of them!	我以前都不知道，看來失去一個顧客還挺昂貴的！
Cliff	It is. Now you see how important you are!	是的。現在你知道你有多重要了！
Fred	So do you. Thank you, Cliff.	你也是啊。謝啦，克里夫。
Cliff	Anytime.	不客氣。

知識補給站

　　顧客關係管理（Customer Relationship Management，簡稱 CRM）的定義是指透過日常管理以及資訊科技，將行銷、客戶服務等功能加以整合，提供顧客量身的服務內容。目的在於增加顧客滿意度與忠誠度（increase customer satisfaction and improve the loyalty），以提昇顧客服務品質（improve service quality），達成企業經營效益的提升

　　簡單來説，我們到百貨公司、餐廳、美容店或 3C 通路，購買了一項商品或服務之後，店家在取得我們認同後，可以透過留下的顧客資料，透過手機簡訊、E-Mail 郵箱、地址信箱（mail address）等管道寄送促銷活動訊息（promotion information）、新品訊息、折價券（coupons）、企業刊物（business magazines）等資料。或者提供消費累積（cumulative consumption），達到不同會員等級後，享受不同折扣或特殊待遇。其實，消費者經常暴露在 CRM 活動的訊息中，例如，賓士車主可以享受每年一次的音樂會，或微風百貨公司一年一度的封館 VIP 之夜…等等都是。

　　顧客關係管理的最終目的是獲取更多銷售量，如果顧客數量多了，或者每人貢獻額度增加了，都可以協助達成這個目標；怎麼樣讓顧客人數增加呢？有下列三種方式：

　　第一，獲取新的顧客（gaining new customers），企業以各種方式創造顧客，必須先創造出顧客，才有銷售與收入，有了顧客才能談 CRM。

　　第二，保有現在的顧客（keeping the current customers），但是增加購買率或購買金額；此部份是 CRM 核心部份，需要企業創造更深一層互動關係。

　　第三，由現有顧客創造出新顧客（creating new customers through the former ones），此層級是 CRM 概念的發揮，如果一個顧客介紹另一個新顧客，就創造了兩倍的收入，介紹十個就是十倍效益，這就是為什麼忠誠顧客能帶來巨幅效益的原因了。

Related Word 相關詞彙

1. You are looking really good　你看起來氣色真好

    文法加油站：本句也可以縮寫成 You're looking good，同義詞還有 You are looking great、You look great。

2. keep early hours　早睡早起

3. classify　分類，分層級

4. frequent buyer　經常性買家，主要購買者

    文法加油站：frequent 是經常的、頻繁的、密切的意思，加上 buyer（買家）組合而成，也可接 customer（顧客），亦即經常光顧的客人。

5. personalize　個性化

    文法加油站：此作動詞。形容詞為 personalized（個性化的）。

6. potential customer　潛在的顧客

    文法加油站：potential 也可作名詞，表示潛力。

    You got potential.　你是具有潛力的。

7. inexperienced　涉世未深的，沒什麼經驗的

8. indifference　忽視，默不關心

9. former　原先的

    文法加油站：這個詞還有之前的、過去的、舊有的，和過世的意思。

10. cumulative　累積的

Exercises 練習題

Please complete the word or sentence by filling in the blanks.

A：I went to A Supermarket today, and they gave me this!

B：It's a _____ key ring. Why they gave you that?

A：Because I am their _____ .

B：Or you spent a lot of _____ there.

A：Maybe both.

B：By the way, I will start to _____ from today, could you please turn off the light from 9pm for me?

A：Ok, I will do my best.

請填空完成下面句子或單字

A：我今天去 A 超市，結果他們送我這個禮物耶！

B：是個性化的鑰匙圈。為什麼你有呢？

A：因為我是他們的經常性顧客啊。

B：或者你累積的消費額度很高。

A：兩者都有吧

B：對了，我從今天開始要早睡早起，可以請你晚上九點後不要開燈嗎？

A：好，我盡量。

Answers to the Unit:

personalized

frequent buyer

cumulative consumption

keep early hours

Unit 24 Customer Relationship Planning
要想乘涼，先種樹

Background Introduction 背景介紹：

Juliana and Scott are co-workers at the Marketing Department, and they are planning for a new CRM plan.
茱莉安娜與史考特是行銷部的同事，他們正在商討該如何提出一個新的顧客關係計畫。

Conversation 對話

Juliana	For example, did you check on the other competitors yet?	舉例來說，你確認過其他競爭對手了嗎？
Scott	Do you mean **investigating** how they handle customer relations with their customers?	你是說調查他們怎麼處理顧客關係的嗎？
Juliana	Correct.	對呀。
Scott	No, I haven't done that yet. But, thank you, I will.	沒有，我還沒進行。但是，謝謝你，我會的。
Juliana	Besides, you need to construct a policy to manage consumer communications.	除此之外，你需要規劃一個管理和顧客溝通交流的政策。

Scott	Do you mean plan the tools of communications? Aren't we already doing this by EDMs, Facebook, even the official website?	你是説規劃溝通的工具？我們不是已經用 EDM、臉書和甚至官網在進行了嗎？
Juliana	Then I think you could add **SMS**. By the way, did you set financial budgets for your customer relationship management plan?	那我想你應該增加手機簡訊服務。對了，你為這個顧客關係管理計畫設定了財務預算？
Scott	I didn't know I need to.	我不曉得我需要這樣做。
Juliana	Sure you do. I thought you attended the internal training last month.	你當然需要。我以為你參加了上個月的內部訓練。
Scott	Sorry, I went to do the **OTJ training** at one of our counters. I think I am going to be **dizzy** soon.	抱歉，我當時去其中一個專櫃進行了在職訓練。我想我就快要頭暈了。
Juliana	Not finished yet. You will also need to describe how you will measure results. For example, asking customers to participate in customer satisfaction surveys.	還沒完呢。你還需要描述你要怎麼衡量計畫結果。好比說，請顧客參與填寫滿意度問卷。

Part I

Part II

Part III

Part IV

Part V

Part VI

Scott	My conclusion to this is I think writing a CRM plan is not only our department's job, but also needs help from other departments.	我的結論是，我想寫一個顧客關係管理計畫不只是我們部門的工作，應該需要其他部門的協助。
Juliana	Yes, I think you are right. Based on my experience, you probably need help from departments such as sales, finance and repairs.	我想你是對的。根據我的經驗，你大概需要例如，銷售部門、財務部門和維修部門的協助。
Scott	Could you help to set up a project **coordination** meeting for me, please?	可以請你幫我組織一個協調會議嗎，拜託啦？
Juliana	**Don't get that look**, it's your project, not mine.	別給我那種表情，這是你的專案，可不是我的。

知識補給站

顧客關係管理計畫的成型，有時候牽涉到跨部門的通力合作（**cross-sectoral** cooperation）。例如，蒐集與分析顧客資料可能需要資訊部門（IT department）的設計與參與；活動設計需要行銷或銷售部門（Marketing or Sales Department）的參與；獎項購置需要財務或採購部門（Financial or Purchasing Department）參與；遇到顧客的商品出現問題，可能還需要維修部門（Repairs Department）參與。

曾經有一支電視廣告，拍出了「凱莉想要什麼包」的廣告，就是描述顧客資料管理與預測消費行為的重要性；原來凱莉購物的時候不僅要看到各式各樣手提包，連她最愛吃的小籠包也要出現在購物商城畫面。這支廣告充分體現了顧客關係管理的精髓（**essence**），可以說是經典範例（**classic** example）。

顧客關係管理的工具很多，大多是利用軟體來進行資料蒐集和分析。另外，行銷上講的顧客關係維繫，很多時候的是指推出哪些活動，或者是回饋方案（feedback program）給顧客，讓他們持續感覺和這個品牌或產品維繫感情是有必要性的。例如，積點或積分（points）、折扣、生日卡片、生日優惠（birthday discount）、特殊禮遇（special treatment）…等等。生活中小至買一本書後填寫個人購買紀錄上網回傳或寄回函，大至購車之後的關懷服務等等，不一而足。

總而言之，透過顧客關係管理，企業或品牌才能達到永續經營（**sustainable** management）的目標；換句話說，要想享受更多的顧客消費，那就先搞好顧客關係吧。

Part I　Part II　Part III　Part IV　Part V　Part VI

Related Word 相關詞彙

1. investigating　調查

   文法加油站：美國著名影集 CSI 犯罪現場的原文就是 CSI: Crime Scene Investigation。

2. SMS　手機簡訊

   文法加油站：SMS 是 Short Message Service 的簡稱，全文稱作短訊服務。

3. OTJ training　在職訓練

   文法加油站：OTJ 是 On-the-job 的縮寫，也就是在工作中的意思。

4. dizzy　頭暈的

   文法加油站：頭暈還可以說成 I feel dizzy 或 My head is in a whirl。名詞則是 dizziness。

5. coordination　協調

   文法加油站：動詞是 coordinate，協調、配合、接應的意思。名詞 coordinate 則有座標的意思。

6. Don't get that look.　別這樣看著我，別擺出這種臉色

7. cross-sectoral　跨部門的

8. essence　精華

   文法加油站：這個單詞也是保養品中精華液的單字。

9. classic　經典的

   文法加油站：作為形容詞還有第一流的、古典的意思。名詞為 class，有階級、班級、種類的意思。

10. sustainable　持續的，永續的

Exercises 練習題

Please complete the word or sentence by filling in the blanks.

- One _____ song could be _____ .
- A marketer's _____ ability is important.
- I felt _____ since finished the _____ .
- I need to put this bottle of _____ every morning and night.
- _____ . I don't like a business trip either.
- After the _____ , police found out that he is not the killer.
- SMS is a _____ for sending _____ to mobile phones.

請填空完成下面句子或單字

- 一首經典的歌是可以持續流行的。
- 行銷人員的跨部門協調能力是很重要的。
- 我今天上完在職訓練後就感覺頭暈。
- 我每天早晚都要擦這瓶精華液。
- 別這樣看著我。我也不喜歡出公差。
- 經過調查以後，警察發現他並不是兇手。
- 手機簡訊是一種傳送簡短訊息到手機上的服務。

Answers to the Unit:

classic, sustainable
cross-sectoral coordination
dizzy, OTJ training/ on-the-job training
essence
Don't get that look
Investigating
Service, short messages

Part I
Part II
Part III
Part IV
Part V
Part VI

Unit 25 Customer Interaction Tools
如何與顧客互動？

Background Introduction 背景介紹：

Josephine is the Store Manager of a jewelry shop, Ernest and Luke are the store staffs. Now is their morning meeting, and they are talking about how to improve the ways of interacting with customers.

約瑟芬是珠寶店的店長，歐內斯特與路克是店員。現在是晨會時間，而他們正在討論該如何增進與顧客的互動方式？

Conversation 對話

Josephine	Hi, guys.	嗨，夥伴們。
Ernest/ Luke	Hi, Josephine.	嗨，約瑟芬。
Josephine	Today, we will focus on finding the ways of how to interact with our customers.	今天，我們要專注在發現如何與顧客互動的方法上。
Ernest	I wanted to discuss this since weeks ago.	幾個星期前我就想討論這個話題了。
Luke	Didn't we already interact with them through EDMs, birthday cards, SMS and phone calls?	我們不是已經透過電子廣告郵件、生日卡片、手機簡訊和電話和他們互動了嗎？

Ernest	Don't forget Facebook and blogs. What else can we do?	別忘了還有臉書和部落格。我們還能做些什麼？
Josephine	It is a good question, that's why we are here this morning.	好問題，這就是為什麼今天早上我們聚在這裡的理由。
Ernest	I remember we sent some discount leaflet by post to our VIP buyers.	我記得我們郵寄了些折價宣傳單給 VIP 的買家們。
Luke	That's right. It's also a tool of interaction.	對呀。這也是一種互動方式。
Josephine	I **assume** you all know that we are going to publish our company's seasonal magazine from next month?	我猜想你們也已經都知道從下個月開始公司將出版季刊？
Ernest	Yes, and I think the idea is great.	是，我個人覺得這個點子很棒。
Luke	Can we provide some services in the store?	我們能不能在店裡提供一些服務呢？
Josephine	What do you mean?	什麼意思呢？

Part I

Part II

Part III

Part IV

Part V

Part VI

Luke	I mean, for example, offer them cookies, coffee or juice. Anything that can help them feels more comfortable.	我是說，例如，提供他們餅乾、咖啡或果汁。
Ernest	Maybe also invite them to attend a charity event? This can not only help bring in new customers, but it will also help show the **community** we care about the people who live in it.	或許也邀請他們參加社區慈善活動？這不但可以帶來新顧客，也可以向社區展示我們對住在這邊的人的關心。
Josephine	That is a wonderful idea, Ernest! I wrote it down this morning, and guess which one of you may mention it.	這是個絕妙的想法，歐內斯特！我今天早上寫下來，想說你們哪一位可能會提到這個建議。
Ernest	That's because I am the **idea hamster** in this team.	這是因為我是團隊裡的點子王啊。
Luke	Do you think an **open house** will help, too?	你們覺得參觀日也會有幫助嗎？
Josephine	**I have reservations about this**, I mean, we are a jewelry shop.	我對這個建議持保留態度，我是說，我們是一家珠寶店。

Part I
Part II
Part III
Part IV
Part V
Part VI

Luke	Yes, that may be very risky.	對喔，可能會很危險。
Josephine	But it's a good idea, **though**. Thank you, Luke.	然而這是個好主意。謝謝你，路克。
Ernest	Maybe we also can provide various ways of payment?	也許我們也可以增加多樣化的付款方式？
Josephine	I couldn't agree with you more, but could you be more **specific**?	再同意你不過了，但是你可以說得具體一點嗎？
Ernest	I will say we need to handle the payment procedure more quickly and **accurately**.	我的意思是我們需要把付款程序處理得更快和準確地。
Luke	How about also setting up a **credit card terminal** instead of accepting cash only?	不如也設置一台刷卡機而不是只收現金？
Josephine	Let me write it down, so I can report to the **head office**.	讓我記下這個，好報告給總公司知道。

Part I
Part II
Part III
Part IV
Part V
Part VI

Ernest	There is one more thing, Josephine. Can the people from Marketing or Sales Department send someone to change the window display every three months or some? It hasn't been changed for half a year already!	還有一件事情，約瑟芬。行銷或者銷售部門可以派人每三個月或什麼時候就更換一下櫥窗佈置嗎？已經半年沒有更新了耶！
Luke	One time, a client asked me if we had nothing to change for it.	有一次，有個客人問我我們是不是沒東西可以展示了。
Josephine	That's really bad, isn't it? I will **make report** today, and hopefully, they will send somebody in this month.	真糟糕，不是嗎？我今天就會上報公司，然後希望這個月他們就可以派人過來。
Ernest	That will be great.	那就太好了。
Josephine	I guess that's all, guys, thank you for your opinions and have a nice working day.	我想這些就是全部啦，夥伴們，謝謝你們的建議也祝你們有個愉快的工作日。
Ernest/ Luke	You too, Josephine.	你也是，約瑟芬。

Part I
Part II
Part III
Part IV
Part V
Part VI

308

知識補給站

如何與顧客互動，也可以解釋成如何維繫和顧客的關係（how to keep an relationship with customers）。從以往的生日賀卡，到手機的簡訊、EDM，再到今日的臉書、部落格、App…等等，提供給企業許多的工具選擇可以即時與顧客保持訊息的傳遞。

但是除了溝通（communication）這件事情本身，還有許多地方也成為與顧客溝通的細節，卻被忽略了。例如：門店的櫥窗展示、門店或專櫃的佈置（decoration）、人員提供服務的速度和態度（speed or attitude of providing service），甚至室內設計（interior design）、動線（movement）、燈光與音樂（lighting and music）…等等，都是與顧客互動的展現。

有些顧客會在門外或專櫃稍遠一點的地方，稍微觀察後再決定要不要走進或靠近，甚至也有顧客已經到店內了，店員們卻都聚集在一起聊天而沒有人發現。這些都是與顧客互動的細節，雖然大多屬於現場人員的職責，行銷人也需要在規劃活動的時候留意，是不是會造成現場人員在與顧客互動的時候，感覺不受尊重（not respected）或被打擾了（disturbed）。

Part I

Part II

Part III

Part IV

Part V

Part VI

Related Word 相關詞彙

1. assume　假設
   文法加油站：同義詞還有 suppose、presume。

2. community　社區，鄰居

3. idea hamster　點子王

4. open house　參觀日
   文法加油站：如果用在機關、學校單位，指的是開放參觀日；如果用在房地產上，指的是隨時可進入參觀的出售中的房子。

5. I have reservations about this　我對此持保留態度
   文法加油站：reservation 也指訂位時保留、預約的意思。

6. though　然而
   文法加油站：放句中，有不過的意思；放句尾，則是然而的意思。例如：
   (1) The overall standard is low, though it varies from area to area.　整體的標準是很低的，不過也視地區而定。
   (2) I could have asked him to take the cakes with him, it's too late now, though.　我本來可以請他把蛋糕帶走的，不過現在太遲了。

7. specific　具體的，詳盡的，詳細的

8. accurately　準確地

9. credit card terminal　刷卡機
   文法加油站：也可以寫作 credit card machine。

10. head office　總公司
    文法加油站：head quarter 是總部，並且有 CEO 坐鎮的地方。有時候總公司等同於總部，但是對比較龐大的體系來說，總部有可能在一地，而不同國家則分別有當地總公司。

11. make report　向上呈報

Exercises 練習題

Please complete the word or sentence by filling in the blanks.

● After I _____ to the _____ , we have a _____
in the shop finally.

● Today is the _____ day of the chocolate factory, all the family in
_____ will go there.

● This report neither accurately or _____ .

● _____ about whether she is a good person or not.

● I _____ my daughter finished her homework yesterday, but she
didn't.

● John is the _____ of our Department, he always can come up with
some unique ideas.

請填空完成下面句子或單字

● 在我向總公司呈報後，店內終於有了一台刷卡幾。

● 今天是巧克力工廠的參觀日，我們 C 社區的家庭都會前往。

● 這份報告既不具體也不詳盡。

● 我對她是不是一個好人持保留態度。

● 我假設我女兒昨天完成了回家作業，但是並沒有。

● 約翰是部門裡的點子王，總是能想出與眾不同的點子。

Answers to the Unit:
make report, head office, credit card terminal
open house, community
specifically, accurately
I have reservations
assumed
idea hamster

Part I
Part II
Part III
Part IV
Part V
Part VI

Unit 26 Setting up a Customer Loyalty Program 讓顧客愛上你！

Background Introduction 背景介紹：

Laura and Penelope are co-workers at the CRM Department from an Airline Company. They are designing a new customer loyalty incentive program.

蘿拉和潘妮洛普是一家航空公司顧客關係管理部門的同事。她們正在設計一個新的顧客忠誠獎勵計畫。

Conversation 對話

Laura	Hi, Penelope, did you see my lunchbox and coffee **mug**?	嗨，潘妮洛普，你有沒有看到我的便當盒和馬克杯？
Penelope	You were in employee lounge, **is it coming back to you**?	你剛才在員工休息室，有沒有想起什麼啊？
Laura	Right, thank you so much.	對喔，謝謝你啦。
Penelope	I think you can get back lately, because we already behind the schedule and I really need your help in this program.	我想你可以等會兒去拿，因為我們的計畫已經落後進度，而我真的需要你的幫忙。
Laura	Sure, no problem.	當然，沒問題。

Penelope	First of all, the customer loyalty program needs to add something new.	首先，顧客忠誠計畫需要增加一些新的東西。
Laura	I personally think it is perfect already. You see, we are now offering frequent passengers points with each purchase which can be **cashed in** later for rewards.	我個人是覺得它已經夠好了。你看喔，我們已經提供給經常搭乘的乘客可以兌換成獎品的積分。
Penelope	I know, but this has been done for five years and our customers need new attractions.	我知道，但是這個已經進行了 5 年了，而顧客需要新的刺激。
Laura	You are right.	你是對的。
Penelope	So, what's in your mind?	所以，有什麼建議嗎？
Laura	How about we partnering with other brands?	不如我們和其他品牌合作吧？
Penelope	Do you mean something like **alliances**?	你是說像聯盟一樣？

Part I
Part II
Part III
Part IV
Part V
Part VI

Laura	Yes. For instance, we can partner with restaurants or hotels to offer co-branded deals for **mutual benefits** for our customers.	對。舉例來說，我們可以和餐廳或飯店聯合推出互惠方案給我們的顧客。
Penelope	That's a wonderful suggestion!	真是個絕妙的建議！
Laura	You are welcome.	不客氣。
Penelope	But I think we need a plan which encourages more purchases from current or future customers.	但是我想我們需要一個能夠鼓勵現在或未來顧客消費更多的計畫。
Laura	Not only rewarding them?	不只是獎勵他們？
Penelope	No. So, that's the most difficult part.	不。所以，這是最困難的地方。
Laura	It is difficult to make a linkage, because we don't know what kinds of incentives they like or don't like.	的確是很難製造關聯性，因為我們不曉得他們喜歡或不喜歡什麼樣的誘因。
Penelope	I can go to IT Department to get more detail analysis, but before that, I need some possible ideas.	我可以去一趟資訊部門取得更多資料分析，但是在那之前，我需要一些可行的想法。

Laura	Let me think. How about we provide three levels of incentive, so frequent passengers can be treated differently? For example, Club Blue members carn miles on flights and get discount on hotels. Club Gold members earn 50% more points on flights, expedited check-in, and get discounts on rental cars and hotels. Club Diamond members get double miles, priority boarding, and access to exclusive VIP room where they can get a massage before the flight.	讓我想想。如果是提供三種層級的誘因呢，讓經常搭乘的乘客可以享受不同待遇？例如，藍色俱樂部會員可以贏取飛行里程，並且享受飯店折扣。金色俱樂部會員可以贏取多 50% 的里程，優先登機，和租車與飯店優惠。鑽石俱樂部會員可以贏取兩倍里程，優先登機，和在登機之前享受 VIP 空間的沙龍服務。
Penelope	It sounds a terrific plan, isn't it?	聽起來是個了不起的計畫，不是嗎？
Laura	I am glad that you like it. So, what's next?	我很高興你喜歡。那，還有什麼嗎？
Penelope	I need your help to write this program for me.	我需要你幫我寫下這個計畫。
Laura	Oh my God, **here we go again**!	老天啊，又來了！

Part I

Part II

Part III

Part IV

Part V

Part VI

Penelope	I'm **older and smarter**.	請容我倚老賣老一下囉。
Laura	**Could you at least** bring my lunch box and coffee mug for me?	可以請你至少幫我拿便當盒和馬克杯給我？
Penelope	Where are them?	它們在哪裡？
Laura	At employee lounge!	在員工休息室裡！
Penelope	**On my way** now.	現在就去。

知識補給站

Part I

Part II

Part III

Part IV

Part V

Part VI

　　推行顧客忠誠度計畫，是顧客關係管理的一部份，所以也可能需要其他部門的參與；資訊部門、財務部、銷售部、行銷部、行政部（Administration Department）…等等。

　　按字面意思解釋，計畫施行的最終目的，是讓顧客對品牌或企業保持一定的忠誠度（loyalty），不會有機會在購買相同產品的時候，選擇其他品牌；如此一來，可以確保企業或品牌有一定的獲利。經常出差旅行的人，對於航空公司的獎勵飛行計畫（Frequent-flyer program）一定不陌生，另外酒店、租車業（car rental business），甚至連鎖飲料店（chain **bubble tea** shop）的集點換一杯飲料或贈品，都是顧客忠誠度計畫的展現。

　　忠誠度計畫需要推陳出新（find new ways of doing things from old theories）而且設定的門檻（threshold）要合宜，否則經過長時間後，顧客可能會對品牌產生疲乏，甚至覺得老是達不到獎勵的標準，就會選擇離開，投入其他品牌的懷抱。

Related Word 相關詞彙

1. mug 馬克杯

2. Is it coming back to you? （回）想起來沒有？

   文法加油站：it 在此指記憶、回憶。

3. cashed in 兌換

4. alliance 聯盟，結盟。指兩家以上的企業或品牌聯合推出的活動，例如，到便利商店買周刊送一杯咖啡。

5. mutual benefits 互惠互利

6. here we go again 又來了

7. older and smarter 倚老賣老

8. Could you at least… 可不可以請你至少…

9. on my way 在路上

10. administration 行政、管理

    文法加油站：企業管理的英文就寫作 business administration，常聽到的
    MBA 就是 Master in Business Administration（企業管理碩士）
    的縮寫。

11. bubble tea 泡沫紅茶

    文法加油站：取中文意思直翻的英文，bubble 可以形容泡沫紅茶上層的泡沫，
    也可以拿來形容珍珠奶茶（bubble mike tea）裡的珍珠。

Part I
Part II
Part III
Part IV
Part V
Part VI

Exercises 練習題

Please complete the word or sentence by filling in the blanks.

A：Hi, I would like a cup of _____ , please.

B：Any sugar?

A：Just half.

B：What is your major, kid?

A：_____ .

B：I remember when I studied at the same University as you are, and⋯

A：_____ , I have heard of this for dozen times.　Please stop being

_____ .

請填空完成下面句子或單字

A：老闆，來一杯泡沫紅茶。

B：要加糖嗎？

A：半糖。

B：你是念什麼科系的，小子？

A：企管系。

B：想當年，我跟你念同一間大學，那時候⋯

A：又來了，我已經幾十遍了，老闆。請不要在倚老賣老囉。

Answers to the Unit:

bubble tea

Business Administration

Here we go again

older and smarter

Part I

Part II

Part III

Part IV

Part V

Part VI

Unit 27 Key Points of Hosting a Meeting
主持會議要點

Situation 情境：

Annabel is the Manager of CRM Department. She is explaining the importance of CRM, as well as the new customer loyalty incentive program to her colleagues from the same department. She hopes that her colleagues can discuss the plan and raise questions.

安娜貝兒是顧客關係管理部門的經理。她正在向部門同事解說顧客關係管理的重要性，以及新的顧客忠誠獎勵計畫。她希望同事們討論計畫內容，和針對計畫提出疑問。

Key points for your conversation 對話急救包

🖇 說明簡報內容

Today I would like to provide a brief overview of the importance of CRM. After the overview, I will describe the new customer loyalty incentive program and raise a discussion based on the program.

今天我想針對顧客關係管理的重要性提供簡短的介紹。然後，我想說明新的顧客忠誠獎勵計畫和針對這個計畫的討論。

I would like to take this time to have an overview picture of the importance of CRM, and the new customer loyalty incentive program.

我想利用一點時間介紹一下顧客關係管理的重要性，以及新的顧客忠誠獎勵計畫。

Let me touch on the importance of CRM briefly, then I will go into the new customer loyalty incentive program in more detail.

讓我簡短說明顧客關係管理的重要性，然後我會詳細描述新的顧客忠誠獎勵計畫。

激起討論

Perhaps we can start with **John**?
也許可以先從約翰開始？
小貼士：想要指名或點名某人時常用的句子。

To begin with, we might spend a few minutes discussing the disadvantages which this program may have.
一開始，我們先花點時間來討論這個計畫可能有的缺點。

John, how do you feel about this new customer loyalty incentive program?
約翰，你覺得新的顧客忠誠獎勵計畫怎麼樣？

I would like to ask John first and then Jimmy to tell us if they agree with Lisa's opinions.
我想問約翰，接著是吉米關於他們對麗莎的意見有什麼看法。
小貼士：同時點名兩人（或以上）對另一人陳述後的意見時的用法。

簡化、終止討論

Please be brief, since we have limited time.
請簡短發言，因為我們的時間有限。

I like your discussion here, but in all fairness I think I should hear some opinions from others.
我喜歡你的發言，但是為了公平起見，我想應該也聽聽其他人的意見。

Let's get back to you a little later. I think we would be interested in having as many opinions as we can get.
讓我們待會兒再回到你這邊。我想我們都很有興趣盡可能多聽些意見。

I think I would like to put this issue aside for the moment and concentrate on the point under discussion.
我想把這個議題暫時擱置，專注在我們要討論的話題上。

Part I
Part II
Part III
Part IV
Part V
Part VI

Part VI

Brand Management
品牌管理

Unit 28 Brand Naming and Identity Design 製造一個人人愛的品牌

Background Introduction 背景介紹：

Colleen is the Brand Manager from J Company, and Walter is the Art Director of U Design Company. They are talking about how to design a new brand image for J Company.

可琳是 J 公司的品牌經理，華特是 U 設計公司的藝術總監。他們正在討論該如何替 J 公司設計一個新的品牌形象。

Conversation 對話

Colleen	Hi, Walter, **congratulations on your new baby**.	嗨，華特，恭喜你喜獲麟兒。
Walter	Thanks. By the way, do you know that X Company decided to **exit the market** last week?	謝謝。對了，你知道上週 X 公司決定要退出市場？
Colleen	**So I have been told.**	我聽說了。
Walter	That's terrible, isn't it?	真是糟糕，不是嗎？
Colleen	That's why I set up this meeting for us, I think it's better we sort something out as soon as possible.	這就是為什麼我安排了今早的會議，我想我們最好盡快開始解決一些事情。

Walter	Sure. What would you like to discuss?	當然。妳想要討論什麼呢？
Colleen	As you know, brand **identity** design is to graphically represent the company's or product's character.	你也知道，品牌識別設計是用圖形設計傳達公司或產品的特色。
Walter	Very true. And it's not complete without a brand name and logo.	很正確。如果缺了品牌名稱和標誌也就不完整了。
Colleen	So, I am thinking maybe you can help us to convey the value we are prepared to deliver.	所以，我在想或許你可以幫我們傳達我們準備要傳遞的價值。
Walter	What values are they?	這些價值是什麼呢？
Colleen	Trustworthy, eco-friendly, and advanced.	值得信賴的、環保的和先進的。
Walter	That doesn't sound very complex. Do you need me to develop any **personification character**?	聽起來不是很複雜。妳需要我發展任何擬人化的角色嗎？
Colleen	Like animals or talking vegetable?	是像動物或者會說話的蔬菜？

Part I

Part II

Part III

Part IV

Part V

Part VI

Part I Part II Part III Part IV Part V Part VI

Walter	Very funny! But something like that, what do you think?	妳真好笑！但是差不多意思，妳覺得呢？
Colleen	I prefer not.	我傾向不要了吧。
Walter	OK, no problem at all.	好的，沒問題。
Colleen	I just hope this logo can be **tangible** and hopefully **memorable**.	我只希望這個標誌是有形的，並且難忘的。
Walter	So the customers will remember your product once they need the service your company provides.	所以消費者才會記住你的產品，一旦他們需要貴公司提供的服務的時候。
Colleen	Absolutely correct. Can you do that for us?	完全正確。你可以幫我們做到？
Walter	Are you kidding me? I am **making a living** from this.	妳在和我開玩笑嗎？我可是靠這個謀生的呢。
Colleen	Great!	太棒了！

Walter	I think you also need to know that the logo should **evolve** when the product or company policy changes. Off course, we can design one now and then **modernizes** the logo as visual trends change.	我想妳應該也要知道標誌應該跟著產品或公司政策改變而進化。當然啦，我們可以現在設計一個，然後隨著視覺潮流改變而現代化。
Colleen	What do you mean by that?	這麼說是什麼意思呢？
Walter	I mean, for example, even Coca Cola changes its logo design several time since 1930. Modernizing logo could involve varying things, such as color scheme, font, **tagline** and overall design.	我是說，舉例喔，即使可口可樂的標誌也自從 1930 年以來換了好幾次。現代化標誌可能包含幾項事情，例如配色、字型、標語和整體設計。
Colleen	**It rings my bell** that Apple computer also changed his logo sever times.	我想起來蘋果電腦巾換過標誌好幾次。
Walter	There are plenty companies are doing this, simple because they don't want to look **over-dated**. They want to keep providing a fresh and vivid image to their customers.	還有很多公司這樣做，就是因為他們想要看起來不是那麼過時的。他們想要持續提供他們顧客一個新鮮和有生氣的形象。

Part I

Part II

Part III

Part IV

Part V

Part VI

Colleen	It's like they are saying "Hey, look at me, I am still alive".	就好像他們在說：「嘿，看我呀，我還活著呢」。
Walter	Pretty much like that.	大概是這個意思吧。
Colleen	OK, so you are clear about what you are going to do?	好啦，所以你都清楚將要做什麼了？
Walter	Sure, you shouldn't worry.	當然，妳不必擔心。
Colleen	Good. I'd better be going, it looks like it's going to rain.	好的。我最好該離開了，看起來好像要下雨的樣子。
Walter	I see you two weeks later.	兩週後再見。
Colleen	Thank you, Walter. Just let me know if you have any question.	謝啦，華特。有任何問題儘管告訴我。
Walter	Will do. **Let me walk you out**.	我會的。讓我送妳出去吧。

知識補給站

　　品牌管理的第一步，是命名與設計；一個好的品牌名稱和標誌設計，通常有下列幾點特色：

1. 暗示產品特性（characteristic）或利益（benefit）。例如，翻譯機品牌「快譯通」就很清楚的展現產品特色。
2. 符合目標市場特性。例如，零食產品取名可以偏向可愛、通俗、易懂、易叫的；高檔精品品牌取名可能就要雅緻（elegance）一點的。
3. 好記好唸。例如，「蝦味先」是從台語「呷未嫌（吃不膩）」發音而來。必勝客比薩的原文是「PizzaHut」、搶佔特殊節慶市場的米果品牌「旺旺」…等等。
4. 避免不當諧音。尤其是跨國品牌進入當地市場時，應該先做好文字或翻譯上的功課；行銷界眾所周知的典型案例是，美國通用汽車公司當年在墨西哥推出一款「NOVA」的汽車，但是按照當地語言（西班牙語）的意思，卻是跑不動的意思。
5. 合法性。在國際環境日益開放的今天，品牌取名或設計也要避免抄襲（copy）才能走得長久。

　　品牌命名是長久之計，設計卻應該與時俱進，給人耳目一新之感。不過，如果品牌或產品訴求復古（retro），那麼經典的復刻版也沒有什麼不可以了。

Related Word 相關詞彙

1. congratulations on your new baby　恭喜你喜獲麟兒

   文法加油站：經常祝賀的場合還有：

   (1) Congratulations on your graduation. 恭喜學成畢業

   (2) Congratulations on your promotion. 恭喜升官 / 升遷

2. exit the market　退出市場

   文法加油站：進入市場則是 enter market。

3. So I have been told.　我聽說了

4. identity　辨識

   文法加油站：我們常說的身份證（個人識別證）英文就叫做 Identification

   　　　　　　（ID）Card。

5. personification character　擬人化的角色

6. tangible　有形的

7. memorable　可記憶的

8. make a living　謀生

9. evolve　進化

   文法加油站：此為動詞，名詞為 evolution，進化、演化的意思。

10. modernize　使現代化

11. tagline　標語

12. It rings my bell.　我想（記）起來了

13. over-dated　過時的

    文法加油站：同義詞還有 dated、old fashion、bygone、antique。

14. Let me walk you out.　讓我送你出去，讓我陪你走出去

Exercises *練習題*

Please make a line match then English and Chinese.

連連看。

- tangible
- over-dated
- evolve
- tagline
- personification
- modernize

- 標語
- 有形的
- 擬人化
- 使現代化
- 過時的
- 進化

Answers to the Unit:

（依照英文的順序）
- 有形的
- 過時的
- 進化
- 標語
- 擬人化
- 現代化

Part I

Part II

Part III

Part IV

Part V

Part VI

Unit 29 Brand Story 說動聽的故事

Background Introduction 背景介紹：

Ivy and Jessica are Brand Assistants of an organic skin care product company, and they are planning a new brand story for the brand.
艾薇和潔西卡兩個人是有機護膚用品的品牌專員，他們正在替公司規劃一個新的品牌故事。

Conversation 對話

Ivy	Just tell me again why we need a new brand story? I think the original one is already enough for me.	再說一遍我們為什麼需要一個新的品牌故事？我覺得原來這個已經夠好了。
Jessica	That's because we need to evolve when strategy changes.	那是因為當策略改變的時候我們也需要進化。
Ivy	OK, that could **convince** me.	好吧，這可以說服我。
Jessica	You see, creating a brand story is not about getting noticed, but about building something that people care about and want to **buy into**.	你看喔，創建一個品牌故事並非只是告知，而是建立人們會關心和想要接受的東西。
Ivy	It sounds like a big project.	聽起來是個大工程。

Jessica	Not really, just **put yourself in the customers' shoes**. Let's try it step by step. First of all, do you think when a consumer sees our logo, visits the official website, or experiences our **interaction**s on social media will **affected** by a brand story?	也不盡然，就讓自己站在顧客的角度思考。讓我們試著一步一步來。首先，你認為顧客看了我們的標誌、造訪我們官方網站、或與我們在社交媒體上互動的經驗，會被品牌故事所影響？
Ivy	I think so, I mean, at least when I see the appeals from their FB or website, I have some expectations from the brand story.	我想會吧，我是説，至少當我看了某些品牌的臉書或網站，我會對品牌故事有所期待。
Jessica	Good. So, this means how or what to tell in a brand story is the combination of an overall company image.	很好。也就是説，這表示一個品牌故事怎麼説或説什麼，就是企業整體形象的結合。
Jessica	You just gave me an inspiration of the contents of a great brand story. I think we can focus on our product features.	你剛才給了我一個品牌故事絕妙的靈感。我想我們可以專注在產品特色上。
Ivy	Organic?	有機的？
Jessica	Yes. Look, we have our own farm in the USA, workers from multicolor race, nature **ingredients** and **handmade** manufacturing process.	對呀。你看喔，我們在美國有自己的農場、工人來自不同種族、天然的原料和手工的製造流程。

Part I
Part II
Part III
Part IV
Part V
Part VI

Ivy	Basically, it's making **relevance**.	基本上，就是創造關聯性。
Jessica	Yes, and the **founders** of our company. We didn't mention them, but now they can make this story **livelier**.	是的，還有我們公司的創辦人。之前我們都沒有提到他們，但是現在他們會讓故事增色不少。
Ivy	That sounds really cool!	聽起來真的很酷！
Jessica	And I think we also need to change the way of writing. We should consider that we are talking to our customers, making ourselves real, **accessible**, and approachable.	我想我們也需要改變寫法，我們應該想成是在和顧客們說話，使我們聽起來真實、合宜的和易親近的。
Ivy	I think this revision will be perfect.	我想這個版本應該是完美的了。
Jessica	Nothing is perfect, darling, only keeping trying to be perfect.	沒有什麼事情是完美的，只有不斷試著達到完美的境界。
Ivy	**That's the spirit!**	就是這個精神！

知識補給站

　　想好了品牌命名與設計後，給品牌一個出生和成長的背景，行銷上稱為品牌故事。

　　品牌故事的創造十分不易，既要寫得真實，還要打動目標消費族群的心；一個品牌故事的誕生，往往考驗著行銷人員的創造力（creativity）和筆下功力（writing skill）。雖然說是不易，但是也有下列幾個方向可以參考：

1. 創辦人的故事（story of the founder）。品牌是創辦人的縮影（**miniature**），從取名、顏色、線條到故事的背景，往往可以看到創辦人如何影響著品牌的走向（direction）。從知名的精品品牌 LV、Chanel，到黑貓宅急便的品牌故事，都和創辦人形影不離。

2. 特殊的想法或夢想（unique dreams or thinking）。之所以想要發展品牌，不外乎產品獨特，想要與更多人分享；所以描述這樣的想法或夢想產生、執行（execution）、挫折（setback）、實現（dreams come true）⋯也是一種打動目標消費群的故事。

3. 獨特的作法（unique production）、獲利模式（business model）。例如，天然的原料、手工、回饋社會（contribute to the community）或與幫助弱勢團體（support on disadvantaged groups）⋯等的部分，也容易成為一篇打動人心的故事。

Related Word 相關詞彙

1. convince　説服

　　文法加油站：同義詞還有 *persuade*、*talk over*。

2. buy into　接受，相信

　　文法加油站：除了有買進的意思之外，也有相信或接受某事物的意思。

　　　　　　　　Why people buy into conspiracy theories?　為什麼人們要相信陰謀論？

3. put yourself in the customers' shoes　站在顧客的角度想

　　文法加油站：這句話原本寫作 *put yourself in my shoes*，意思是站在我的立場想一想。

4. interaction　互動

5. affect　影響

6. ingredient　原料、成份

　　文法加油站：食譜（*recipe*）裡面的原料也是用這個英文單詞表示。

7. handmade　手工的

8. relevance　相關性

9. founder　創辦人，創始者

10. livelier　活潑

11. accessible　合宜的

12. That's the spirit.　這樣就對了，就是這種精神

13. miniature　縮影，縮圖，袖珍物品

　　文法加油站：縮小展現某東西樣貌的意思。例如，袖珍博物館就翻作 *Miniatures Museum*。

Exercises 練習題

Please complete the word or sentence by filling in the blanks.

- I will never get tired of enjoying_____.
- You cannot_____me to_____there is an alien living outside the planet.
- There are many contaminated_____inside Taiwan food.
- Her novel is_____and that's why she won the prize.
- The_____between our_____is not so good and peaceful.
- What he said has no_____to what we were talking about.

請填空完成下面句子或單字
- 手工的袖珍物品真是百看不厭。
- 你無法說服我相信有外星生物這件事。
- 台灣食品有許多原料受到汙染。
- 她的小說非常活潑，這也就是為什麼得獎的原因。
- 我們的創辦人之間互動並不怎麼融洽。
- 他說的和我們在討論的並無相關性。

Answers to the Unit:
handmade miniatures
convince, buy into
ingredients
livelier
interaction, founders
relevance

Unit 30 Brand Attributes, Functions, Benefits, Personalities
有知性，更具感性

Background Introduction 背景介紹：

Phil is a student of Graduate School of Marketing, and Samson is a Brand Manager. Today, Phil comes to Samson's office and interview him.
菲爾是一名行銷研究所的學生，薩姆森是一名品牌管理經理。今天，菲爾來到薩姆森的辦公室進行訪問。

Conversation 對話

Samson	OK. Let me start share with you the **fundamental** principles, which we call them the four **dimensions** of a brand.	沒問題。讓我先和你分享基本的原則，我們稱為品牌的四大構面。
Phil	Yes, I have heard of them at the class. They are brand attributes, functions, benefits and personalities. Brand attributes are a bundle of characteristics that highlight the physical and specifications of the brand.	是的，我在課堂上聽過。他們分別是品牌屬性、功能、利益和個性。品牌屬性是一些物質上和規格方面的描述。
Samson	True, for example, our products are **sparkling beverages**. Brand attributes can be the color of bottles, how much **capacity**, taste etc.	對，例如，我們的產品是氣泡飲料。品牌屬性就是瓶子的顏色、有多少容量、口味…等等。

Phil	Brand functions are the extension of brand attributes.	品牌功能是品牌屬性的延伸。
Samson	The brand functions of our drinks could be bringing our customers more fun and more choices, since we have the most complete **product line** in sparkling beverages. What about brand benefits and personalities.	我們飲料的功能可能是帶給消費者更多樂趣和更多選擇，因為我們有最完整的氣泡飲料產品線。那麼品牌利益和個性呢。
Phil	They are as easily understood as their names. Brand benefit means, for instance, what consumers get from your sparkling drinks?	它們就像字面上易懂。品牌利益表示，舉例來說，消費者從你們的氣泡飲料獲得什麼？
Samson	I will say they are the joy of sharing with friends, or the fun of the drink popping in your mouth.	我會說是與朋友分享的樂趣，或飲料在你口中跳動的快樂。
Phil	Brand personalities are a set of human characteristics that are under a brand name. I can **make a guess**. I will say they are joyful, interesting and **easy going**.	品牌個性就是在一個品牌名字下面的一組個性。我可以試著猜一猜。我會說是歡樂的、有趣的和隨和的。

Part I

Part II

Part III

Part IV

Part V

Part VI

Samson	Easy going! You really consider it as a person, don't you? OK, let me ask you who or which Hollywood star you will think of when mention our brand.	隨和的！你還真把它當成一個人了呢，是不是啊？好，讓我問你，當提到我們品牌時，你會想到誰或哪一位好萊塢明星？
Phil	Maybe Reese Witherspoon, because in Legally Blonde, she is really cute and sweet.	也許是瑞絲薇絲朋，因為她在「金髮尤物」電影裡真的很可愛與甜美。
Samson	I see, well, there is no right or wrong answer here. But you have to know that if a company spent a lot of money on building the brand image or personalities, it is a pity if their customers always give not relevant words when asking about this kind of questions.	了解，嗯，無所謂對或錯。但是你要知道如果一家公司花了一大筆錢在建立品牌形象或個性上，但是當問到這類問題時，消費者給的是無相關的字詞時，那就很遺憾了
Phil	That's pretty risky.	的確風險很大。
Samson	Indeed. Sorry, young man, time's up. I hope **it pays to** interview me, and good luck with your assignment.	確實。抱歉，年輕人，時間到了。我希望你訪問我是值得的，還有祝你的作業有好運。
Phil	Sure, thank you for your time, Samson.	沒問題，謝謝你的時間，薩姆森。

Part I
Part II
Part III
Part IV
Part V
Part VI

實際上發展一個品牌時，會從四大構面來做串聯。

1. 品牌屬性。通常是肉眼可以看出來的，例如，尺寸、長短、顏色、寬窄…等等。以電風扇為例，品牌屬性可能有大中小、紅色、藍色、涼風扇（cooling fan）、暖風扇（warm fan）等等。

2. 品牌功能。在品牌屬性之下所帶來的功能展現，例如，卡車（truck）可以載貨，房車（sedan）讓人乘坐舒適，越野車（SUV）可以走在顛頗的路面…等等。

3. 品牌利益。在品牌屬性和功能之下，所帶給目標消費群體什麼好處；這個好處可以是功能面的也可以是情感面的。例如，輕薄手機（slim mobile phone）的推出，解決了很早以前攜帶大型手機（黑金剛）的困擾；選擇喝一杯星巴克有時候是向身旁的人炫耀（show off）「我喝得起昂貴的咖啡」。

4. 品牌個性。在前面三個構面的情形下賦予的人格化特質。例如，幫寶適給人一種可愛的印象，德芙巧克力好像是都會女性的化身，蘋果電腦是時尚和潮流的代名詞…等等

　　按圖索驥規劃品牌不難，難的是在環環相扣（all linked together）的情形下不出現矛盾的語詞或定位。這時候 也就是考驗行銷人或品牌經理的關卡了。

Part I

Part II

Part III

Part IV

Part V

Part VI

Related Word 相關詞彙

1. fundamental　基本的，根本的
   文法加油站：同義詞還有 basic、essential、foremost。作為名詞則有基調、基本原理的意思。

2. dimension　構面

3. sparkling beverage　氣泡飲料
   文法加油站：sparkling 原意是閃閃發光的、有氣泡的意思；亦可指氣泡水，或氣泡酒。

4. capacity　容量

5. product line　產品線。依照產品價格、功能、通路或銷售對象不同而組成的產品。例如，某車廠有三條產品線，分別生產休旅車、跑車、房車，其中還可能依照汽缸數不同再分類。

6. make a guess　猜一猜
   文法加油站：也可以說成 take a guess。

7. easy going　隨和的

8. it pays to…　值得…
   文法加油站：pay 有付錢、付出的意思，所以此句解釋成值得為某事付出。
   It pays to go to university.　上大學很值得。

9. SUV　越野車
   文法加油站：SUV 是 sport utility vehicle 的字母縮寫。另外，前一陣子常聽到的 RV 車是一種長型的露營，全名是 recreational vehicle。

10. show off　炫耀
    文法加油站：同義詞還有 peacock（此單詞也是孔雀的意思，取其開屏時吸引人目光的引申意思）、flaunt。

Exercises 練習題

Please complete the word or sentence by filling in the blanks.

● In his report, he analyzed the two_____of products.

● I am a_____man, but this doesn't mean I have no_____.

● How many different_____of_____do you have?

● Jack just joined the_____（SUV）Racing Competition last month.

● _____visit Paris.

● Amy is a girl who loves to_____herself.

請填空完成下面句子或單字

● 他的報告裡分析了產品的兩大構面。

● 我是個很隨和的人，但不代表沒有基本原則。

● 請問你們有多少不同容量的氣泡飲料？

● 傑克上個月剛參加了越野車大賽。

● 造訪巴黎是值得的。

● 艾咪是一個很愛炫耀自己的女生。

Answers to the Unit:
dimensions
easy going, fundamental principle
capacities, sparkling beverage
sport utility vehicle
It pays to
Show off

Unit 31 Branding Decisions
品牌，怎麼擺才恰當？

Background Introduction 背景介紹：

Nigel, Millie and Nicole are colleagues at the Marketing Department, and they are arguing what is branding decisions as well as how to do it.
奈杰爾、米莉和妮可三人是行銷部門的同事，他們正在爭論品牌決策是什麼，以及如何做比較恰當。

Conversation 1 對話1

Nigel	Sorry. What are you doing?	抱歉。你在做什麼？
Millie	**Are you spying on me**?	你在偷窺我嗎？
Nicole	Hi, **guys**, what are you doing here? Look, I have a problem and maybe need your help. Do you guys know what brand decision is?	嗨，夥伴們，你們在這裡做什麼？嗯，我有一個問題可能需要你們的幫忙喔。你們知道品牌決策是什麼嗎？
Nigel	Sure. It means when a firm decides to brand its products or services, they will choose which brand names to use.	當然。就是當一家公司決定要推出產品或服務的品牌時，他們會選擇要使用哪一種品牌名字。

Millie	There are usually three types of them. First, individual brand. Second, family brand. Third, **hybrid** brand.	通常有三種型式。第一，個別品牌名稱。第二，家族品牌。第三，混合品牌。
Nigel	The classic example of individual brand would be Procter & Gamble, also known as P&G, has several individual brands such as Pantene, Head & Shoulders, and Pampers. One bigger advantage is that the company doesn't tie its **reputation** to the brand, if any brand fails, the company's name or image is not hurt.	個別品牌的經典範例可能就是寶僑公司，也叫做 P&G，就有幾個個別品牌，像是潘婷、海倫仙度絲和幫寶適。其中一個最大的優點就是，公司不用將它們的名聲和這些品牌綁在一起，如果任何一個品牌失敗的話，公司的招牌或形象也不會受到傷害。
Millie	Companies usually use different brand names for different quality lines within the same product class, in order to reduce the risk.	公司也通常在同樣產品類別裡，使用不同品牌名稱在不同品質的產品上，以減少風險。
Nicole	I see, very clear.	懂了，很清楚。
Nigel	Family brand is like SONY. For example, they have digital camera, notebook, MP3 etc. etc. all under SONY's brand name.	家族品牌就像索尼。舉例來說，他們有數位相機、筆記型電腦、MP3 等等，都在索尼的品牌名稱之下。

Part I

Part II

Part III

Part IV

Part V

Part VI

Millie	This could be risky if a new product launches and then fails. But it is a good way to notice or **separate** them **from** competitors on the market.	如果新產品上市然後失敗的話就很危險了。但是這是一個在市場上受注意或與競爭者區隔的好方法。
Nicole	What about the hybrid brand?	那混合品牌呢？
Nigel	That's easy, they combines the company's name and individual brand name. For example, a Honda Civic car.	很簡單，它們結合公司名稱和個別品牌名稱。例如，一台本田 Civic 車。
Nicole	I see. But when we decide to choose which one?	了解。但是我們什麼時候選擇哪一個呢？
Millie	I think that's company's decision, however, we can suggest. You know, through a **risk measure** or evaluate pros and cons.	我想這是公司的決定，但是，我們可以建議啦。你知道的，透過風險衡量或優缺點評估。
Nicole	I think I need to **digest** the information from you guys.	我想我需要消化一下你們的資訊。
Nigel	I bet she will **fall apart** soon.	我打賭她很快就會崩潰了。
Millie	You are really a mean person!	你真的是一個很壞的人耶！

Part I

Part II

Part III

Part IV

Part V

Part VI

　　品牌取名字時，如果現在有許多產品或將來準備推出很多產品，不管同類或不同類型，企業（母公司）都會面臨要怎麼取名字的問題，在行銷上我們稱之為品牌決策。通常有下列三種方式可以參考：

1. 個別品牌名稱，就是單獨幫每一個產品取名字。以知名的寶僑家用品企業來說，光是洗髮精品牌就有沙宣（Vidal Sassoon）、海倫仙度絲、潘婷等品牌。採用這種方式最大的優點就是，當新產品在某一領域表現不佳時，並不會波及母公司本身的企業形象，但是相對的，缺點也是新品牌必須在市場上單打獨鬥（fighting alone），沒有母公司形象的庇蔭。

2. 家族品牌名稱，就是企業內所有產品一律使用同一個品牌名稱。例如，BMW 公司旗下車全部為 BMW 品牌，分成不同系列；SONY 旗下不管是收音機、隨身聽、相機或筆電，手機品牌則是併購了易利信品牌後採合併品牌名（索尼‧易利信）。通常是在企業取得某一單一領域的成功後，慢慢延伸（extension）的取名方式，可以讓消費者在腦海中產生「他在這個領域做得不錯，那麼在那裡應該也不差」的印象。

3. 混合品牌，就是以公司名稱結合個別品牌名稱。例如，統一企業旗下多個產品都採用這種命名方式，有統一麥香、統一滿漢、統一純喫茶…等等。

　　品牌決策端視企業文化而定，沒有絕對要採取哪一種形式；只要事先規劃好品牌的發展路程，和思考不同品牌決策的優缺點，就應該可以得出答案。

Related Word 相關詞彙

1. Are you spying on me? 你在偷窺我嗎？

2. guys 夥伴們，大夥們

   文法加油站：同行人當中若有男有女，也是使用 guys。

3. hybrid 混合的

   文法加油站：這個單詞也拿來形容油電混合車（hybrid car）。

4. reputation 名聲，聲譽

5. separate A from B 將 A 從 B 中分開，從 A 從 B 中分別出來

6. risk measure 風險衡量

7. go for 支持

   文法加油站：另一種用法是鼓勵對方勇敢去做的意思：

   Go for it! 去吧！去試試看吧！

8. naive 天真的

   文法加油站：也有幼稚的意思。

9. digest 消化

   文法加油站：此作動詞，名詞則有摘要的意思。

   (1) I don't eat beef because my stomach cannot digest it. 我不吃牛肉因為我的胃無法消化它。

   (2) This is the digest of this week's news. 這是本週新聞摘要。

10. fall apart 崩潰

    文法加油站：也有四分五裂的意思。

Exercises 練習題

Please complete the word or sentence by filling in the blanks.

- I_____Japan as the location for corporate travel.
- _____car will become eco-trendy.
- As long as making sure of_____, we can reduce the investment risk.
- John's personality is too_____, that's why he is keeping be cheated by people.
- When hearting her son passed away, she_____.
- A Company remains good_____among the industry.

請填空完成下面句子或單字

- 我支持公司旅遊去日本。
- 油電混合車是環保趨勢。
- 只要做好風險衡量，我們就可以降低投資風險。
- 約翰的個性就是太天真了，難怪老是被人騙。
- 當聽到兒子突然過世的消息，她崩潰了。
- A 公司在業界一直有很好的聲譽。

Answers to the Unit：
go for
Hybrid
risk measure
naïve
fell apart
reputation

Part I

Part II

Part III

Part IV

Part V

Part VI

Unit 32　Key Points of Hosting a Meeting
主持會議要點

Situation　情境：

Andrew is giving a presentation to board members about this year's brand development plan, as well as answering their questions.

安德魯正在向董事會成員簡報今年的品牌發展計畫，並且回答在座成員提出的問題。

Key points for your conversation 對話急救包

敘述簡報的內容

What I think I would like to do today is to show a few problems that we are facing right now.
我今天想做的，是指出我們正在面臨的幾個問題。

What I would like to do this morning is to review with you some of the concepts for brand naming and identity design, and give you my own viewpoint on that.
今天早上我將帶各位一起檢視品牌命名與標誌設計的概念，然後提供各位我對此的看法。

This afternoon I would like to present the present state of brand development plan for this year.
這個下午我想要簡報關於今年品牌發展計畫的最新情況。

補充說明論點

I shall return to this point later.
我等會兒會回到這個議題上。

It is a special problem with brand alliances, and if time permits, I will return to it in a moment.
這是一個關於品牌聯盟的特殊問題，如果時間允許的話，我稍後會回到這個議題上。

The major disadvantages are a variety of untoward situations, I am sure that we will discuss more in a few seconds.
最大的缺點就是各式各樣難以應付的情況，我確保我們再過一會兒就會深入討論到。

📎 有限的論點說明

I would like to confine my presentation to the most recent progress made in the brand story which my team just came out.
我想將簡報的重點，放在我團隊剛完成的品牌故事的最新進展上。

I am not going to talk much more about the concept of brand naming, I just want to focus on what we are going to do in the events for creating a new brand image.
我並不打算說太多品牌命名的概念，我只會專注在為打造新的品牌形象而即將要做的活動上。

For the sake of time, I cannot show you too much detail about the new brand image design.
因為時間的關係，我無法呈現關於新品牌形象設計得太多細節。

📎 歸納與總結

My presentation this afternoon will not be complete without mentioning the **new brand development strategies**.
我今天下午的簡報，如果不提到新的品牌發展策略，就不算完整。
小貼士：接著就說明上述提到的新品牌發展策略，或者其他替換的資訊。

In closing, I would like to common on the brand decisions our team made.
結束前，我想要評論一下我們團隊規劃的品牌決策。

Allow me to conclude by thanking you once again for this opportunity.
最後，請容我感謝各位讓我有機會在這裡簡報。

Part I

Part II

Part III

Part IV

Part V

Part VI

用英語說出行銷力
Speaking Marketing in English

作者	胥淑嵐
發行人	周瑞德
企劃編輯	倍斯特編輯部
封面設計	King Chen
內頁構成	華漢電腦排版有限公司
印製	世和印製企業有限公司
初版	2013 年 09 月
定價	新台幣 349 元

出版　　　倍斯特出版事業有限公司

電話／（02）2351-2007 傳真／（02）2351-0887

地址／100 台北市中正區福州街 1 號 10 樓之 2

Email ／ best.books.service@gmail.com

總經銷　　商流文化事業有限公司

地址／新北市中和區中正路 752 號 8 樓

電話／（02）2228-8841 傳真／（02）2228-6939

國家圖書館出版品預行編目（CIP）資料

用英語說出行銷力／胥淑嵐著 .
-- 初版 . -- 臺北市：倍斯特 , 2013.09
面；　公分
ISBN：978-986-89739-2-3 （平裝）
1. 商業英文　2. 會話
805.188　　　　　　　　　　　　102015645